# DEADMEAT

## Q

Front cover and flaps: Al Oliver
Backcover Art Direction: Q
Styling of author photograph: Darren White
Dancing Figures: Q
Author photograph: © Q

First published in 1997 by Hodder and Stoughton
A division of Hodder Headline PLC
A Sceptre Book

10 9 8 7 6 5 4 3 2 1

A CIP catalogue record for this book is
available from the British Library

ISBN 0 340 68558 1

Typeset by Palimpsest Book Production Limited,
Polmont, Stirlingshire
Printed and bound in Great Britain by
Clays Ltd, St Ives plc
Bungay, Suffolk

Hodder and Stoughton
A division of Hodder Headline PLC
338 Euston Road
London NW1 3BH

Jane

Yaw, Alice, Amma for everything

Don't be afraid. The devil can't harm you until you open the door and let him in. He could be outside your window holding all the jewels and money in the World. But you are safe. Once you let him in, he'll tell you where he wants to sit and what he wants you to do ...

# SIDE 1

*Soul. Soul. Soul.*
*You gotta have soul.*
*You gotta have soul.*

Prison is an artificial world. The eighteen months of slow-paced agony I'd spent inside made me feel ... empty. Real empty. I was not the same guy. I'd changed, big time. I'd had a lot of time to think and the question I always asked myself was, 'Why the fuck did I get locked up in the first place?'

The answer was always the same. I went inside because of my own stupidity or bad luck. Whatever the reason, it was still down to me 'cos I was the one who went to prison.

*Soul. Soul. Soul.*
*You can't fake it if you want to make it.*
*Get in step pep up the rep and take it.*

S I D E  2

## Caption: Friday 10am

I woke up from the hellish nightmare with a start.
My nerves jumped, my stomach tightened and air
ricocheted through my system. A thin film of sweat
lined my brow and I was mouthing the words 'Wayne?
Wayne?' My voice felt ice cold.

I wanted to curse. I could still feel the shock
waves rippling, rumbling, roaring, tearing through
my body like an earthquake. My eyes darted around
the compartment. My mind working like a machine,
my lips parted. Everything was sketchy, grainy, black
and white, then I relaxed ... The tension drained
from my face, to be replaced by a hot flush. I felt
awkward and embarrassed, like a child who had

been caught in the bedroom by its parents, doing something naughty. But it was still comforting to see the colourful faces of the other passengers on the train.

I stared into their eyes. Maybe I was mad but I thought there were smiles flickering below their smooth, deceptive surfaces. I zipped up my black leather jacket, slipped on my Dior sunglasses, put a salsa tape into my Walkman and chilled.

*How do we get rid of rats in the ghetto?*

Thatched-roofed cottages, cows, horses, sheep, meandering streams whizzed, swooshed, fast, past the window like images in a kaleidoscope. Excitement flickered, the flames strong, gold, hot enough to set a house on fire. I began to perspire as the inferno raged and burnt the ugly shadows of pain that caged me and made me insane in the brain, that made me a slave to time, pay for a crime in a prison so Gothic-horrific. There was no one else to blame, full of shame, no other player in the game. Cheers replaced fears, and diamond tears were standing, shining bright in the corner of my eyes. The fight was done, won, freedom was now my prize, someone up there had heard my cry, that I could not deny.

The biography of Muhammad Ali was on the seat next to me. I had wedged a pile of letters into the middle, of the book along with photographs of Bones, my brother, Froggy, my friend, and my parents. Muhammad Ali was a role model of mine. I was choked when he lit the Olympic flame in Atlanta 1996; I smiled when he was given a replacement gold medal. It told me a lot about America.

*I float like a butterfly and sting like a bee.*

I'd lost weight in prison but I made up for it by reading – Plato, Socrates, Aristotle, Egyptian mythology, the life and crimes of Don King – and listening to various tapes by ultracosmic thinkers. I was armed with knowledge but my body felt as tight as a ball of wire.

I needed to stretch my legs and piss like a race horse. I was wearing a baseball cap, the black leather jacket over a T-shirt emblazoned with a London Monarchs logo, baggy jeans and white Nike trainers. I noticed a smudge on my trainers. I licked my finger, wiped it off and made my way down the aisle towards the toilet.

*How do we get rid of rats in the ghetto?*

The mirror was cracked, the cubicle felt tight. I wanted to piss so bad, I was doing a war dance. I placed my hand on the cold metallic surface to steady myself and sighed as I relieved myself. I had a week's growth of stubble and one of those faces people refer to as hard. I prefer to call it well-lived in. It's not wrinkled up like a prune, just one of those faces that people associate with a tough guy. When I was at junior school, the older boys teased me in the playground and called me sleepy, or Mr Blind Man, because of the way my eyes were set. They also made fun of my Afro. Many a day I ran home from school with tears streaming down my cheeks. The Afro went and I can remember my Mum picking me up, sitting me down on her knee and telling me that I shouldn't worry about the children's comments because when I grew up my eyes would be beautiful. She said my eyes would make people so jealous that they would be forced to ask me about them, and then, and only then, I could tell them that they were a gift from a stranger from a far-off land, a king, who loved children.

Her words comforted me, I mean everybody was teased or teased somebody at school about something; you know, for being too black, for having big teeth or ears. However, to be told that your eyes were special at such a young age meant a lot to me, even though it was by my mother.

When I arrived at secondary school, nothing changed really. I was older and a little bolder but the girls still didn't want to go out with me because my eyes made them feel uncomfortable. If I went out to house parties and asked a girl to dance, everything was OK, everything went to plan until she saw my eyes. She might be in my arms already but, when she saw them, she'd instantly stop dancing and walk off or make a feeble excuse like she didn't feel well. I wasn't good looking but I refused to believe I was ugly.

Things changed dramatically when I was about twenty when the very feature that I had been derided for in my youth started to work for me. Women started saying that my eyes were sexy and that the way I looked at them turned them on, a whole new world suddenly opened up for me, and I wasn't knocking it.

I'd be in a club and a woman would walk past me and smile in a real cute way. When I got talking to her, I would find out that the thing that had attracted her to me was my sensitive eyes. Can you believe that? Now my eyes were a talking point. It was all in the eyes. Looking back I think those kids in the playground did me a favour, because if I had grown up thinking my eyes were an asset I might have used them in the wrong way. Now I was enjoying them. But the damage had already been done, because I wasn't very academic at school, I was hardly there.

A lot of time has passed since school days but once in a while I still find my eyes annoying, because people think I'm taking drugs or I am tired when I'm fine. On the other hand, I'm real lucky because I'm not the type of guy you'd walk up to in a bar and pick a fight with. If I put my eyes on you and squint, they tell you directly that you're about to make a very serious mistake.

## Freeze frame: Caption Clarkie

I flushed the toilet, washed my hands, dried them with my handkerchief and felt the back pocket of my jeans, checking the piece of paper with my fantasy list was still there. I'd taken the time to write out ten. Number one was to make love in a boxing ring. I knew exactly how I was going to run it when the time came. I'd gone over it a million times in my mind.

Some deep Detroit techno would be playing, something by Mad Mike or Nu Era. I take the girl by the hand, real gentle, we're both naked. She closes her eyes tight. But it's dark. I turn on the light. She opens her eyes, sighs, as she sees the surprise. The ropes are blue and red, the seats yellow. She smells like a summer meadow. Fresh from the dew a dream come true. We climb into the ring, each take a corner. I'm full of fire, her eyes twinkle with desire. I look at every curve, the swerve of her hips, the shape of her lips, she is what I deserve. Her eyes are locked on me, I am bursting, she's swimming on the inside, waiting for a grind, a ride, a dream trip in the mind. We're not wearing gloves, our hearts are coated in love. We walk towards each other and when our lips touch. It's ... it's like ... like ... mmmmmmmmmm. Lightning on a summer night. She smells so ... so ... so ... I feel her hot butter rolls. We melt into each other's hips and let our imaginations grow, show as the feelings flow.

# S I D E

*Gotta say it loud. Gotta say it loud.*

Men in orange uniforms picked severed legs off the railway track. They placed them on a stretcher. A person had jumped in front of an incoming train on another platform. The men covered the remains with a blanket and put the individual's shoes on top. Looking at the bundle it was hard to believe that underneath the grey cloth there was a human body.

The arrival and departure board at Charing Cross flickered and rattled. I shouldered my way through the crowd, carrying a clear plastic bag with my personal belongings. A cleaner was sweeping rubbish into a pile. I noticed an empty Harrods bag, picked it up and poured the contents of my plastic bag into it. The

bag sporting the words Her Majesty's Prison Parkhurst
I deposited on the floor.

S I D E

I could have caught a tube from Charing Cross and
gone straight home, but that would have been too
quick. I wanted to feel the big buzz of the hot city.

As I walked down the tunnel, the sound of the
traffic was like music to my ears. I felt like a shaken
bottle of champagne, full of bubbles, I couldn't contain
myself and punched the air with delight. It was such a
big feeling.

A man with a mahogany complexion was standing
at the traffic lights, holding a dictionary and singing
in a Latin tongue. I couldn't understand what he
was saying but he looked happy. He tapped his
feet along to his words, the rhythm lifted my heart.
I stamped my feet on the ground and started a
salsa shuffle.

*One two three five six seven.*
*One two three five six seven.*


He looked down at my trainers and said, 'Yeh, mon.' We exchanged smiles, the communication was complete.

I lost track of time wandering the streets.


*You got to do your best.*


There were women in high heels and mini-skirts, convertibles pumping music, sunglasses, coffee tables on the pavements just like in Paris and Amsterdam, giving off a continental vibe, beautiful flowers, people sharing cigarettes, mobile phones. Banks had turned into pizza parlours, the shop windows in Tottenham Court Road had changed, hi-fi's were in the back or downstairs and computers were up front, the smell of hot bread, Chinese, Indian and Italian food. The scent of women's perfume, the sound of hard belly laughs, flamenco guitar, jazz piano, couples kissing, parents feeding children, wiping their mouths, bright lights flashing above theatres, cinemas dripping with blockbusters, clowns, buskers, *Big Issue* vendors, art galleries, new magazines, billboards, people selling second-hand bus and underground travel cards, traffic jams, horns blaring, raised voices, fists shaking, strong beaty music coming out of doorways, bottoms wiggling, children giggling, ice-cream, cold drinks, red, green, amber lights, see-through dresses showing knicker lines, bare torsos, shorts, sexy shop assistants, money for goods, goods for money. A corrugated iron fence was smeared with graffiti and a line of posters saying 'Wanted Cyber Vigilante. Calling card, a dead white rat. Phone police on (0208)01814503240. URL – http://www.cybervigilante.com Reward: £10,000 for information leading to arrest.'

The warm wind stroked my face as I looked through the drum 'n' bass CDs on a record stall. I was familiar with some of the DJs, Doc Scott, L Double, Stretch, T-Bone, Bukem, Grooverider, Randall, Kemistry and Storm, 4 Hero, DJ Ink, they all coated the styles I liked.

*SexmeeeeeSexmeeeeeSexmeeeeeSexmeeeee.*

A shop in Savile Row caught my eye, the sign above it read Oswald Boateng, the clothes weren't boring, they screamed of sex. They were pucker not for suckers, you could admire them in the same way you would a painting in the Louvre, or a good body. They were definitely the sort of garments that would do something for me, make me more approachable, give me an elegant look; the fabrics shone bright in the light, it was no hocus pocus business, I knew it was the real deal, delivered and sprinkled with energy. I just had to put one on then I could walk strong and feel like a don.

A cafe stood next door it, I could see people inside clicking on mouses and tapping keyboards, the screens of their PCs jumping with sexy colour graphics. I'd never seen a place like this in Zone 1 before, where people sipped drinks and were totally engrossed in technology.

I sighed as I realised that I had stepped in dog shit. You know, in a funny kind of way I enjoyed scraping it off at the edge of the kerb and cleaning my trainers with a tissue. I was free again, back on the street, ready to link up with the world.

*Baby baby baby baby baby*
*babySexmeeeee.*

# S I D E  5

The barber shop was packed. A television tuned into MTV was showing a U2 video. I sat confidently in the chair, relaxing as the razor hummed over my head and my hair fell to the ground. I looked in the mirror in front of me and watched the TV mounted on the wall behind me. I smiled as I saw lines of text racking up.

:-(
What a wanker!
I don't like his hat
What is this shit?
:-)

It was going so fast, my eyes were not accustomed to the pace, no one was censoring it, the teenagers in the shop nodded and laughed, they understood the shorthand. I wanted to know what was going on so

I asked a youth in the chair next to me. He told me that the kids were sitting at home dialling into MTV over the Net and getting involved in IRC, Internet relay chat, and everything was scrolling and happening in real time.

'Who's the Cyber Vigilante?' I asked the barber, looking at his reflection in the mirror.

The barber laughed. 'Where've you been? Don't you read the papers?'

'I've been real busy the past few days,' I replied. 'Away on business.'

'TV, you must have a TV or a radio?'

'My company has taken up all my time. We're restructuring, forward planning.'

'I understand. You've got to look after number one,' said the barber, blowing hair from the electric razor. 'It's a serial killer. There's a big police hunt.'

'I've seen the posters.'

He held my head steady. 'The Cyber Vigilante don't joke. It hangs its victims and leaves a dead white rat with a URL burnt into its flesh as a macabre calling card, then it sends messages to the address. The police have logged in and watched the graphics, now they're throwing out the drag net and giving out the address to net-heads, hoping someone can understand the images on the screen. You know, maybe recognise the style or give them a pointer in the right direction. Are you wired?'

'Pardon?'

'Are you connected to the Net?'

'Not yet.'

'It's a good site. Whoever this character is, they know about technology. There are cookie files, but their own version. I was up half the night browsing through the pages and copying source codes. Real interesting. The site got so many hits, advertisers and marketers logged in and were trying to negotiate with the police to sell their products. You know, they reckon the police can use the money to solve crime.' He looked at me and said, 'What do you think? Should they take the money?'

I shrugged my shoulders. I was a newcomer to this world.

The barber sprinkled some talcum powder on a bristly brush and flicked it quickly around my neck. 'They're not sure if the killer's male or female,' he said, holding up a mirror so I could see the back of my head. 'No sightings have been made but the victims are always savagely strung up. A lot of people are staying indoors, they're frightened to go out after dark.' He loosened the cloth draped over my shoulders.

I felt my head, the skin was soft, bald, just the way I liked it. The barber accepted my tip and raised two bottles in my direction. I chose Eau Sauvage by Christian Dior because it was French, exciting, it had a touch of class.

I shoved a couple of coins into a machine in the wall and purchased a packet of ribbed condoms.

*I wanna freak you.*
*I wanna freak you.*
*I wanna freak you.*

I stepped out of the shop and caught sight of an old school friend. Back in the day, he'd had one of the greatest minds I'd ever come across. He walked towards me, no shuffled towards me, he wore shoes without laces, his clothing was dirty, dishevelled, I thought he must have been in some sort of accident. I greeted him with a warm smile.

He grunted, threw a violent hand in the air, his

voice had a callous edge to it as he muttered, 'Fuck off and leave me alone.' He didn't have to say another word, I got the message loud and clear, his digi eyes gave him away. He'd joined the growing numbers of people who'd been given a liquid lobotomy. He had no identity, he was turned inside out, and now the world could watch him die.

> *I wanna freak you.*
> *I wanna freak you.*
> *I wanna freak you.*

S I D E  **6**

A sea of feet rushed up Oxford Street, it was high tide. I wanted to post a letter, but all the post boxes had been removed because of IRA bombing campaigns. So I had to walk up to Holborn post office where I slipped in the letter addressed to Clarkie, 87 Olive Avenue, London, NW10.

# SIDE 7

A few rent-ah-bwoys were spread out on street corners in Soho, ready to sell their dicks and holes for money. I knew the name of the game. They'd get rarsed up the batti in a car, a toilet or a disused car park, get their dollars, buy some plug or crack, get high. Then they'd be back on the hoe stroll. It was a real vicious circle, a hardcore lifestyle.

An amusement arcade was packed with teenagers playing electronic games. I whistled softly as I walked past, sniffed the hot air and glanced at the address on the back of my fantasy list. An inmate had recommended the establishment to me; he said everything was live and it had a 21st century sexy vibe.

A chubby man with short dreadlocks was standing in the doorway, his oblong face looking like it was bursting with fibre optics. He was in the shade, watching a Casio mobile TV, its aerial sticking out.

His eyes were submerged in a pool of imagery, he used one big hand to keep the light off. He looked happy, soaking up the rays. He wasn't in his house, paying tax, connected to a wall; nobody knew who he was or where he was and the Boring Broadcasting Company were not saying show me your TV license. I nodded, he grunted, the sound metallic and coarse. I entered.

*oooh la la laaaaah*
*oooh la la lah la la lalah la la lah.*

Two potted rubber plants sat on the dusty windowsill, facing the sun. Sexy women played pool. I inspected their shoes. The woman I chose was playing barefoot, her ankle bracelets gleamed, her red toe nails were finely painted. She was black. The short, flimsy white dress barely covered her tight butt, every time she moved it made you think of two puppies playing under a blanket. She looked fit, lissome, like she could radiate tropical heat. I paid the craggy-faced owner the money. She smiled. Her teeth looked like a computer keyboard, she had a nose like a Microsoft mouse and a thin line for a mouth, just like a floppy disk.

She was burning a big head, her lips were wet. I took a deep breath and followed the red toenails into a poky room. My fingers were trembling.

*oooh la la laaaaah*
*oooh la la lah la la lalah la la lah.*

The woman looked about thirty years old, three years older than me. She had a small head, her dark hair was pulled back and tied with a black ribbon in a girlish fashion. She had a quiet smile on her lips. She pulled her white dress over her head, I stayed motionless, watching. I consciously controlled my breathing. She had laughing brown eyes, winegum-shaped nipples and a pierced tongue with two silver studs. Just looking at her made me feel free. She kissed me on my cheek, her lips were soft and smooth, she had a delicate throat.

The walls of the room had different surfaces – metal, foam, glass, brick – and various objects were fitted to them; hand clips, foot grips, back rests, running shoes, leg extension machines, metal step crawls, starting blocks. A Kaboom trapeze was hanging down from the high, mirrored ceiling. A massage table stood underneath it. The inmate had told me all about it, the pictures he'd painted on the canvas of my mind matched the reality, fitting like a glove.

She moved like a dove, a gift from above, she asked me if I wanted her to use any tools. Equipment was laid out on a table in the corner. Whips, cockrings, magicbars, cripbods, hurtzippers, virgin tongues, a plastic doll with a tag which said Lorna the Sauna.

I grinned pointlessly, lit a cigarette, thought about using a condom but decided against it. She was standing in front of me, long legs, pert breasts, skin glistening, listening, wondering what was missing, baiting me, waiting for me to tell her to make a move, waiting for me to take her, so she could use her groove. It had nothing to do with her it was just me, she was the honey bee, with a sweet hive, tantalising, mesmerising, there to help me survive, her stomach a washboard of muscle, proud and naked, nothing too sacred. She licked her lip, tempting me to take a dip, but my mind didn't flip, my dick was not that quick, all I did was sit on a seat. I told her that I just wanted her to massage my feet, she looked at me through inscrutable eyes. The smoke from the cigarette curled into the air, she ran her fingers through her hair. She must have thought I was a joke but still she pulled forward a black stool, sat on it. I could see the hood that covered her clit, I put my leg on her lap, the pink tip of her strong tongue peeped out of her mouth, heading south as she concentrated. There was disappointment in her eyes, she had taken it personal, she felt rejected, wanted, expected me to use my arsenal.

*oooh la la laaaaah*
*oooh la la lah la la lalah la la lah.*

I loved the soft feel of her hands on my skin. Strong. Confident. I could feel the tension leaving my body. The room was warm, 'Let's get it on' by Marvin Gaye drifted in through the open window, the sound of the city rose to meet my ears, clouds were rolling in the blue sky. The woman's eyes flashed over me quickly, asking me if I wanted more, just checking the score.

*Come on, come on, oh, come on.*

The song gave me confidence, it reminded me of when I was fourteen and lost my virginity to Jean Carty, a sweet-smelling, pretty girl who lived at the top of my road.

*Aaaaaaaaaaaaaaaaaaaaaaaaaaaaaaaah baby.*

The record was playing in her bedroom. Jean was seventeen, a prefect, and to me her body was like water to a fish. She was the postman's daughter.

*Get it on, Sugar.*
*Wooooooooooooooooooooooooooo.*
*Ahhhhhhhhhhhhhhhhhhhhhh.*
*Ahhhhhhhhhhhhhhhhhhhhhh.*

S I D E  8

When I stepped out of the erotic building I noticed a blond-haired man standing in the doorway of a sex shop across the road. The scumbag owed me money.

He was a shoplifter and I'd given him £80 to get me some jumpers from Selfridges a couple of months before I went in the clink. When I came back on the night we had arranged to collect my goods, he'd gone. I searched Zone 1 for him, no one in the West End could tell me where he was, and now there was the little shit-cunt smoking a cigarette. It was a beautiful day, almost noon, the sun was hot and there he was laughing, suntanned, wearing white Reebok classics, blue jeans and a Ben Sherman shirt.

I walked across the road and asked him for my money. He was an arrogant punk. He played it real cool, like it was just another day; to him the two years were like twenty-four hours. He was lippy and gave me some cock and bull story about how he'd been looking for me as well. Looking for me for two years. I didn't like his attitude, he was going on like a bad guy. I cut him short and said I was coming back later that night. He got hot under the collar, his voice had a dirty tone as he said, 'If I see yah I see yah.'

I asked him if he would have my money.

'I dunno, like I said mate. If I see yah I see yah.' A hard expression drifted across his face. 'I can't tell you any more than that.'

S I D E 9

*Things ain't right.*
*Things ain't right.*
*They just ain't right.*

A group of winos were hanging out in Soho Square, some were arguing, others had pissed and defecated in their pants and were fast asleep on the grass or the concrete. A female wino with saliva-coated lips caught my eye. She was on the ground breathing heavily, puffing her cheeks in and out, using her buttocks to move along the path, her wiry arms and legs supported the motion, she had trainers on her feet. I didn't notice the brand, just her brown skin; she looked past me, somewhere over my shoulder. I felt sad, helpless, guilty; she was old enough to be my mother. I mean, if I went over and picked her up and put her on the seat where would it end? It wouldn't have bothered me if other people stared at me carrying her. But would I have to take her home? If I did, then what? I stepped out of her way and let her engine roll.

*Things ain't right.*
*Things ain't right.*
*They just ain't right.*

S I D E **10**

Yani, a sixty-year-old Maltese man with dark poker rings under his eyes and jet black hair, slicked back and tied in a ponytail, gave me a tight bear hug. He slipped his pipe into his thin mouth and showed me to the best table in his restaurant. The place was jammed.

*You're the one I wanna romance 'n' slow*
*dance with.*

Yani prepared the food himself and bombarded my senses. Pasta, with a rich sauce of meatballs, garlic bread, olives and imported French wine – I would have preferred beer but I didn't want to offend. The colouring of the food made me feel warm and alive. Yani's wife Ester was on the till keeping an eye on me; when she wasn't looking I slipped some bread and cheese into my pocket. It was a bad habit I'd picked up in prison, it was nice to have something to nibble at night, I hated it when my stomach was knotted up tight.

*You're the one I wanna romance 'n' slow*
*dance with.*

Ester had a false smile pinned on her face, her grey eyes searching mine. I grinned at her. She was wearing canvas sandals and they had grown roots. In all the years I had known her, she hadn't changed; she wasn't going to leave her spot behind the cash register until night fell and every customer had left. Ester wanted to make sure everything went into her pocket. Yani could make his money after 4am. That was his time behind the till, because every penny he earned was used to play poker or went to buy his rocks. Yani's Bentley was parked outside, he stood at the window, one hand in his pocket the other holding his pipe. The white Bentley was the only object that reminded him of the high days in his past.

I decided to share a laugh with him. 'Yani, listen, I wannai borrow your Bentley.'

'No way. I drive,' he said firmly. 'You can take my wife but not my Bentley. Take my wife but not my Bentley.'

'Yani don't fuck me about. I've jus got out, I need a ride.'

'It's a good car, £70,000. I love it, the biggest high I get, better than fuckin coke, better than plug.' He moved over to my table. Very quietly he said, 'On my life. Driving down Kings Road. I let them see. I spit.' He transferred me into the scene. 'Hey, you punks. Hey, you shit-cunts. Hey, fuckin old bastards get out the fuckin way.' Yani put a warm hand on my shoulder. 'You wanna drink the best champagne I have in the house, fine, Clarkie. You wanna get drunk with Yani, fine. But my Bentley, no.' He squeezed my shoulder affectionately. 'It's nice to see you Clarkie, but the streets have changed.'

'They always change, Yani.'

He grunted under his breath. 'But things are bad now. In the old days, any trouble, I pick up the phone and things would be sorted. Now I could get a knife in the heart before I put the receiver down. The kids are crazy.' He let out a terse laugh.

His face tightened into a mean grimace. I'd never seen him look like that before. It must have been hard for Yani to adjust, the smallest movements on the streets rocked his world. In the old days, when he was the Mack Daddy, help was always waiting at the end of the line. He only had to smell trouble. But to do those things he had to have money; now the money was no longer there and the help had drifted away. So the only thing Yani was left with was his Bentley and his memories and in his head they played happy melodies, he sucked on his pipe, he was as a high as a kite.

*Hold me tight right in your arms tonight.*

I finished my meal and felt like a fat rat in a cheese factory. Yani handed me a wad of money. I tried to refuse but he shoved it in my pocket. That was what was going to happen. As I visited my old haunts, everybody would greet me and put dollars in my pocket. It would only last a month or so. Then after that I was on my own. Because nothing lasts forever. Nothing lasts forever.

*Baby I got to say I never knew I could feel this way.*

S I D E  11

My next stop was the illegal gambling club that Willow ran. He was from the West Indies, in his early fifties, a tall man with four fingers missing on his left hand. He'd got into a rumble with some Eyetalian nightclub owners a few years back, and they'd chopped them off with a butcher's knife. He escaped, they chased him, but he'd been a 400-meter runner when he was younger. If they had caught up with him in their car, heaven knows what would have happened.

Willow was wearing black patent leather Guccis,

his blue suit smelt of mothballs. He didn't dress up often, so today something big had happened or was about to occur. Normally, he liked to look like an ordinary working man, but even when he was dressed down the brother was together, he could look like a beggar but operate like a city slicker, or top seller, he was very, very clever. He was studying the form in the *Racing Post*. He marked the paper, took out some money and gave it to an obese youth, who waddled out of the club to place the bets.

Willow lived well, he went on holiday three times a year. He had big houses all over the place as well as flashy cars and slick boats. He always had a smile on his face because he was selling ki's and making money. His boats travelled to far off places. Sometimes they went to Amsterdam, but it wasn't like they blew a whistle and let Customs know they were coming into harbour. He'd done time just before the law of seizure came into effect, so when he came out all his property was still intact and he'd built up from there.

*The harder you come the harder you fall.*

Willow took me into his office and thrust a large glass of whiskey in my hand. He wanted to toast my freedom but I wasn't getting it for free – he was having some personal problems and figured I could help him iron them out for a fee. He opened a drawer and took out a gun. He wanted me to make a hit just to see if he could still trust me. I knew what was really going on – Willow just wanted to have something on me. Something he could remind me of, something he could use against me if I wanted to leave his fold. I refused to take the gun and told him that I was no longer in that line of business. I didn't want no more bandulu runnings.

*The harder you come the harder you fall.*

Willow led me to the kitchen. A woman wearing white backless heels was busy putting coke powder into bottles of various sizes. Boiling pans of hot water stood on a little stove, she popped the bottles inside and took out others which she placed in cold water. I knew what she was doing. She was recycling, washing, getting the dirt and the impurities out of the coke, stretching it to bring it back to its natural state. She was so busy she even had the microwave in use. When the bottles had cooled down, she sprinkled the contents out and they were ready for action, the rocks had been born.

Willow picked some up and offered them to me. I declined the offer, I didn't want my heart to be torn. There was no way I wanted cocaine running around my brain.

*Cocaine runnin' around the brain.*
*Cocaine drivin' me insane.*

S I D E

*My sweet dove fly with my love.*

The interior of the payphone was plastered with a rainbow of cards displaying women offering all kinds of fastlove. Shopping bags were at my feet, the receiver was to my ear, Bones, my younger brother, was on the other end of the line.

A plastic football crashed against the phone box.

I couldn't believe what I was hearing, so I wanted to make double sure, '... I'm stuck here in prison and you're telling me you're too busy to talk to me? Is that what you're saying?'

'... Well, yeah, but I don't mean it that way, I'm in the middle of something, I'll call you back,' said Bones.

'... In prison? A'right, fuck you,' I said, slamming down the receiver.

I could have belled him when I stepped off the train at Charing Cross, but the city was my real home. The place where I felt safe, the flavour I had to taste before I went back to base.

*My sweet dove fly with my love.*

The street was nearly empty of cars. Yellow cones stretched out on either side. Teenagers ended their game of football, kicked over the cones they had used as goal posts and sat on a red brick wall. I exited the payphone and approached them. One of them was building a spliff. He had a scar down his face and the bony knuckles of a fighter. He took off his bogus Versace glasses with gold medusa heads on the sides of the frame, wiped them on his track suit and put them back on again.

'You smoking outside my house?' I asked, nothing pleasant in my expression.

His eyes were lazy. He did not respond. A loathsome grin pulled at his mouth. I wanted to knock it north then south-east, but he was a minor and looked like he was suffering from a mental disease. He was sad, I didn't want to hurt him too bad and make him RIP.

'You smoking outside my house?' I asked again. This time a little stronger. 'What's my Mum gonna say if she sees you doing that? Why don't you do it on your own block?'

The teenager kept his eyes locked on me as he took two steps towards me and picked up the ball. He was loose-limbed, had a bounce in his stride, but it was all false pride. He walked away, his gang followed him, disgust and sarcasm written all over their faces, taking sloppy paces with sneakers with fat laces, a bunch of headcases. I'd thought

South London was bad; things were getting worse in my own neighbourhood. To be honest, the only real difference between South London and Kensal Rise where I lived on north-side was that they were just louder. And they had a tower block for a police station in Tooting Broadway. The station had stables, dormitories for the riot police and police bird nests on top of the building. The crime rate was low in that neighbourhood, everyone went further afield. In the north we had Paddington Green police station on the corner of the Harrow Road and Edgware Road. It was a more compact building, the place where they held the IRA.

From where I stood, I was shocked by the untidy state of my front garden. There were cigarette stubs everywhere. I opened the dustbin and saw lots of empty beer and wine bottles. It didn't take long for me to put two and two together. A party must have gone off.

My next door neighbour was laying his patio. I wondered who he was burying underneath it.

I took out a bunch of keys and was just about to open the door, but I changed my mind and rang the bell instead.

# S I D E 13

Froggy swung the door open. 'ROCKSTONE!'

That was the first thing that shot out of his mouth.

'Oh bwoy, OH BWOY, oh bwoy,' he said, grinning from ear to ear. 'My good godfarda. Di ORIGINAL rudebwoy FREE like Nelson Mandela.'

## Freeze frame: Caption Froggy

He was holding a SuperVHS camcorder and wearing a baseball cap, a Brazilian football shirt, shorts and trainers. He moved to hug me, I pushed him back a bit.

'Watch the threads, skipper. Don't crush the threads,' I said.

Well, I'd gone back into that Oswald shop and bought me two suits, shirts, ties and cuff links with the money I'd collected around town. The suit I was wearing was two-toned; when the light hit it the grey faded and the purple flickered. I'd crowned it off with an orange shirt and purple tie. It was a killer. You had to see it to believe it. Guys like Mick Jagger were wearing his clothes, so if it was good enough for me, it was good enough for Mick. Yeah, I had to big-up my status.

Froggy eyed me up and down. 'Where yu get di suit, bro? OXFAM?' He chuckled. 'Yu shoulda CARL an seh yu ah cum hout. Ah WOULDA pick yu up.'

'Not in that battered tractor disguised as a Jeep.'

'EAR WHA, ear wha, ear wha. Ah ave ah LIMITED edition Karmann Ghia now, RUDEBWOY.'

'Yeah right.'

The corridor was full of cables and photographic lights.

'What's goin on?' I asked.

'Bones! BONES!' shouted Froggy up the stairs. His voice was packed with excitement.

I put one hand over Froggy's mouth and with the other put my finger to my lips. I didn't want him to spoil my surprise.

Froggy caught the vibe.

His eyes reached out to me and he nodded, lowering

his voice. 'Ah Japanese magazine AH do ah story pun Bones. Is works, di new game. E's HOUTTANATIONAL. Arn ah PROPA multi-media RINSE. Yu get me? PROPA. Im hopen up is own clothes shop, an night-club carl Chameleon. E's CANEING it. An me HINVOLVED tu di maxi. Everyting cook 'n' curry, we deh pun ah crusade.'

'Your nose is sweating.'

'It sweat WEN mi tink bout moni. Yu noh SEH me's ah man ooh like im pockets FAT not flat.'

I laughed. 'You're still off key and after the quick buck.'

A beautiful, breathtaking woman emerged from the living room. Neat, short Afro. Good figure. Pleasant smile. She was the living boom. She gave Froggy a coy smile, a soft peck on the lips and spoke to him in a foreign language.

I flicked a glance at him. 'Is she talking fast or slow? That's the kind of language that walks up to you and just slaps you right in the face.'

She continued talking to him.

'Yah. YAH. Yah Vol,' said Froggy, waving her up the stairs. 'Danya, she German, an tahl, jus ow mi like dem. Nice beany. DON'T speak DI lingo.' Froggy's mouth tightened. He stared at Danya, her hips rolled as she climbed up the stairs. He sighed, licked his lips and started singing. 'God is TRULY amazin. My God is amazin.'

'When did you learn to speak a foreign language?'

'Ah can't. But ah can fuck een HENY language, rudebwoy. Yu get me? Met har LAAS nite. We did ave ah PARTY ere. It wuz di bomb, ah ego trip. Tings wuz RUNNIN. As soon as mi SET eyes pun Danya ME WUZ een DERE like swim WEAR. Ah didn't ave tu LYRICS har tu tuff, didn't use no Keats an Brownin.'

'How do you communicate?' My tongue ran over my lips.

'Don't worry yuself bout DAT. We jus plug 'n' play, yu get me? We got HOUR own ting goin arn. Vibes. Vibes talk.'

Danya turned, her eyes dancing. 'Vibes? Vibes? Yah Vibes,' she said, excitedly. She hurriedly made her way back down.

Froggy waved her back. 'NO. NO. NO not now, we do vibes LATE-AH, vibes late-ah.'

She hugged him and kissed him on the lips.

'Not NOW, Danya.' Froggy turned to me. 'Sorry bout

DIS. Yu noh di coup. She JUS ah look ah LIKKLE mout wash an ting. Ah go BOUNCE har late-ah. She's GZIPPED.'

'Well, I suppose there is only so much English a man can teach a woman. But I don't think this relationship is based on verbal communication.'

Froggy ushered Danya towards the stairs. 'Late-ah. VIBES soon.'

Danya looked real disappointed; she managed a crooked smile as she walked upstairs.

Froggy turned to me. 'Ah mix up een PROTOCOL.'

'Protocol. What's that?'

He paused. 'One ah di new WORDS Bones an me ah fly round di hood. Computa language, BRO.'

'So how's the family? How are Tina an the kids?'

Froggy shrugged and laughed at the same time. 'Good. We split up. Ah get SOMEONE helse pregnant.'

Froggy was a pace or two ahead of me as we entered the kitchen. A bald-headed woman with shaved eyebrows was sitting at a table fixing some papers to her clipboard. One of them read, 'DeadmeatChameleon guest list'. She glanced at me. 'Who are you?' she asked, her face wrinkled up. 'The models were here yesterday.'

'Who are you?' I countered.

'Im A'RIGHT. E's wid me. Don't carry ARN stush. Yu tink yu bettah dan everybaddy helse,' said Froggy, casually. 'Ah fi im YARD.'

The woman was wearing biker boots, I gave her a cold glance. She looked like a speed freak. I wasn't going to let her question me in my own territory. As far as I was concerned she was the stranger.

Froggy's mobile phone rang, he smiled. 'Somone ah TINK bout me.' He put it to his ear. '... Yeah, yeah, yeah. Ow much we TEK een di shop? ... Wooooooh! SI MI NEVA TELL YU, dat's business ... Ah bell yu ina LIKKLE while.' He shook his head, grinned, flicked the phone shut and opened the fridge. There was no food inside, just alcohol. He mumbled to himself, doing some rapid mental calculations.

Froggy took out two beers, handed me one. Sadness creased his mouth momentarily, then he picked up the conversation. 'Mi honly grind di UDDER woman once. Di baddy wuz ripe. She ad AH nice yard. It big, yu si. Two floors, but she lonely. Jus di TV. Not even ah pet fi keep HAR company. No, tell ah lie, she did ave ah budgie. She wuz ready, low light, music. It WUZ ah good long session.'

'It sounds like you're still enjoying life.'

'She FLING mi hall ova di place. An me jus boos har ead, tell har dis, tell har dat. Den she ben ova an kiss di bed, ah put one knee down, one up an gi har ah back shot. Yeah like mi ah seh, me honly TOUCH it once. But wen ah CUM it ain't no TADPOLE business. Mine cum hout wid dem eyes HOPEN an legs RUNNIN. It's an army.'

'You didn't wear a condom?'

'Yu noh somtime ah DO an somtime AH don't.'

'So it's like the lottery, you might win and you might lose?'

He frowned, like I had hurt him. 'Me HALWAYS ave bad luck wid dem EEN som positions. Ah wine mi WAIS an dem jus bus. Me's ah dutti dawg. Ah need fi wear two, YU get ME rudebwoy? Anywhey Bones pay fi di habortion. Bail mi hout. Wen Tina FINE hout she DASH me.' He shrugged gently. 'Ah still ave tu get mi forty-inch TV back from HAR DOUGH. She can keep DI settee.'

'You're so materialistic.'

Froggy turned his back to me. He placed his SuperVHS Camcorder on the table and glanced at the guest list the bald-headed woman was compiling.

'Metalheadz twenty passes, dat's fine. A, A, A, A! OW cum DEM Movin Shade fucks is down ere?' he asked, sternly. 'Strike DEM ARF.'

'They're my friends. It's too late to get a hold of them,' said the bald-headed woman.

'Well YU ave tu pay fi dem. Deh ain't gettin no FREENESS. An, F. One TEK im arf as well. E want im name ARN every flya. Like im ah di man.'

'He's got his own radio show.'

'So ave pirate DJs. Fuck im. If im an is GYAL, is agent cut up bout it tuff.'

'Are you sure?' asked the bald-headed woman, nervously.

'Yeah. Yeah. DAT'S why me book som ah di up an cumin DJs like DJ Ink an Loxey give dem som props. An wen DEM Movin Shade people CUM tu di door ah won't feel no way. Tell dem DAT Froggy said deh CAN'T CUM EEN. Yu get me? Deh halways ah go arn like DEM busy. Well MI fuckin busy tu. Yu get me? Ah soon rarse dem een dem ead. An mek sure VIP passes ISSUE tu VIPs. Ah don't want no STREAGGE gyal ah fool fool bowy een dere.'

I quickly opened the cupboard under the sink and felt around; my fingers touched the cold steel of a gun. It was taped to a pipe. I'd left it there before I'd gone inside.

Froggy turned to me.

'Sounds like there's a lot of politics going on, blood.'

'Yu si dem man dere. Dem ah bwoy. Yu get me, bro? Mi an Bones WUZ hout flyin one nite before Chameleon hopen up. An we see one ah dem KISSMEARSE Movin Shade man. E look ah me an Bones an SEH, "What the fuck are you guys doing out here? I don't do that. I pay people to stand on the street and hand out flyers." Im ah GWAAN like ah big shot. Ah ready fi DRAPES im up an put chokey pun im.'

'He must've really upset you.'

'Bones stop me from kickin IM ina im SEED. Well im an is KRU can fuck ARF. Yu get me, bro? HOUR kru cum from di DRAMA STREET AH LIFE. Bones like fi keep EEN contact wid im audience, mek IMSELF haccessible. Richard Branson do di same ting.'

'I hear you, bro.'

'An ah so we do FI WE tings. An now ah ave fi mek dem OVASTAN. Yu get me?'

S I D E **14**

*Baby Float on, float on.*
*I'm floating on your love.*

I stopped outside my bedroom door, looking in unnoticed by Bones. Canvases were stacked facing the wall. There were SiliconGraphics computers, Hayes ACCURA ISDN terminal adaptor, CD ROMs, samplers, TV and sound cards piled up high, lights flashing, fans humming. It was the height of technology. *Akira*, the cult Japanese animation film, was playing on two computer terminals. Some of the equipment had been there before I went inside. But now there were new units, it looked like the intestines of a time machine that had transported itself into my space, and I wasn't happy about that.

Bones was wearing a Deadmeat baseball cap, glasses with gold chameleons on the sides were perched on his head and he was fingering his diamond-studded earring. He had an air of elegance about him. He used his asthma inhaler and scratched the bouquet of barbed wire tattoo on his arm as he studied a game of chess on a computer screen. 'Nice trap,' he muttered to himself as he took off his cap. His hair was growing in tight twists, he hated having it cut.

A Japanese photographer puzzled over Polaroids on a small laptop computer connected to a camera. Hunter, Bones' art dealer, was looking over his shoulder. He was wearing a checked jacket, white shirt, black slacks, brown suede shoes, tortoiseshell spectacles, his eyes betrayed the fact that he had had too little sleep. Hunter kept in shape by burnishing the handshakes of rich men. He'd made some of the sweetest deals in the thin, selective art world community. His sexual preference was for men and he had prostrate cancer. Just before I went to prison he'd undergone a chemotherapy bombardment and the cancer had gone into remission. Hunter appeared shy on the surface, but was very single-minded and spent a lot of quality time with accountants and lawyers.

Danya was wearing wooden glasses with slits. She

was playing the Deadmeat computer game, the logo flashed across the screen.

Hunter faced Bones, studying him, and sighed with pleasure. 'Your work in the last year has been sublime. The collectors are high on it.' He nibbled his lips nervously. 'The Deadmeat computer game is going to sell. You can compete because you've got a point of view that is special.' He paused. 'You haven't got your knees under anybody else's table, have you?'

The telephone bleated.

Bones didn't even look at it. 'The press have been biting my dick all day. I want them to get off it.' His frown deepened and he waved his hand in a dismissive manner. 'The fax, telephone and my mobile have been going off all day, all at the same time, I'm sick of it. Tell them I'm in a meeting and then plug in the answerphone.'

## Freeze frame: Caption Bones

The photographer picked up the receiver. Hunter moved over to the chess game and showed Bones the images on the laptop.

'This is what we're working towards. It's very fluent.

Better than Schnabel, Basquiat, Haring,' said Hunter, smiling.

'No, no, feature the game, and we should have more of my paintings in the background. It should be hard and punchy.' Bones picked up a pen connected to a computerised drawing pad, his movements swift and definite. 'That's better. I've used the air brush to colour in the letters,' he said confidently. 'Save it onto the syquest. That can run. I can do some rendering later and link in some animation. Make it a pastiche of comic imagery. I love using the computer, it's so much faster.' He looked troubled. 'Has anyone seen the dictionary? I want to find a name for this piece of work.'

'Why don't you make one up?' asked Hunter.

'Last time I did that everybody came up to me and said "What does that mean?" I can't be dealing with those Dufus Pixel heads.'

*Above the law everything remains raw.*

I let my eyes travel over my younger brother. Bones had spent most of his youth holed up in his bedroom, drawing. He'd even gone as far as stuffing towels under his door to block out the sounds and voices from the outside world. He spent all his money on spray cans, he was utterly fascinated by paint, it was his way of escaping into another world, his partner in crime. The colours helped him to shrug off a few of his insecurities and to visualise his fantasies. When he had a spray can in his grasp he could visit far away places, go to other planets, meet, greet and talk to aliens, he could stretch reality, get away from house work, get away from school where the art teacher terrified him, from me and our old-fashioned parents who frustrated him because they couldn't understand his love of colours. They despaired, feared he was wasting his time. But Bones was making time stand still, gravity was suspended as he put his fears and the unearthly creatures that inhabited his mind on pads. It was not a passing fad, they crawled and sprawled, multiplied onto patchy walls and the iron bridge in our neighbourhood. He breathed, sprayed life into their nostrils, they knew their drill, some were programmed to kill. They were drawn so they would never die. This was the way Bones exorcised the demons.

*Good God!*

He spent his time in record shops studying album covers, he wandered around art galleries, listened to diverse music, watched movies and cartoons and read comics and books to increase his references. He came back to the room stuffed with towels and spent hours and hours creating mood boards before he started work on a painting. He wrote down everything he possibly could about the piece of work he was about to embark on, family, friends, music, colours of places, the feel, clothes, images, the record covers. They were all used in abstract ways.

*Above the law everything remains raw.*

When it came to art work he was supremely confident, he had no qualms, no worries. Back in the day when he was starting out, things were a bit like the weather for him, some days he was up some days he was down. But his heart was always in it. He became enterprising and made up a range of t-shirts with various characters and sold them on a stall in Portobello Market on Saturdays. He kept plugging away at it and eventually got a break and started doing work for DC comics and just carried the swing. He had a fat ideas book, which he flicked through constantly, absorbing, checking to see if he had missed anything because he was moving so fast. Everything was fresh, he loved slapping his ideas across any artistic medium.

*Your voice reminds me of*
*sugar you're my choice.*

I stepped into the room, my voice was firm as I said, 'Yo. Mr Busy.'

Bones turned his head in my direction and nearly fell out of his chair with shock. Froggy laughed.

Hunter's face showed his displeasure. 'Look what the cat's dragged in.' His tone was derisory.

I looked down at his shoes and said, 'I thought you'd be dead by now, you muppet.'

Hunter's eyebrows went up in mock surprise, he shook his head slowly. 'That's a very reductionist thing to say.' He used a finger to push his Joe 90 style glasses further up his nose.

'Fuck you,' I replied. 'You still wearing those Joe 90s?'

'Bones has got a gold pair. You don't say anything to him about them.'

'That's because he looks good in his. As a matter of fact, he'd look good in yours.'

'You're so tedious. Your brother is the only one I can relate to because he's got O levels,' said Hunter with a smirk.

There was no love lost between the two of us. We'd never got on, he didn't like Bones to be around me too much.

Bones shot across the room and gave me a solid bear hug. 'A'right geezer. Only you could do a stunt like that.' His voice was full of joy. There was new light in his eyes. 'You were in the call box up the road?'

'So is this why you're too busy to talk to me?

'Does Mum know? Did you phone her as well?'

'Nope. I jus wanted to slip into town, no fuss. You look stressed out. Are you growing a beard?'

'Nah. I haven't had time to shave the last couple of days.'

I looked around my room. It wasn't anything like I remembered.

'It's jus for today,' said Bones, letting me out of his warm grip. 'The light is better in here.'

A photograph of a lean, dark haired guy with glasses was hung above the fireplace.

'Who's that?' I asked.

'Bill GATES,' said Froggy. 'CEO ah MICROSAAF.'

'What happened to my Muhammad Ali poster?'

Bones and Froggy looked like they had both lost their tongues. I noticed a framed photograph of Froggy hugging his wife, Tina, and two children on the mantelpiece.

'What's that doin in here?'

'You're so sensitive. Froggy's been stayin over for a while,' said Bones, as he took a long, deep pull on his inhaler.

'Time's going,' said Hunter, impatiently. 'Bones. Can we get on with it?' he chewed at his lips again.

He was beginning to get on my nerves. 'Hold your corner.'

Hunter ground his teeth.

Bones came to his rescue. He put his arm around Hunter's shoulder. 'I need a break for just a few minutes.'

'You've only got one brownie point in this game,' said Hunter, adjusting his tie and looking across at me with fire in his eyes.

I decided to rub some salt into the wound. 'Still scooping up the talent from the street, buying a bit of soul to smooth over the evil?'

Hunter opened the door dramatically like a drama queen bitch, cut his eye at Bones and said, 'Call me when you've finished your reunion.'

Bones snapped his fingers together, Danya and the photographer left the room. I shut the door behind them. Bones breathed out heavily. Softly he said, 'There was no need for that.'

I shrugged nonchalantly. 'He's had a privileged education but that doesn't make him smart. I know about them public school boys, you remember a couple of their rejects came to our school. They was always in the toilet.'

'Haul an pull up. Hunta like YU,' said Froggy, smiling. 'E LUV yu hattitude. Yu noh wha E remine me arf? One ah DOZE tiny dolls. Ah TROG. IS di whey im TEET stick HOUT. Yu si DEM before yu si im.' He let out a throaty laugh. 'E's like one ah dem man dat escape from London Zoo.'

'That kind of animal eats its own arse. It turns around and realises it has bitten off half its face.'

Bones sprung to his dealer's defence. We all knew

Hunter was a raving queen but he wasn't going to let me say a bad word and get away with.

'Pause, pause,' said Bones, his eyes full of steel, his attitude strong. 'Nobody fucks with Hunter. When he writes a letter his double first Cambridge comes out and he makes people feel this small.' There was very little daylight between his thumb and forefinger. He waited and watched me. Challenging. I didn't say a thing, I just let the moment pass.

Froggy walked over to the terminal, he studied the chess board, clicked on a pad and his king moved forward.

Bones grinned and made a move.

Froggy smiled. 'Yu want di quick HEXCHANGE?'

Bones looked at me, he made a wry face. 'His wife did it, Tina booted him out. So I let him st . . .'

I interrupted him. 'So that's why there are suitcases and bin liners in the corner?'

'Yeah, DEH mine,' said Froggy, he shrugged his shoulders and scratched the back of his head. 'Ah went tu ah DRUM 'N' BASS rave een Camberwell. Ah get back tu mi GATES bout six een di AM. Di milkman pass me, buds wuz singin een di trees.' His voice was now a whisper. 'As ah put di key INA DI lock, mi stomach start rumble. Ah hungry yu si. Believe dat. So mi creep up di stairs.' His eyes darted between us. 'Ah didn't want tu wake Tina. Firs stop WUZ DI KITCHEN. AH TEK AH LEG AH chicken houtta di pot. Mi hopen up di fridge, tek hout di carrot juice, get ah glass fill it tu di BRIM, believe dat. Ah TILT it tu mi EAD tu kill it. Yu get me? Wen AH light jus lick me een mi face. BOOM!' he grunted. 'Like ah shot gun. Tina AH SIT dere. Jus sittin dere wid har mout CURL up.' He shook his head. 'OLDIN ah torch. Mi suitcase pack halready.' He looked at me silently a moment, then his voice filled with emotion. 'Dus bin bahg dem full ah mi BES garments. Dat's di trute.' He lowered his eyes. 'Ah CUM ere ova ah month ago tu feel DI strength an LUV dat is ere right now. Til me get miself togetha. Ina time ah need where else can ah man go if he can't CUM TU im two bes spars yard?'

I wasn't having any of it. 'There's your aunts in Brixton. You can go and get yourself together down there. We're friends. Don't do it here.'

'That's cold,' said Bones.

'I don't wanna hear it,' I said. 'He's disorganised. He'll jus put his foot bottom on my good table. You guys . . .'

'Pause, pause, pause.' Bones glanced at me shrewdly. 'Froggy is a brother.'

'Then the brother should understand.'

Froggy's jaws dropped open for a brief second, then he shut his eyes. It was all too much for him, but that was the thing about Froggy, he had no inhibitions. He wasn't cautious about coming into other people's homes, you paid the rent and he kicked off his shoes, made himself comfortable and drank your cans of beer. He didn't think twice about it because he loved loafing. He was gravalicious, lazy, lived for his dole cheque, did anything for a quiet life and loved draining your time and energy. But he covered all of that with a great sense of humour, which outweighed a lot of his faults.

Bones was caught in the middle and trying to wiggle out of the situation. He shook his head. 'If I had had some warning.'

'Froggy's jumped into my life,' I said, forcefully. 'I've been sleeping in a cell this size.' I spread my arms out to the sides. 'Am I using the wrong protocol here?'

Bones glanced at Froggy, their eyes gave the answer. They both sucked in air like vacuum cleaners and raised their hands to their foreheads and said, 'Learn!!'

It was a gesture that was used by deaf and dumb people.

'I need some breathing space,' I said. I looked at the computer screen and began to take an interest in the chess game.

'We've got to help him out,' said Bones 'I couldn't leave him homeless. I can't make him homeless now. That's what friends are for.'

'A'RIGHT, a'right, a'right, a'right, a'right, a'right, a'right. If yu nah gi mi ah BLIGH dat's cool. AH don't wanna cause heny static,' said Froggy, with a lost boy look on his face. 'Ah go sleep PUN di sofa.'

'No. You wretch. I jus bought it.' Bones was not falling for Froggy's hard done by attitude. 'You look ugly when you snore. When that bottom lip of yours starts going and you start dribbling down the side of your face. It's like Freddy Kruger having a nightmare.'

Froggy made a motion with his shoulders. 'Don't worry bout me. Ah be fine. Ah got AH Billie Holliday tape EEN mi bahg.' Froggy picked up his plastic bin liners. 'Ah jus fine MISELF een di nearest bed an breakfas, play me som blues an TINK bout pain an poverty.'

He was so suddenly serious that I had to stop myself from laughing out loud.

'Ah come on, Clarkie, he'd do the same for us. Froggy can sleep on the living room floor,' said Bones, looking intense.

Froggy seized his opportunity. 'TRUS me. Ah be as quite as ah CHURCH mouse.'

'Froggy, spell Dad backwards,' said Bones, his eyes laughing now.

The room went quiet for a second. I could almost hear Froggy's brain ticking over.

Bones creased up with a hard belly laugh. 'See how confused you've made him, Clarkie, he's so confused he can't work it out. Let him stay, he'll give you some jokes.'

I had to laugh. Bones' joke broke the ice. Maybe it wouldn't be such a bad thing to have Froggy around.

Froggy was not amused. 'Yu tink YU funny? Yu jokes so DRY.'

Bones slapped Froggy playfully on the back. 'Dufus.'

I grinned as I noticed a sticker with the words EDIOT on his back.

'Froggy when you're annoyed your words are data economic and very quick to download. Did you know that?' said Bones, touching the electronic pad. He was just about to move his bishop.

I held his hand. 'No, no. Bones you can't put the bishop there ... Slide the castle up instead.'

Bones took my advice.

Froggy buried his head in his hands. 'Ah ATE dat. Clarkie yu halways MESS up mi plan.'

'Checkmate.' Bones punched the air. 'Yes. Yes. Yes. Thanks, Clarkie. Froggy is rubbish at everything else but he always beats me in chess. Froggy is not a gamester, he's always got his cheat book with him when he's playing against the computer,' he said, dancing in his seat. 'Froggy. Where are those games I wanted to swap with the contacts over the Internet?'

'EEN yu room PUN di desk nex tu di computa.'

'Good, there's some kids that have been sending me emails. They've got some serious games. Trus me. I was playing Deadmeat with them over the Net this morning. Testing it out. I've set it up so you can have teams in different countries. I'm gonna beat all of them and get the trophy.'

'Yu even cheat wen yu ah PLAY yu own game.'

'Froggy you wanna play Tekken? Let me kick your arse. I'll click into it.' Bones' face hardened. 'Have you been moving things in my room?'

'No. WHY?'

'Well somebody has. And there is only me and you in the house.'

'Ah di Jugs A YU AH SMOKE.'

'I'm serious. I left some disks and bits and pieces in a cupboard and they're not there. Someone's been in there.'

'OOH?'

'If I knew that, Dufus, Pixel head I wouldn't be asking you.'

'It MUS be ah poltergeist.'

'Maybe I left them at Mum's house. Yeah that must be it,' said Bones, picking up a joy pad.

The theme music to Tekken began to play.

'OK. Get ready to get destroyed,' said Bones.

A host of characters appeared on the screen.

Froggy wiped his hands on his shorts and held his joy pad loosely between his fingertips. He pointed at the terminal. 'We program it fi di news, games an sports. We jus type wha we want een tu di menu an it cum up. If we wanna watch it we do, if we don't we jus click ARF an continue wha we ah do. Ah LUVE GADGETS. Ah can connect mi video camera tu it.'

He could sense I was feeling left out. I'd just got out and I felt like a time traveller, I didn't know what to hold on to and what to let go of in this new world.

'It's a good service,' said Bones, 'It's an interactive terminal, a bit like the old television, but now we might be watching a baseball game, and we can click on statistics and we get real time stats on the players, we can check background information on the player that is batting, at the same time I can watch music videos on MTV, and select information and find out all the tour dates of the band whose video we are watching, as well as order concert tickets.'

They pressed their joy sticks and the game sprang into action. Bones was the Drunken Master, Froggy the Silver Ninja.

'Yu guys AVE ah really nice drum ere. Cable jus CROWN it arf big time,' said Froggy, as the Silver Ninja kicked the Drunken Master in the face. Froggy smiled. 'Ah mean wha is ah OUSE wid hout cable?'

'One that's out of touch.' Bones laughed as the Drunken Master flew through the air and landed on the Ninja's head.

'You must be twins,' I said. 'You're still both MTV-watching Sony-playstation-meatheads. The only thing you both think about is the next pair of Filas you're getting.'

'Right, RIGHT, right. An di moni mi ah save tu buy di Nintendo Ultra 64,' said Froggy, making himself feel at home again.

A new box sprang up in the right corner of the computer screen, it squashed the game. Bones and Froggy stopped playing.

A female newscaster appeared above the word NEWS FLASH.

*The search for the killer who leaves a rat as a calling card has intensified. Another male victim has been found hanged in a flat in West London today. This makes the total five. The victims are all male and Scotland Yard has just released the fact that they all have some connection with paedophile activities operating on the Internet. There is a strong possibility that the killer may be some sort of Cyber Vigilante. A spate of similar murders took place earlier this year in the USA. The Cyber Vigilante may be operating in the UK or the murders are possibly the work of a domestic copycat.*

The box disappeared and an advert came up.

*Wanted Cyber Vigilante. Calling card, a dead white
rat. Phone police on (0208)01814503240. URL –
http://www.cybervigilante.com Reward: £10,000 for
information leading to arrest.'*

Bones, sucked his teeth and continued playing the
game. 'The police shouldn't arrest whoever it is that
is doing them killings. They should let that guy wipe
them all out, that is what I say, he's doing a good
service for the community. Anybody who's luring kids
or looking at their images over the Net deserves it.'

*I wanna know a lot about a lot of little things
and sing about the joy they bring.*

Froggy nodded his head in agreement. 'But ow can ah
cyber vigilante hoperate hout dere?' said Froggy with a
big smile on his face. 'Een dat WIDE space? If di police
can't control it OW can DEH?'
    The Ninja knocked the Drunken Master out. Froggy
jumped up in the air. He growled, hunched his

shoulders over and posed like he was in a bodybuilding competition.

Bones threw the joy pad down. 'He must be a sniffer, and a pretty good one.'

'That's if it is a man,' I said, choosing a character on the screen. The joy pads were lighter than I'd expected.

'Yeah you're right, it's transparent, you're learning quick.' Bones took a moment to gather his thoughts. 'They've got to be a sniffer, a network sniffer. You know, they most probably work for some large organisation and have access to the technology, but they could even be set up in a garage. Then they play possum, that's what I would do.'

'Possum?' I inquired as the game started.

'Play dead, infiltrate the network get in there, pretend to be into whatever they are doing then eliminate them one by one.'

I got up. Froggy's character had knocked me out with a single blow. It would take me time to get used to the game. Froggy strutted around the room.

I cottoned on to what Bones was saying. 'Just like the police do when they want to bust a drugs ring.'

'Yeah, you have to consume the product, sell it, so

they don't think you're a grass.' Bones had a glint in his eye. 'But the possum or cyber vigilante can operate like the IT department to find the main source, they can hook up into the network, get some sort of search engine and send it out into cyberspace and it will sniff out, look for large collections of pornographic images.'

*I wanna know a lot about a lot of little things*
*and sing about the joy they bring.*

I opened the wardrobe and felt my clothes.

'No one's been wearing your clothes,' said Bones, putting his inhaler to his lips. 'Everything is where you left it.'

I picked up my sports bag, unzipped it and looked inside. Boxing gloves, head guard, bandage, shorts, skipping rope, pads, groin protector. I was ready for action.

'Keep tomorrow night free, we're gonna see a band called Ibex at my magical rinse, Chameleon. I'm having a special night. You'll love it. It's got that old school vibe.'

'Where is it?' I asked.

'South London.'

'South?'

'Yeah, don't sound so amazed. It's a good venue. Tucked away in a warehouse behind a petrol station. It takes ages to find it if you don't know where it is. And it's open on real obscure days of the week. Full of manic ravers.' Bones sounded excited. 'Things are gonna be running later tonight, though. There's a party. It is just gonna be the three of us riding together again, rudebwoy.'

'I'll see how I feel.' I slung the bag over my shoulder.

S I D E **15**

Through the window, I saw Melanie, Bones' girlfriend, getting out of a Citroen 5 super D. 'I Will Survive' by Gloria Gaynor blasted, she was wearing a cut-off Posse top and a short jeans dress. A tattoo of a red rose was just visible above her belly button.

## Freeze frame: Caption Melanie

Melanie had been in my dreams the previous night. I was dancing with her in a darkly lit boxing ring, the street lights striping our naked bodies.

I looked at Melanie's butt as she walked towards the boot of the Citroen, her cheeks swinging from side to side, like they were saying 'Good morning, good evening, good morning, good evening, good morning, good evening.' Her way of walking was concentrated, straight, brisk, like a supermodel's. Her favourite film was *Breakfast at Tiffany's* with Audrey Hepburn, the one set around a jeweller's shop – which told you a lot about Melanie. She put some shopping bags into the boot.

*Kookai*
*Tiffany & Co.*
*Emma Ryce*
*Sactta Valbonne*

She slammed it shut. My neighbourhood wasn't full of thieves but Melanie was a shopaholic and didn't want people to know where she bought her clothes.

*Good morning, good evening, good morning,*
*good evening, good morning, good evening.*

Melanie took a long, slim tube of lipstick out of her handbag and began to apply it, she bent down and checked the line in the wing mirror. She ran her tongue over her mouth to wet the lipstick.

*Good morning, good evening, good morning,*
*good evening, good morning, good evening.*

As if he was reading my mind Bones clicked into another programme on the computer and said, 'How's the girl situation?'

'I'm staying celibate,' I replied.

'Hall DI bes,' said Froggy putting down the joy stick. 'Yu stay DERE an masturbate.'

'Your problem is you don't know how to treat a woman, Dufus,' interjected Bones, as he browsed a page.

'Yu should concentrate arn YU own woman. An don't carl me Dufus,' countered Froggy.

There was a mean note in both their voices that I'd never heard them use on each other before.

Bones took out some dollars and handed them to Froggy. 'I need some tweed for tonight. I don't want no rocks.'

'Whodayah TINK me is? Fred FLINTSTONE?' asked Froggy as he slid the notes into his back pocket.

There was static in the air.

Bones was obviously showing him who was boss. He slipped into official mode. 'Have you organised the computer party for tomorrow?'

'Yeah, mi book hall di top DJs een di UK, MARK, DEGO and IAN from 4 hero, Grooverider, Kemistry and Storm, DJ Stretch, Randell. Kaizen een Japan, Moby 2 een New York, Sarah een Venice. AN dem hall hinvolved een di Tekken competition.'

'What about Doc Scott?' asked Bones, turning away from the terminal to face Froggy.

'Ah bin workin like ah TEGG REGG tu get old ah im. No one knows where im deh. Di DJs houtside di country ah send dem tunes, visuals an graphic packets down DI LINE. It hall link up tu di Deadmeat. Everyting will be put arn di WEB. So DAT man een Russia an France can download di drum 'n' bass beats, an di vibe dats cumin from di Chameleon.'

Bones softened slightly. 'Good, good. I want you to

bring your camera and film it. MTV are coming down but I want my own footage. Hey listen Froggy, I'm sorry I was so sharp with you. I shouldn't have talked about the way you treated Tina.'

He was forever the diplomat.

'I never really thanked you for all the work you did, assisting me on my art pieces.'

'Feel NO way,' said Froggy, stiffening visibly. 'Is jus like school daze. Ah DO di work. Yu get di CREDIT, rudebwoy. Di honly difference now is DAT yu don't really need tu OLD ah paint brush.'

That comment got Bones' back up. School days was something Bones hated to think about. Froggy and Bones were in the year below me. There wasn't much of an age difference so we found ourselves doing things together. Art was Bones' favourite subject but the teacher never encouraged him, she spent more time with the white kids so Bones didn't bother, because when he did she marked him down. No one could understand it but that was the way it was. I mean, how could he argue? It was all subjective, down to her opinion. So Bones eventually learnt to believe in himself and his work and not to look for a pat on the back from a figure in authority. Froggy didn't give a shit

73

about the teacher's point of view on his work, he joined a street writing crew and bombed trains, buildings and bridges. He built up quite a reputation, everyone in our manor knew his tag. When people talked to him about the pieces, he always brought Bones in and said that Bones had inspired him or done some of the work.

But now I could see the roles had reversed, money was involved and Bones was not as forthcoming with his compliments. His voice was firm with an undercurrent of rage. 'I'm selling ideas and you're getting paid in full for executing some of them. You get me?'

'What's my HINVOLVEMENT een DI future? Mi ah SCAN fi different hopportunities.' Froggy spoke to Bones, but his eyes were on me, checking my reactions.

'You're a technician, a box bwoy,' said Bones, the corner of his mouth twitched. 'You gotta fucking problem with that? T. E. C. H. N. I. C. A. I. N. Technician.'

'Yu spell it RONG.' Froggy rubbed his jaw and frowned

'How would you know, you read backwards, Dufus Pixel head.' Bones' head wobbled, he looked at me then back at Froggy. 'I'm fronting everything. The shop. The nightclub. Your habit. Your lifestyle.' Bones let the hardness drift out of his face, it turned into a grimace.

'Yu stay deh. Yu HALWAYS ah big UP YUSELF.'

'And you're a technician,' he said simply. 'You complaining? You wanna go back to cuttin sandwiches in your parents' restaurant for a living? I don't need any more distractions around me. The only thing you're good at is downloading girls and bathing in my light.'

Froggy threw the money Bones had given him onto the floor. 'Yu is ah dead loss rudebwoy, yu still DEH PUN ah solo deal. Ah ain't no technician Me is ah creator. CREATOR. FUCK YU moni. Ah don't need dis pussyclatt shit. ME'S not ah novice. MI ah go start mi own concept.' Froggy stormed out of the room. A beat later he came back in and picked up the money.

'ARN secon thoughts DIS might CUM een andy. Mi nah TEK it personal. Mi ah go TU di top,' he patted his chest proudly. 'Yu ah chat hall dis SENSE now but ah rememba yu wen yu ah CHAT nonsense. Pure fart. Watch dis space, RUDEBWOY. Mi ah get HOUTTA dis shell.'

Bone cut his eyes at Froggy. 'You're so slow getting things started people just blow past you. Stick to spraying walls, leave the computer art alone. And remember you're either in or out. I ain't into all this jumping on the bandwagon gang bang business.'

Froggy bumped into Melanie as she walked into the room. The EDIOT sticker was still on his back.

S I D E **16**

*Good morning, good evening, good morning,*
*good evening, good morning, good evening.*

Bones turned to Melanie and smiled. She gave him a soft peck on the lips, looked at me and extended a hand. 'Nice to see you again, Clarkie.' I detected a ghost of a smile pass across her face. 'Just been released from prison have you?' Her voice was low and warm, her lips exciting, she had flecks of fire in her eyes. Her soft, cool fingers grew hot in my palm, she pulled gently.

I said, 'Yeah. I've got to go.' I wanted to say something else but the words stopped in my throat. My breath just hung in my chest.

She handed Bones some documents. 'That's everything as you requested, your will and all the other matters. I saw Hunter downstairs, he's looked them over and signed the ones that concerned him. You'll never guess what he was saying about you, I overheard him on the phone.'

She walked over to the door and made sure it was firmly shut. Her clothes strained against her body.

'Bones, you've got to change galleries,' Melanie lowered her voice. 'He was saying that you are doing so much drugs that he doesn't think you've got long to go. He was encouraging a collector to buy now while it's cheap, saying it's got to go up in value.'

Bones sighed. 'You must have misheard.'

'He didn't say anything about the quality, just that it's different and nobody else is doing quite the same thing.'

'I'll have a word with him in a roundabout way.'

'Talk to him directly. You're producing all this work, you're working so hard. How many paintings have you done this month?'

'Fifty,' said Bones, running a finger tenderly down her arm.

'How much did Hunter sell them for?'

Bones gave her a long, enquiring look. 'He said he was going to be getting £10,000 for each one.'

'So that means you should be getting £4,000 for each of them.'

'But Hunter told me that Akio, a really important character, came in and he had to sell them to him at £3,000.'

'What?'

'Don't worry, he said he'll take most of the risk.'

'I wish you'd spoken to me beforehand.'

'He persuaded me.'

'Had you been taking drugs?'

'I just had a little draw ah tweed, no plug. I don't touch plug any more; the buzz is good but it makes me wake up with a headache. Anyway I accepted that, I accepted what Hunter said.'

'You thought it was great because it was Akio?'

'Yeah. That's the gig.'

I made a move to leave. 'Lissen I gotta fly.'

Bones stretched out a hand and said, 'Nah stay, lissen to this.'

Melanie paced the room. She tightened her body, then shook her hands to release the tension. She pulled a silver hip flask from her back pocket and took a small mouthful. 'Bones.' Her tone was rough at the edges. 'What you don't realise is that most of your pictures aren't being offered for sale.'

'I know they are jus going into storage.'

'Because it's in the gallery's interest,' said Melanie.

Bones picked up a Manga comic. 'Hunter's interest. To let only one or two out at a time to build up the hype, to let the prices go up,' he said, leafing through the pages.

'Have you done another deal with him?'

'Yeah, we've agreed in principle.'

'What?'

'Look it's simple, if he sells the stuff I get forty per cent. But if I really want a cash advance, say for something special, you know a new flat, a car, he'll buy them, but then he'll only give me twenty-five per cent up front because he's taking the risk and maybe he won't be able to sell them.'

'Are you crazy? What do you need up front money for? To buy more drugs?'

'No. I've bought Mum and Dad a house, you know

that. It's all gone through, she's already moved in, did it at the beginning of the week. I haven't seen you to tell you, there's been so much going on this week.'

Bones had promised our parents when he was fourteen that he would make money and buy them a big house with marble pillars and a big garden. He'd kept his word. I felt happy for my parents. They'd worked real hard since coming to England and they deserved nice surroundings. I only wish I could have contributed towards it.

Bones placed the comic on a table. 'Two television companies have approached me about having my own chat show,' he said. 'Another wants me to do a lifestyle thing. Hunter's having another exhibition next week. It's all going off. We're shipping shit out. I just haven't had time to tell you everything.'

'How much is it worth?' Melanie's voice was calm.

'What?'

'The house.'

'Only £180,000. Well, a little over that.'

'I thought we decided that you were going to go for something cheaper. How much did you take from Hunter?'

'Seventy G, well just a little over that, 'cos that way

it means the mortgage is real low for them. They'll get money from selling the old house. It all came through so quick they still haven't done that yet. But if anything happens to me they're covered. Clarkie's name is on this place so he's safe, and the will means the tax man don't get shit. The only shit I'm interested in is avoiding tax.'

Melanie rounded on me. 'Clarkie, talk to him, I don't know what he's doing any more. Bones!! What is the matter with you? The next thing is you'll be turning into a crazy plug head.'

'How do you work that out?'

'Because you can't handle the fame. Your life has changed out of all proportion. You've got no control over the events.'

'So the drugs are another weakness. Is that it?'

'Hunter is buying up most of your work this way. That's why he's giving you all these advances.'

'Fuck it, Mum needs another house, I'll make it back.'

'You'll never be able to leave Hunter.' She took his hand. 'Do you realise that? You'll be stuck with him for life.'

'You're going on. He doesn't own me. I've just sold

him some paintings. Sold him a pair of shoes, that's the way I see it.'

'You're talking in tongues again.'

'You go into Ravel's, you buy a pair of shoes. You don't own the shop. I've got an ace up my sleeve. Forget all the paintings, they're just shoes. I'm into computer art. I've developed a hammer code,' said Bones, authoritatively. 'People think they're hunting me, they don't know I'm hunting them.'

'I don't care about that,' she said, releasing his hand. 'Hunter is organising your life.'

'He can't feed me into an equation and expect me to come out jumping through hoops. I don't have to impress anyone, prove myself. I ain't like his other artists and Froggy, all eager to please. I'm a player. He may not like it but other players know who I am. They know I exist.'

'He owns over 300 of your works. Your shoes. And about 150 are in storage. He's just waiting to reap the benefits later on. They'll be going for £50,000 each and he's bought them off you for £2,500 or £2,000. How are you going to feel? Because there'll be nothing you can do. You'll have to sit and watch while these pictures just go.'

Bones said very softly, 'I know what I'm doing.'

Melanie shrugged. 'And when you get really angry and pissed off and finally decide that you are going to leave his gallery and go somewhere else, it will be too late.'

'It's never too late.'

'All the other galleries and critics are his friends and they'll try to fuck up your reputation. London isn't like New York, there aren't enough galleries in competition with each other.'

'Then I'll leave the country and go to New York.'

'Bones, you're destroying your fucking career. And another thing. I know Froggy thinks I'm the Queen Bitch. I don't care if he doesn't talk to me. I've recommended a solicitor to Tina, she's filed for a divorce, they've got a custody hearing next week. I don't care what anyone thinks. Froggy's undynamic, flawed, flaky, everything he does dies or is destroyed. As long as I'm taking care of your legal affairs in my own time and you're making money, I feel good.'

'You're always on about money and power.'

'Money is honey, unfortunately.'

'You should take a leaf out of Clarkie's book.'

'Are you insane?' Melanie glanced at me. 'I don't mean to be rude but that's how I feel.'

I could feel my stomach tighten, but I decided to let the comment pass. I didn't want to add more fuel to the fire.

Melanie sucked her teeth. 'How could he treat the mother of his children like that? Froggy's a backstabber.'

'He's a good person to bounce ideas off,' said Bones.

'Mark my words. He'll deny that you ever helped him. The best thing that has happened is that Clarkie is here now, you've got your own flesh and blood at your side. Even Froggy's father said he was an idiot.'

'An ediot.'

'Idiot, ediot, it's all the same thing to me. That's how Hunter is treating you now. Get a grip, stop taking plug, and start TCB. Taking care of business.'

'I'm a NBP. Natural born professional.'

Melanie's face was sour. 'You don't have a crisis, you just give other people them,' she said, coarsely.

She looked like she was going to hit him but Bones didn't seem at all worried.

I excused myself and left them to it. I didn't want to get caught in the crossfire.

*Nothing comes from nothing. You gotta do something, anything. Be a Queen or a King.*

S I D E **17**

The sound of a saw buzzed. A man was strapped to a tree, cutting down the branches. His partner picked them up and threw them into the hungry jaws of a van.

Froggy was sitting on the wall with Danya, speaking to Hunter. His camcorder was perched beside him.

'My MISSION is tu please yu,' said Froggy. 'Henyting ah can do jus LEK me noh.'

'Now Bones' bint is here we'll never get any work done. She's so anally retentive,' said Hunter, sounding irritated.

'She's ah CLOSET drum 'n' bass ead.'

'There are a couple of things you could do. What's your mobile phone number and URL?' asked Hunter, taking out his electronic organiser.

Froggy was about to download the information, but hesitated when he saw me. 'Where yu off tu, BLOOD?'

'The gym.'

Hunter ignored me.

'Ah pick yu up AFFTA. We can link up an NYAM somting,' said Froggy.

'A'right, bro.'

'Mek sure yu don't spar WID Joey Blade. Yu jus CUM hout yu noh ready fi im yet.' Froggy took off his Deadmeat baseball cap. His hair was in funki dreads, exactly like Bones.

'You copy everything he does,' I said, in a tired voice.

Froggy smiled. 'Only di GOOD TINGS. OLD it down, bro.'

I walked towards the phone box. I wanted to speak to Mum, to talk to her about the new house and the neighbourhood. To catch up on the local gossip.

*Nothing comes from nothing. You gotta to do
something, anything. Be a Queen or a King.*

S I D E **18**

The gym was above the regal-looking King Edward pub
in Willesden Green. Light shone through the windows,
casting my shadow along the wall opposite.

The punch bag swung towards me. I feinted to
the right, moved to the left with lighting speed
and hit it with well-timed combinations. I was a
little rough at the edges but I was still composed. I
hadn't lost anything drastic. I did some skipping and
shadow boxing, then I moved into the weights room.
I warmed up with power-lifts of 80kg, then started
off with 100kg decline bench-press and ended my full
body work out with 200kg squats, then rounded it off
with gruelling sit-ups. Sweat was dripping off me. It
felt real good when the cold jet from the shower hit
my face, turning me into a new man. I felt the scar

on my stomach, it had been made with a knife, I'd
had a misspent youth. My knuckles were also scarred,
fresh marks from an encounter in prison. I'd come off
best. There was no sign of Joey Blade. If he turned up
I wasn't frightened of taking him on.

*That, that does not kill you will make you stronger*

S I D E **19**

Froggy picked me up in his Karmann Ghia. He'd bonded
with the car, he was really sweet on it. He kissed
the steering wheel and said, 'She ave an UNKNOWN
quality.'

He put on his sunglasses, pretended he was blind
and felt for the steering, rocked his head from side to
side like Stevie Wonder, then drove off at high speed. A
monster track by Dillinja pumped out of the speakers.
It was a brutal high roller. Froggy wasn't into no slow
R 'n' B shit. He liked the fast drum 'n' bass licks.

Froggy rewound the Dillinja tune. 'Dis track is di BOMB. Yu can BROK hout tu it. Yu get me?' He was killing it. He loved the flavour and he kept chopping it back, he couldn't get enough of it. 'Ah want tu die LISSENIN tu music,' said Froggy.

We drove past the Mozart housing estate; no greenery or breathtaking sights, just bricks and mortar. A couple of youths were standing on the corner outside the Lancer Pub. Crack and plug dealers.

'SKITTLES?' asked Froggy, offering me the bag of sweets. I took a small handful. 'Deh jus TANG up yu mout. Especially di red ones.'

Two fire engines turned the corner, their sirens blaring. Froggy put his foot on the accelerator and slipped behind them. The cars in front pulled over to the side.

Froggy chuckled to himself. 'Ah hope dem ah go tu Ladbroke Grove, we'll ave ah smooth ride. HALL ah need now is ah blue light arn top ah dis car an we safe.'

I asked Froggy to pull over on the Harrow Road, I wanted to drop in to a pawn shop so I could pick up my gold Patek Phillipe watch. It was hallmarked and full of diamonds. I'd purchased it a few years back for two Gs but it was worth a lot more. I'd left it in the shop and got some money on it, so I could settle a few debts before I went inside. I knew the Asian man who ran the place, Mr Patel was his name, I'd done him a few favours. So the deal was he'd give me the money as a loan with no interest, but if I didn't come out in eighteen months he could sell it. I'd just made it by a day or two.

I gave him back the ticket and money I'd borrowed and slipped the watch onto my wrist. It was 5 pm. I could tell from the way Mr Patel adjusted his turban that he was not happy. Froggy drove into the Grove. He popped into 192 to see a waitress who owed him money. Then he parked outside the Chameleon clothes shop in Portobello Road. It was a few doors away from the Electric cinema. Deadmeat and Chameleon merchandise was being displayed in the front window. PC disks were attached to each garment.

The shop assistant, a stringy brunette, was reading a book by Jenny Diski. I looked over her shoulder. The SiliconGraphics computer on her desk was collating orders from the Internet via the Deadmeat web site.

'We jus' add DIS tu di network an me hinvolved,' said Froggy proudly. 'Wid di Chameleon nightclub an Bones' computa art we'll HATTRACT hall di right people

EEN di media. Everyting is digital. An we ah go mek sure everyting copastatic.' Froggy's face suddenly lit up. 'Di paintings PUN DI WALL OVA DEH SO are Bones' an arn di LEF is my works.' Froggy moved over and admired his work. It was abstract, the colours were loud.

'It's got juice. I like it. Is Bones happy?'

'Yu noh, Bones is mo ah less di same. But di HONLY ting rong wid im is dat im spen tu much time ARN di Hinternet. Ah keep tellin im if E really want tu chat tu people E should put arn im shoes, hopen di door an go hout. E use it tu much. It's like somtime E'S afraid tu talk tu real human beings. Di honly time E talk TU real human beings is wen im ah talk bout di Hinternet an dat is ridiculous,' said Froggy, picking a piece of paper off a table. 'Wha yu TINK BOUT dis flya me design fi Bones' club?' He slipped it in my hand. 'Yu tink IT TU black?'

As I looked over it, I noticed Froggy open the cash till and take some money out in a very casual manner. Like it was an everyday thing. The brunette gave him a piece of paper with a list of names and phone messages. They were from five females.

Froggy had a big grin on his face. 'Di tree P's. Paper, power, pussy. Ah wanna show yu dis new business me ah set up. Ah BIN sittin an waitin fi di right TING. Now it pop up an mi READY. Ah got firewalls up.'

The brunette lowered her book, her bright blue eyes sized us both up and then settled on Froggy. 'I've been here since ten. Are you gonna spend some time in the shop so I can get something to eat?'

Froggy didn't even look at her, he just walked out. Her eyes moved over to me. I shrugged my shoulders. I felt for her but there was nothing I could do.

*Keep the good dump the garbage.*

S I D E  20

Portobello Road was alive, exciting. People were enjoying their food in the Makan Malaysian cafe under the flyover, others were bustling up and down in stylish clothes. The market traders were doing brisk business.

'Portobello Dave' was sending out soulful vibrations

from his tape stall. He was shaking his tambourine and singing along to the track. The stall was surrounded by punters who wanted to take the music that jumped out of the speakers to far off places around the globe. I glanced at the selection he had compiled.

*Funkie Hippie Shit part I & II*
*Gimme Some 2*
*Peppers part I & II*
*Mind Funk*

My friend Dave smiled, slipped four tapes into my pocket, gave me a box of ginseng and said, 'Enjoy.'

Froggy had his camcorder with him and was filming randomly. I noticed a woman changing her child's soiled nappy. She put it in a plastic bag and was about to throw it in a bin. I took it from her and held it out to Froggy. 'Do you want a beef sandwich?'

Froggy reached out for the bag, clocked the woman and the baby, looked at me and we started laughing. I took out a stick of gum, put it into my mouth and threw the paper on the ground.

Froggy shook his head in the negative. 'LITTABUG.' His mobile phone rang. '... Ello babe ... ah glad yu

HINJOY it,' said Froggy, speaking into his phone. '...
No, no, we might be AVIN anada rave but DIS time
it's ah wash AH car party. Nex week, so don't forget
tu bring yu bikini. Yeah yu noh me it's goin tu be fat.
We'll ave AH barbecue goin een di GARDEN ah DI same
time. Burgers an chicken, EVERTING. Tell di res ah yu
gyal Kru, si yah.'

*Do it yourself, you are better than these guys.*

S I D E  **21**

A computer-animated gang of bad guys ran across
the screen firing their laser guns. Froggy and I shot
them up. The sound effects were wild. The amusement
arcade was packed.

I wiped the back of my hand across my mouth as the
tension in the game increased. Froggy's mobile began
to ring. He ignored it.

'Aren't you going to answer it?' I asked.

'No. Me ah play ah computa game. Deh can CARL back.'

'How's your mum and dad?'

'OWARD SELL di restaurant.'

I ran out of ammunition, a bad guy buried a hatchet in my character's head before I had a chance to reload. The phone stopped ringing.

'An buy ah property EEN Hell's Kitchen. Shirley like New York. Ah should really go an see DEM but ah don't wanna spen di price of ah air ticket tu ave AH hargument wid mi madda an farda. Ah wish dem luck.'

Froggy's phone rang, he finished the game and answered it. '... A. A. A. baby, baby, BABY, baby.' He pressed the receiver to his ear. '... Ow yu DOIN, sexy? So yu ear halready? RAAAAAAH. News travel FAS. Yeah we might be havin ah party nex week. Oh dere ain't no real hoccasion. Jus tu celebrate di fact DAT Clarkie's back. Yeah, im jus step een tu di LAN ah di brave. Me wid im now. We preparin fi di Tekken competition. Ah don't care ooh enta. Ah goin whip Goldie's arse een di firs roun,' said Froggy winking at me. '... Is ah good ting yu phone, YU AH GO LIVE LONG. Ah seh is ah good ting yu bell me.

Ear wha, EAR WHA, ear wha, ah got anada club carl di SAAF warehouse. No STRICKLY my runnins, yu get me? Ah draw hout di battle plans. It's ah fresh RINSE, yu get me? AH GOIN be arn di box, famous, jus like Bones. No one use di venue. It's jus bill. Yeah, yeah, yeah. Dat's wha ah waan talk tu yu bout. Yu can work di GUES lis. Wen it lick arf yu ah go get yu moni. Ah carl yu ah ome lateah. A'right, bye. Yes, sweet HEART. No, DARLIN. Maybe HONEY. Bye, SEXY.'

*Do you trust anyone to run your life?*

S I D E  22

The sign above the restaurant read 'Howard and Shirley's Crib'. Froggy was greeted by a waiter, who promptly showed us to a table. On the lower level. A salsa dance class was in progress, the Latin music drifted up. A sexy song was playing.

*I'm never gonna give you up.*
*I'm never gonna give you up.*

I leaned over the banister and watched the routine.

'Can yu still FLY, rudebwoy?'

'Une petite peu.'

'Oward wuz halways tryin tu teach mi. Ah WUZN'T
hinterested. Ah still ain't. But yu TEK tu it,' said Froggy,
waving to a Nubian woman in the class. He blew a kiss
at her. She smiled. Froggy put the camcorder to his eye
and pressed *record*.

'Dat's rong. Dat woman's bin een mi DREAMS tu
NITES een AH row. CUMIN towad me like ah VRML
Robot. Me ah go fine har source code.'

'Who is she?'

'Ah frien ah YU madda.'

'My mother's got friends like that?'

'Yep, she JOIN ah new church.' He started singing.
'God is TRULY amazin. My GOD is amazin.'

'Cute. Good foot work. She's got the living style. If I
was dancing with her my hands would be up and down
her body like a piano.'

'Primary SKOOL teacha.'

'I wouldn't have to force her into any moves to look

good, it would be flowing, pure showmanship, it would be hot. I'd fling in the American vibe, a little street dance, mix it up.'

'She bored. Is WORK, OME, WORK, OME, WORK. Mum's bin stickin tu har like Supaglue.'

'Does she live in the neighbourhood?'

'Dress nice. Halways well pruned, olda DAN she looks dough. Louis Vuitton.'

'Louise?'

'No. Dat's wha me CARL olda women. Louis Vuitton.'

'Why?'

'Cause deh carry ah LOTTA baggage.'

I laughed.

*Make it last forever.*
*Make it last forever.*

The class came to an end. The students clapped. The woman picked up her coat. Froggy lowered his camera.

'Normally MI prefa di younga ones 'cos deh AVE life een front ah dem. But she high class.'

'So she's not your woman? You're not checking her?'

'Mi ave pussy cumin HOUTTA mi ears, rudebwoy. Ah still WANNA TASE it, dough. Ah ave di right lyrics fi HAR. Ah go gi HAR som Keats an Brownin. Yu noh ow ah work mi lyrics hout? Ah himagine me is Bill Cosby sittin EEN ah big chair. E HEXPLAIN tings wiiiiiiiiicked. Paints ah picture. Watch dis.'

The woman walked up the staircase and came over to the table. Her brown eyes were as cool as her dress, which was simple but dramatic. I could see the edges of her teeth under a smile. Her walk was sedate, she was trying to hide the contours of her body, but it wasn't working.

Froggy leaned back in his chair and started singing 'Lek mi lick YU UP AN DOWN til yu seh stop.'

The woman covered her face. She was even more beautiful close up. Good complexion, high cheekbones, a small diamond-studded watch on her wrist, pearl necklace.

'Tunite baaaaaaby ah wanna get FREAKY wid yu.' Froggy held her hand and kissed it. He raised his eyebrows and puckered up his lips just like Bill Cosby.

'You just like embarrassing me,' said the woman, slapping his hand.

A gentle grin started tugging at my mouth.

'Dis is Daniel Clark, Bones' MADDA'S heldest son.'

A warm smile spread across the woman's face.

'E's jus BIN release from prison.'

I gave Froggy a cold glance. He could see the anger in the tightness of my face. There was no need for him to give her that piece of information. I moved my chair back, stood up and shook her hand.

'Now here is a man who knows how to greet a lady.'

'My friends call me Clarkie.'

She could see the hurt in my eyes.

'My back foot. Ah neva noh DEH TEACH yu eti ... eti ... etiqu ...'

'Manners,' I said.

'DEM teach DAT een prison now?'

I touched a vacant chair. 'Would you like to join us?'

'I've got to pick up my son. Have a nice meal. Bye.' She walked towards the door.

My eyes followed her; they stayed above her waist. 'I never caught your name.' She stopped and turned to face me. 'Pauline,' she said, in a very polite tone.

## Freeze frame caption: Pauline

'I like your dancing style,' I said. 'You're going to be dangerous, a bomb waiting to explode.'

She smiled her smile, her teeth looked like the ones in those commercials that sparkled. PING!

Froggy had a frown on his face. 'Yu feel seh yu large. Where DI FUCK yu get arf bein so FUCKIN polite? Mussi tink me fool.'

'Lighten up, skipper. I jus Bill Cosbyed her.'

He scanned my face. 'Ah NEVA see yu fuckin STAN up fi ah woman een mi liiiiiife.'

'It's all nice. Your mind's playing tricks on you.'

'No YU ah play ME.' Froggy stood up so forcefully his chair fell onto the ground. 'Don't PLAY me.' He winced in pain and held his lower back. He calmed down instantly.

'You told me you're not seeing her. Why suppress feelings? She's Mum's friend. I was just being nice.'

Froggy walked out of the restaurant. Through the window I watched him talking to Pauline. I looked around the restaurant. Everybody was engrossed in their conversations. I took two French rolls from a bread basket and slipped them into my pocket.

Froggy entered. 'Fuck HAR,' he said vehemently.

'I'd like to, twice.'

'She used tu be ah thief ANYWHEY,' he said, coarsely. 'Yu BETTAH check yu wallet. She mos probably TEK dat. She borin. YU NOH ooh mi sunshine is?' asked Froggy, opening his wallet.

He showed me a photo of his five-year-old daughter, Cheyenne.

'Mi youth. Women like Pauline CUM an GO but mi daughta nah go nowhere. Dat's why me need moni tu buy mi children tings ah couldn't hafford before. Tina ah mek dem arks fi di mos hexpensive clothes an Toys.

'It just shows you how much I missed on the inside. Cheyenne's really grown up. She's so tall now. She looks so much like you'

'AH hope so,' said Froggy, with a fixed grin.

I laughed.

'Ah can't MEK Pauline, mi nah lek ah PIECE ah skirt CUM between us. But, yu noh me ah get jealous if ah don't get hattention. Ah ain't changed een dat rispek.'

'Jealousy ain't got no age.'

The waiter whispered real softly in Froggy's ear.

'Let's DUS,' said Froggy.

'We jus got here. It's all nice.'

'We ave tu leave TREW di back.'

Froggy picked up his camcorder and walked into the kitchen. I rose slowly.

S I D E

*The mission is possible.*

I entered the kitchen. Froggy had a big grin on his face. The table was laid out. In the corner there was a small office area.

'Psyche. Dat's mi HOFFICE ova dere, rudebwoy.'

'Your parents sold the business to you?'

'Mi jus ah rent di space. Di KINA coke deh sell HOUT front won't be di kine mi ah sell.'

'Looks smooth. What about your work with Bones?'

'Wha BOUT it?'

'That's dark.'

'If me an yu do somting togetha it's goin tu be big ah can feel it. Ah can cut yu een tu DIS. Ah ave tu mek mi own tracks. Yu get me? Willow ah back mi up im, AH use moni from im plug hoperation ... Ah can use im LOCK-UP an heny ah im car dem. Ah can't LEK Bones jus use mi. Ah want RISPEK.'

'I hate it when you talk like that, it's evil. It's greed. Want, want, want.'

'Ah noh it SOUN vicious but ain't nuttin personal, it's jus business.'

'That's the same shit Wesley Snipes said in New Jack City before he blew his brother's head off. It's like you've sold your soul for seven pieces of silver. Not even gold.'

'It's bout moni an dat is himportant TU me. Ah DON'T want to be poor hagain. Laas year WUZ mi WORST, Neva hagain. Dat don't suit me. Ah got tu do di tings ah got tu do tu get di moni tu Spen. Full STOP.'

'You're always juggling, pulling a skank. You've still got your tongue in everything. If you spread yourself too thin nothing will come of it.'

The waiter gave Froggy a cushion which he placed at the back of his chair.

'Back still giving you trouble?'

'Only WEN ah get angry. It ain't ah big deal.'

The waiter carefully opened a bottle of champagne. It hissed. I took a seat.

'AHHH perfect,' said Froggy. 'Di cork should leave di champagne BUCKKLE like di sigh of ah satisfied woman.'

The waiter filled our glasses.

Froggy raised his glass to the light. 'Yu can tell di quality ah di champagne by watchin di bubbles. If deh rise up di CENTRE is good. If dem rise up di side it bad. Henry Di Eight marry, Marie Antoinette.'

'No. She was Queen of France. Born in Vienna.'

'Or one ah im wives. Anywhey e tell im men dat e wanted tu drink HOUTTA di himage ah she breas.'

'Thank God he didn't like breasts like Roseanne's or we'd all be drinking out of glass bowls.'

'Tu wealth, EALTH an APPINESS.'

We touched glasses.

'So what do you want?'

'We avin ah GOOD time.'

'You do everything for a reason. Even as a kid, you were everybody's friend at different times.'

'Yu use DAT word ah lot.'

'What?'

'Yu'll seh it HAGAIN.'

There was an arrogant expression in his eyes that irritated me. I took out a packet of cigarettes. Froggy was visibly surprised.

'Yu start SMOKE? Mr My Body is my Temple? Tings mus ave bin ARD EEN dere.'

His contemptuous tone riled me. I got up abruptly and exited through a side door.

S I D E  24

*Never give up.*

Froggy followed me out. I scratched a match alight and brought the flame up to my cigarette. The alleyway was littered with rubbish.

The match was burning between my fingers. I threw it on the ground and stepped on it. 'The cigarettes were Wayne's idea, said it would help to calm me down. I smoked the occasional draw.'

'Is E still HINSIDE? Heny baddy dat can hinfluence yu AFFTA ah bit an ah arf is worth talkin tu. Wen yu wuz hinside wha yu tink bout?'

'Coming out. What kind of day it would be.'

'Mi hinjoy vistin yu. Yu SHOW no pain.'

'The screws tried to tempt me over the edge a couple of times in that holiday camp. After a while I gained their respect and then things were cool. They thought I was a mad cat. One day I was reading SAS books. The next children's stories and writing poems. They couldn't work me out. The first day was the hardest. I couldn't sleep. The next day Wayne visited.'

'WAYNE?' he asked, with a slightly anxious note in his voice. 'Who is E?'

'She's a woman. A friend from another time.'

'Dat WORD hagain,' he said, grinning.

'What?'

'Frien. Dat is ah difficult word tu define. Wha WUZ di ardest ting?'

'Being without a woman,' I said impatiently. I looked at my open palm. 'The guy I was sharing my cell with, everytime he went for a shower he said, "I'm goin to fuck Mrs Palmer. I goin to fuck Mrs Palmer." What would you do? It's either that or another man.'

'AH'D fuck Mrs Palmer an hall har daughta DEM.'

'How come you're asking so many questions?' I stared hard at him.

'Yu did hall dat time CAUSE ah Bones. It WUZ is fault, im start di fight. Yu finish it arf.'

I drew a long, slow breath. 'The guy ended up losing an eye.'

'Ah self-defence. Im CUM at yu wid ah buckkle, yu did wha yu ad tu do.' He shrugged his shoulders. 'Ah wuz TALKIN tu Melanie laas nite ah di party. She frustrated.'

My eyes shifted away from his. 'So what's new?'

'Bones don't CHAT tu har.'

'He didn't come and see me and he's my own flesh and blood.'

His voice was sharp. 'Somtime E carry ARN like she ain't even is woman. Yu get me? It's like she een bed lookin ah di ceilin.'

'That's the level you two were on?'

Froggy shyly looked at me. 'Me an she ah talk. Ah tell har bout mi madda an ME childhood. She wuz drinkin ah lot as usual an jus ah LABBER LABBER har mout. She tink she's Bones.'

'I hear you.'

'If yu ARKS me she honly hinterested een im cause ah im credit card, im contacts, an im nice HAIR.'

'That's brutal.'

'For real. Believe dat. Yu should see di gates she ah LIVE een now, rudebwoy. One ah dem luxury business. She ah rent it cheap from one ah Bones' architech frien. But she seh it still nah right. So Bones ah look fi buy property.'

'Melanie does one thing and says something else.'

'HEXACTLY. She's ah graspin fortune hunta. Jus ah look moni. Ah noh she did like yu. Bones did noh as well. But yu is ah relationship phobic.'

'She was my brief. That was it.'

'She wanted tu get een yu briefs. Yu los di AGH case, before yu do time she SWITCH.'

'What are you trying to say? You're quantum leaping.'

'Ah wuz DERE, rudebwoy. Ah wuz dere wen yu cum an tell Bones BOUT dis HOT woman who wuz goin defen yu. OW she ah MEK subtle pass at yu.'

'Melaine just flirts to a certain extent. She likes people to say she's sexy. And I never dip my wick in company ink.'

He patted his chest. 'Ah NOH dat.' He lowered

109

his voice, for effect. 'But DEN she start grindin Bones.'

'Have some respect.'

'Yu look up tu im tu much. Ah did watch har een court, she wuzn't arn it AH hundred per cent. She lek TINGS slip, mus ave bin drinkin. Yu get me? But like mi madda halways seh, if yu can't EAR yu mus FEEL.'

'I'm losing my appetite and that's a problem because I'm hungry.'

S I D E

*It's all good!*

Bones' feet were bare. He was sitting at a computer terminal in his room, downloading files from the Net. His chair got closer and closer to the desk until he was about three inches away from the screen. A picture of Michael Jordan was on the wall above the equipment.

*Fear is an illusion!!*

'Do you know where I could get a hold of Melanie?' I asked.

'Take off your shoes. You've just missed her,' he said, moving over to another computer. 'She's going out of town. She'll be working late at Willesden court tomorrow. She's preparing for a case. A big one. She's a bit nervous, she knows the security guard, he lets her in and she practices. Goes through everything.' He picked up some floppy disks. 'What's the matter?'

The words 'Find a need and serve it' were moving right to left on the screen saver. His Nokia 2110 phone was lying on top of the computer. A label on the computer casing read, 'Bones' moody computer'.

'Melanie did her best didn't she? My case?'

Bones used two fingers to type commands. 'I don't see no reason why she wouldn't.'

'You're not lying to me?' I asked, placing my shoes outside the door.

I got a full blast from his eyes. 'You're paro. She wouldn't behave in that manner.' His searching stare made me feel uneasy. 'Hold on a second. I'm trying to access Denmark, I don't think I've got any more access rights.'

The words 'Welcome to DANTBBS' zipped across the screen.

Bones smiled. 'I'm in,' he said, taking a sip from a bottle of Lucozade.

'Into what?'

'You'll see in a second.' Bones scanned the list of files.

*Night owl.*
*After dark in the Park.*
*Freaky deaky.*

'You visited me three times in eighteen months. I saw more of Froggy. He was there for me, brought me a radio, a Walkman. He was more of a brother than you were.'

'I'm glad you've bonded, you can form a double act.' His tone was abrasive.

'I didn't mean it like that.'

'No, you guys will be good,' said Bones, looking at the screen and writing down file numbers.

'Grow up. You're starting to upset me.'

'Oh, Clarkie's getting angry. I'd better shut my mouth. Who knows what he'll do.'

'You've surrendered yourself to fame.'

Bones stopped what he was doing and turned to face me. He looked at me steadily. 'And you're still seeing things as they were. I've had to become a CSI, creative strategic innovator.'

'OK, so I'm naive. That's me. Mr Naive.'

'You went down but that doesn't mean Melanie had to come and see you. I came when I could. Don't you understand that? OK I'll say it in another language. Ish dab dab dab lab lab nok nok tok tok doj tok, OK? Is that better?'

'What's wrong with pen and paper?'

'I'm a painter, I don't use words.'

'So now you're the biggest nigger in art, that makes you feel good?'

'No, the fact that you're the biggest nigger in my pocket makes me feel even better, Dufus,' he said, turning away from me.

I grabbed Bones by the neck, and before he knew it he was in a tight head lock.

I was part-playful part-serious. 'Mum and Dad wrote

113

every week, came every time I was allowed visitors. I didn't see Melanie once.'

'She's worked hard to get to where she is.' Bones' voice was muffled. 'Why would she give all that up? Do you think she set you up? You think I'd be fuc ...'

I let him go. Bones rearranged his clothes. He picked up his inhaler and took a puff. I opened my arms and moved to hug him. He pushed me away.

I was fast losing patience with him. 'You should have made time. God forbid if something happened to us and we hadn't talked.'

Bones lowered the inhaler from his mouth. He spoke slowly and distinctly. 'You think I'd be party to that?' he asked, covering his annoyance. 'Is that what you're saying? Spit it out, I can handle it.'

'I'm sorry. I didn't mean ... I'm all over the place.'

Bones clicked on his mouse, there was a slight pause, then he said, 'Let's forget it. Let's forget it.'

The computer bleeped and pornographic pictures appeared on the screen.

'Look here,' he said, pointing to a column on the right of the screen. 'I'm the only one calling from London right now, everybody else is calling from Denmark. The SYSOP is the person that runs the bulletin board. Clarkie, sit where you like but don't touch any wires.'

I pulled up a chair and took in the meaty images. 'SYSOP?'

'The systems operator,' Bones' voice crackled. 'You take the S, Y and S from the first word and the O and the P from the other and you get SYSOP, he's on line as well.' He put his finger back on the screen. 'I'm bored of that. I'll just go back to the available menu.' He clicked on the mouse. 'I'll get into a CD ROM file menu.'

'What kind of equipment have they got out there?'

'They've got a machine there with all the different CD ROMS in it. Macro storage.' He picked up a Tribe called Quest music CD and held it up to me. 'One CD out there can hold about 650 of these.' He hesistated a moment, then nodded his head. 'It's loading up the CD for me now. Let's have a look at what's in here,' said Bones as the machine hummed. 'Here we go.'

*Black mini skirt.*

Bones' eyes scanned the list. 'Ohh. Black mini skirt, seen that already, it's sex in the office on the table, that sort of thing, more for women than men. It's made for them to turn them on, but it's good viewing,' he said. 'They haven't got the really hard-core stuff on at the moment, they turn it on and off line on different days. I'll just choose a different CD. I'm going to put Tyra Banks on my screen saver later, she always brings a smile to my face.

'I bet you download all these images and squeeze one off over your keyboard before the whole thing appears on your monitor.'

'Very funny,' said Bones, moving over to the record deck.

He opened a large cardboard envelope and took out a framed gold disc for the album sales of 100,000 records he'd done some work on. He picked up a screw-driver. I thought he was going to find a nice space on the wall to hang the disc. Bones turned the disc over and began to unscrew the frame.

'What are you doing?' I asked.

'Taking it out. The record has to get rinse.'

'You're meant to hang it up.'

'This is Bones you're talking to. Fuck that. It's got grooves in it so it must play. I'll see if my needle will take it.'

'Play it rarse yes,' I said, laughing.

# SIDE 26

*It doesn't really matter at all
really doesn't matter at all if you fall
get up and have a ball.*

The Mind Funk tape 'Portobello Dave' had given me
was playing in the background. I nodded my head to
the flow, the shit was bombing.

I opened my wardrobe and unzipped the carrier that
was holding my other Oswald Boateng garments. Inside
was a pleasure dome. A yellow suit. Dark blue shirt and
tie. I couldn't wait to wear it but I wanted the right
occasion for its debut.

I lay on my bed and took out my fantasy list.

The room had been cleaned up, the poster of Bill
Gates was gone and all the equipment from the photo
shoot had disappeared. It was nice to have my space
back. I was slowly beginning to feel at home. Number

two on the piece of paper was making love in an empty nightclub. I lit a cigarette and took the rolls of bread out of my jacket. I'd also managed to pick up different varieties of cheeses on my journey.

I browsed through the jobs section in a local paper. I underlined a vacancy for a warehouse man, the hours were 7pm to 7am, the money would do. I laid the rest of the paper out on the floor, dabbed a brush in some polish and brought a shine up on my shoes.

Bones popped his head around the door. I hid the cigarette behind my back.

'Me and Froggy are going to a party tonight.'

'You think he's still going to ride shotgun after the way you spoke to him?'

'You wanna hear how he talks to me. It will be alright. I find him or he'll turn up. I'll give him a dong on his moby. I know how to deal with him. So what are you saying? The brothers of the R are having a launch party for their album. You coming?' he asked, holding CDs, a syquest, the Nokia phone and diskettes in his hand. 'It's going to be a big night. Jurassic. Strictly for the bleachers. I did the backdrops and computer animations. We're gonna go out and break some glasses later at some posh restaurant.'

'What for?'

'Froggy says it's good PR.'

'You still on the hellraising tip?'

'The punters will pick up the paper tomorrow and it will say 'Bones loses it in a club'. Then the punters will think Bones? Let's go to his club, let's buy a print of his painting or a Screen Saver.'

'But bad PR can kill you.'

'Yeah, yeah, yeah, yeah.'

'I ain't going nowhere till tomorrow night, star. It's Friday the 13th. You shouldn't be out tonight, you should stay in your yard. You get me?'

'Rebbish, not Rubbish. Rebbish. I don't believe in that foolishness,' he said in a breezy manner.

'A'right, you guys take a drive down South London. I bet all the ruff necks will be inside their gates drinking and chatting, they're gonna come out the next day to see if everybody is alright.'

Bones dismissed me with a gentle wave of the hand. 'So what are you gonna do, go round by Mum's?'

'No. Sleep.'

'Don't sleep, it cuts down your life. Trust me. I thought you were a fully paid up member of the Don't Sleep Ravers?'

'Bones. You know you're making all this money now? What if somebody did you wrong in the past? What if I did you wrong, would you forgive me or would you hold it against me?'

'I'd forgive you. No one is perfect, the only time you're perfect is when you're dead. If you kept fucking with me over and over again, I'd just keep out of your way. I wouldn't want you around me,' he said. 'Are you asking me that because I'm a Scorpio? Do you think I've got a sting in my tail?'

'No. I'm just curious.'

'Did you know that the Scorpion is the only animal that commits suicide. That intentionally kills itself if it is trapped?'

'No.'

'Well it does. It stings itself to death. It would rather that than let something control it,' said Bones, winking at me. He shut the door firmly and left me to mull over his words.

I slipped the shoes onto my feet, put the cigarette between my lips and walked slowly around the room.

I picked up pace and eventually started running. Old habits die hard.

> *It doesn't really matter at all*
> *really doesn't matter at all if you fall*
> *get up and have a ball.*

S I D E

*Deeper love. Deeper love. Deeper love.*

**Caption: Saturday 6pm**

*Deeper love. Deeper love. Deeper love.*

The breeze was cool. I'd slept through the day and now I felt fully charged. McNicholas, a firm of building contractors, had their vans parked on the same side of the road as the Karmann Ghia. Labourers were hard at work digging up the other side and laying pipes for a cable company. I asked the foreman if he had any work going. He said he might have two weeks of work coming up soon. His thick accent told me he was Irish. I inquired about the pay. He told me that it was £300 a week. Not bad, I thought, but the work looked hard. If push came to shove I was ready to do it. The foreman wrote down my details.

I took a letter out of my pocket and walked over to the Karmann Ghia.

Bones was sitting in the passenger seat eating a bagel. Music pumped. He flicked through *Wired* magazine. An Apple laptop computer with a PCMCIA card was on the dashboard. Bones connected his NOKIA 2110 phone to it. He started typing. I sat on the bonnet and laughed as I read the letter.

I glanced at Bones. 'What are you doing?' I asked. 'Can you still communicate with people out here? You don't have to be at home?'

Bones stuck his head out of the window. 'It's all about access. Having multiple access points. 'I'm replying to my email. Some kids in Manchester are interested in what I'm doing. Want me to give them some advice. I'm getting out of paper based communication. There are so many Internet Cafés springing up around the globe, soon I won't even need my laptop to access my various accounts. Wherever I am in the world I'll just pop into a café and move my information smoothly over the Net. I'll be invisible. Cloaked.' He pushed his lips in the direction of my letter. 'You been back a day an you've already got snail mail?'

'Some crazy girl.'

It wasn't a girl who had sent me the letter, it was the one that I'd posted in Holborn. I couldn't bear the thought of coming home and not getting any letters. In prison that was the worst feeling, to see other inmates opening and reading letters when you hadn't received one for months, or those you had got were from people you hadn't wanted to hear from. At least by posting letters to myself, I gave Bones the impression that there were other people out there who wanted me, who wanted to communicate with me, who were writing to me even though they thought I was still in prison. Six more letters were due to arrive the next day.

'How's the woman situation?' asked Bones. 'Is

there anyone you're going to look up now you're out?'

I crammed the letter into my back pocket, opened the door and sat in the driver's seat. 'Do you think I was too hard on Froggy yesterday?' I didn't feel like answering the question about women so I just changed the subject. I was good at that.

'Nah. It was my fault, I shouldn't have let him stay in your room.' Bones put the magazine in the glove compartment. He scribbled some names and numbers into his ideas book. 'We ain't in our late teens any more, with a room and a bed that never got any fresh air,' Bones said, softly.

The memories came flooding back. 'Nineteen Seymour Street, we all chipped in to pay the rent.'

'We had that brotherly love. English boys, English black boys, they don't go on with that nowadays.'

'They don't wanna sleep in the same bed with their spar because they feel it's some gay business.'

Bones chuckled. 'Sometimes when I came back to the room, you or Froggy would be there with your honey and I couldn't hold the bed. Even though I was dog tired, respect was due and I had to sleep on the floor.'

'Even clothes. I'd come back and you'd be wearing my trousers. You'd go to a dance, rock your baby and come in my trousers. I'd go mad because you couldn't afford the dry cleaning bill,' I said.

We laughed.

'That's how close we were,' said Bones.

I was just about to get out of the car when Bones held my arm. 'Are you carrying heat?' His voice was quiet and calm.

'No.'

Bones let my arm go. 'Froggy's still with Willow. Does he know what's going on?'

'Maybe.'

'I'm just finishing off some work on the computer. Tell Froggy I'll be down in a sec. I hope he hasn't spent all my dollars.'

'You won't have much left. You know what Willow is like.'

'Yeah. The tax man.'

I chuckled.

Bones and Froggy had gone to the brothers of the R jam the previous night and now they were tight again, the argument was forgotten, everything had been smoothed over.

*Deeper love. Deeper love. Deeper love.*
*It's a kinda of magic. It's a kinda of magic.*

S I D E

There was a long queue outside a gay drinking club called Spank.

*It's a real kinda of magic.*

A punter was sniffing poppers, getting ready for the House and Garage beats. I scratched the side of my jaw and eyed the crowd.

*It's a real kinda of magic.*

That was the one thing that had really changed in Zone 1 since I'd been inside, there were now more gay clubs. The pink pound was getting stronger and they were obviously paying outrageous rents, but they were bringing style to their venues.

*It's a real kinda of magic.*

They'd moved on from clubs like Trade in the Turnmills area of London, and Queer Nation in Covent Garden, and were now basically spreading the will of gays. They weren't opening businesses primarily to make money, because from my experience the people who opened these businesses already had money, the pink pound had a lot of clout ... Instead, they were just creating a community where they would not feel intimidated by people who were anti-gay or not gay.

*It's a real kinda of magic.*

But that was the thing about Zone 1. To actually survive you had to be, you had to get, you had to reach a point of being nearly international, because if you lived in Zone 6 and you didn't move out of Zone 6 the only mentality you'd have was Zone 6. Whenever I was in Zone 1, I knew I was going to meet people who came from Zone 6, people who came from Zone

3, people who came from Zone 2, people who came from all over the world. And that helped me to become a refined person. That's not to say people from all parts of the world didn't go to Zone 3 or Zone 6, or wherever. But they went to Zone 1 with a certain kind of criteria, they went to Zone 1 to let off, to be creative, to be indulgent. So the people who hung out in Zone 1 regularly, like Willow, Yani and myself, had a different mentality from those who lived in suburbia. We were Zone 1 guys, West End guys, and we dressed in stylish, name brand clothes. We were nice and friendly, but we would still steal your money, because a fool with money is not supposed to have any.

*Brighter days, brighter days.*
*Brighter days, brighter days.*

I walked past Spank. A bubbly character whom I recognised as Patrick Lillie was on the door. Bones had done business with him in the past, Patrick was good at PR and early doors, he'd shown Bones a lot of the pitfalls that were lying in wait. The thing that stood out in my mind was that he had told Bones that, whatever happened, he shouldn't become a media whore.

*I'm trapped. I feel like a man in a cage.*

Patrick shook my hand and I moved easily down the road. A junkie in an alleyway was chasing the dragon, smack was laid out on aluminium foil, he'd made an inhaler and was sucking in the fumes as the hot, liquid brown dot ran away from him.

I entered Willow's smoke-filled gambling club. I was a little apprehensive. Willow had broken my sleep. He'd belled me up in the afternoon, saying that I still owed him a favour from back in the day, and now it was pay-back time. He didn't give a shit that I had just stepped out of prison.

S I D E 29

Froggy was enjoying a game of Kaluki in the corner of the room, being loud and boisterous as usual. He winked at me and raised a fist full of twenty pound notes. His camcorder was on the table.

Yani and a group of people were sitting around a poker table, drinking and smoking. Yani's face was tight with concentration, he lifted his eyes momentarily from his cards and winked at me. He was having a good day. Some of the players looked like they were ready for a two or three day session. They could have been lawyers, doctors, anything. They would most probably creep out early Monday morning, go home and get a few hours' kip before they went to the office. And then, when they got to the office, they would become Mr So 'n' So. But down in the gambling club they were just plain old Alfie and they liked being Alfie.

I recognised one of the guys at the poker table. He was my local butcher, losing a lot of money. He turned and looked at Yani and said, 'All I've got to do is put another two pence on every pound of beef, that will sort the situation out.'

Yani looked across the table at one of the Alfie characters. 'What you do?' he asked, with a dead-pan look.

Alfie was dressed in a pin-striped suit, expensive shoes, a tie, and he had a nice watch. He stirred his orange juice with the arm of his spectacles. 'I'm an accountant,' he replied in a very posh voice.

Yani grunted and said. 'Oh alright. You're an accountant. I've two grand of your money lying in front of me, you have more money on you? Another two grand?'

'No.'

'But you're an accountant. What do you mean you don't have another two grand on you? So what you counting then, fucking flies?'

A roar of laughter leapt up from the table.

Alfie felt really small, his face went as red as a beetroot. He was obviously new to Zone 1, because that was the thing about Zone 1. You never told another person who you were. They made that decision. When Alfie was out in the street he could say shit like, 'Excuse me, do you know who I am? I'm actually an accountant.' In the gambling club we had our own status, the status was actually *you* – and that was what Yani was trying to show Alfie as he took his money.

The gambling club was not a place for schoolboys, it was a place for men filling their egos. Willow had made a lot of money from running the club, all types of people dropped in there from time to time. Personally I felt it was a blessing to pass through there, because passing through there showed me what the bottom of a person's shoes was all about. The people in there were all the product of a fuck, and sometimes the fuck wasn't any good but they were still there. Willow was respected in the diverse Zone 1 community. No one grumbled when he took his ten per cent, he was taking the risk. If the police raided the club, if they threw a spanner in the works because they wanted to show they were maintaining law and order, to make it look official that the club was illegal, Willow would be the first to go down. The way he looked at it was that he could only be illegal if he was convicted. 'People weren't born with convictions, they were given them,' he often reminded me.

The people who frequented his club ran it and Willow was there to keep them happy and to take their money. He made them feel good by creating an atmosphere. Everybody looked upon him as the proprietor of the place but they ran the club, it was theirs for those hours, and they respected Willow enough to run it efficiently. That meant if an outsider came in and wanted to indulge in any nonsense the people would just throw him out. That was the sort of attitude Willow cultivated. It was the psychology of respect.

Willow greeted me with a warm smile. He beckoned

a high yellow woman with purple highlights in her hair and chunky gold earrings over to join us. She leaned against the door, took off her sunglasses, her left eye was swollen. She put her thumbs in the hooks of her jeans.

Willow placed a gun on the table, she reached for it. I stopped her. Willow produced a Stanley knife.

Bones came into the club. He exchanged smiles with Froggy, stuffed his ideas book in his jacket, went straight over to the bar, placed his laptop on the counter and ordered a drink. There was something in his eyes that told me he was not happy with me.

S I D E  30

*I'm superbad with my bad self.*

The Karmann Ghia responded to my touch. I eased my foot off the clutch. The power in the engine was just too much.

*I'm superbad with my bad self.*

The purple-haired woman was sitting in the passenger seat. She handed me an envelope full of money. I could almost taste the honey. She was wearing Escape by CK, the fragrance made me feel sick. It reminded me of a woman in my past who had played a cheap trick.

I glanced at my watch. 'What time you got?'

A packet of salt was resting in her lap.

She raised her wrist. 'Seven on the dot.'

'It's got to be all over in five minutes,' I said sharply.

S I D E  31

*Shaft! John Shaft!*

I slipped on some black gloves, got out of the car and climbed over a six foot wall. I moved through a couple of back gardens until I reached a Gothic-looking house.

The lights were off downstairs. I was going to use a glass cutter to enter the premises, when I saw there was a window half open on the second level, a blue light and music were shooting from the room.

*Wicked, wicked.*

I decided to climb up the drainpipe. It was strong, no rust. I moved carefully, a step and a hand at a time, just like a cat. My nerves twanged like overtuned guitar strings. It had been a long time since I'd carried out a hit and I didn't want to be doing this one. But I had to pay my debt. I wondered how it would all turn out. I shook my head. There was no way I was going to allow the shadowy cloak of doubt to enter my mind. The music was pounding, samples were jumping all over the gaff. The wall was patchy, bad paint work, my rubber-soles slipped a couple of times, but I was a pro-fessional. I just kept getting closer to the blue light. I eventually got my eyes over the sill and looked through the curtains. A guy and a girl were heavy-petting on a sofa. They were both black. It was a beautiful pad, one of them was rich. The flat had the sort of carpets on the floor that made you want to take your shoes off.

*Booyaka, booyaka.*

A spliff lay in an ashtray. The girl had thin long plaits. They were kissing. Her dress was up over her waist. Her knickers were to one side. She was moving to the music. He was sucking her breasts tenderly and getting ready to rinse it.

*Invincible, original, sensational,*
*wicked, wicked.*

She slid her tongue into his ear.

*Bow, Bow.*

The man eased the action down and picked up a glass pipe. He filled the base with champagne and put a rock into the little mould that was designed to hold it. The woman's eyes lit up. She sat bolt upright. The man pecked her on the lips. He had the pipe, he was the governor. She wasn't going to argue with him because she knew she was next. If there had been another person in the room, then she would have definitely made her position known, because the further down the line you went the weaker the power of the rock. But tonight was no problem, it was just the two of them. Hell, if she had been the one with the pipe then she would have been in pole position. The man took out a lighter and heated the rock. He blew, pulled and sucked in his cheeks and inhaled. Her eyes were fixed on the rock.

*Leave some for me, leave some for me.*

The greed was in the rock. The man passed her the pipe.

*Ooooh at last. It's mine all mine.*

He picked the spliff out of the ashtray. She took a lick of the rock, eased her knickers down her thighs and impaled herself on his wood. I could see the muscles on her butt contracting and releasing.

*Slip 'n' slide, slip 'n' slide, slip 'n' slide.*

I was about to climb into the room, but there was a

break in the music. I kept still. A cobra waiting to strike. She arched her spine slightly, threw her head back and gritted her teeth. Her thick butt twitched, her body shook. The silence was broken by the sound of her coming, of her moaning. I waited until the music started up again.

*Booyaka, Booyaka.*

I climbed in, unheard. They were hot for each other. I walked quietly across the room. The guy looked up and saw me over her shoulder. He pushed her off. Her head banged against the edge of the sofa. He stood up. It was too late.

*Booyaka, Booyaka.*

I planted my feet, curled up my fist and threw a solid uppercut to his head. Boom! The sound of his teeth crashing together was like a clapperboard. His brain was instantly divorced from his legs and his lights went out. The girl screamed as his body sank to the floor. She tried to run. I kicked the door shut. She knew she was trapped, she was shivering like a frightened animal, a rat, pressed into a corner of the room. Scratching the wallpaper. I could see her erect nipples through her t-shirt. Under the blue light she was drop-dead gorgeous, nice face, good bone structure, she could have been a model. Her body looked like it had a made-in-heaven label attached to it.

She froze, her eyes darkened. She knew why I was there. I picked up the intercom and pressed the buzzer for the door downstairs.

She started begging and saying all this stuff, but I couldn't hear her properly because the music was so loud. She tugged at my clothes and tried to reason with me. She did everything in her power to soften me up. She even took my hand and put it between her hot thighs. I could feel the juicy fruit. The guy had warmed her up real good. I didn't react. I kept focused. Cold like ice. This made her even more terrified. She suddenly switched tack and picked up a glass from a side table and tried to smash it in my face. I caught her hand an inch from my nose. I applied enough pressure to release it from her sweaty grip. I pushed her away from me, to give me some distance. She paced up and down, shouting, swearing, running her fingers through her hair. I walked over to the stereo and cranked up the volume. She went over to a cupboard. I got to it first. There could have been a gun in there.

But no, there were stacks of plug, the designer drug. Lots of them which she offered to me. She ran over to the guy and shook him. He was out for the count, but she continued to shake him nevertheless.

There was a knock at the front door. I looked through the spy hole and saw the purple head; I let her in and took out the Stanley knife. The purple-haired woman grabbed it from me.

The woman made a dash for the window. It was her only escape route. She was nearly out but I dragged her back inside. I put my hand over her mouth, she was kicking and fighting. I took some black tape out of my pocket and wound it around her mouth and the back of her head and threw her onto the bed.

The purple-haired woman ripped the telephone out of the wall, cut the cord into two with the knife. She tied the woman's hands behind her back, then lifted up her skirt. The music was still playing at over hundred sixty beats per minute ...

*Booyaka. Booyaka. Sensational. Wicked.*

*Wicked.*

Tears were streaming down the woman's exquisite face. Her eyes were coated with fear.

The knife glimmered in the light. The tip dug into the woman's buttocks.


S  I  D  E  **32**


A wild scream filled the night.

The Karmann Ghia pulled away at speed, the city lights reflected in the car windscreen. Whichever way you looked at it, the woman would be grateful that we hadn't done her face. She wouldn't be able to shit or piss properly. Every time she moved to sit, she'd feel the stitches. No more G-strings or doggy-style.

I calmly lit a cigarette. I was a little shaken but I held myself together. I was angry at Willow for getting me to do this job.

The purple-haired woman swayed from side to side and clicked her fingers to the music. She laughed as I stopped the car at a zebra crossing for a black guy carrying an eight foot white cross, who raised his hand in thanks.

'Somebody told him a story,' she said, chuckling, 'and he said yeah.'

S I D E **33**

The blond-haired man was still wearing his white Reebok classics, jeans and Ben Sherman shirt, the sign above the sex shop was ultra pink.

> *Girls*
> *Girls*
> *Girls.*

He had a can of beer in his hand, he was full of smiles. 'I ain't got it, Clarkie. I couldn't rustle the money up.

Fuckin hell, it was over two years ago, can't you put it aside?'

I began to breathe uneasily. I was pissed off anyway about the job and his cocky attitude didn't help matters. I didn't open my mouth. I just walked away. I found myself a 7-Eleven and bought a tin of corned beef. I took off my right shoe and sock, my luck was in, I'd put on a long pair. I put the tin of beef in the sock and made my way back to the sex shop. I fired one shot, BOOM! The sock hit him across his face, his nose busted instantly, blood gushed down his shirt.

He stumbled back and said, 'You've lost it! You've lost it.' He eventually got himself together.

'I still want my money,' I said calmly.

He ran upstairs and within fifteen minutes he had my dollars.

I walked around the corner and got back into the Karmann Ghia. The woman smiled as she felt the leather upholstery. 'This is a nice ride. How much did it cost?' she asked.

'I don't know. I've stolen it,' was my tongue in cheek reply.

I was good with my hands. I could have used them and dealt with the geezer with the Ben Sherman, but boxing is for the ring, not for the street. I'd found myself in a street situation and had to deal with that. Because he could have been tooled up, he could have come at me with different things. I mean, if he put his hand in his pocket, he wasn't going to bring out his cock. I had to hit first and hit hard, so he was left in no doubt what the future held if he decided to get silly. It's amazing what you can do with a tin of corned beef or a tin of condensed milk. If the police came along, what was he going to say? What could he say? 'I got hit by a sock, officer,' that was all he could say. 'I got hit by a sock.'

S I D E  34

### Caption: 7.40pm

Willow was standing in the street with Yani when we pulled up. The purple-haired woman jumped out, kissed Willow on the cheek, handed him a bag with the plug and ran into the club.

'Don't run,' said Willow. 'They're gonna think it's a police raid.'

He gave me another envelope of money, then followed the woman inside. I took my shoes off and used a handkerchief to wipe away the blood.

Bones came out of the gambling club. 'Was it a man or woman?'

'A woman,' I replied.

'What did she do wrong?'

'I don't know. I don't ask any questions. All I do know is that I can't do it any more.'

I threw the blood-stained handkerchief into a bin.

'I think you should pay Froggy to get the car cleaned.'

That was Bones' way of saying he didn't want anything to do with violence.

'How can you stop people from being jealous of you?' asked Bones. The question caught me off-guard.

'You can't unless you're a psychiatrist. To want other people's things is sick.'

'Yeah. I suppose you're right. We'll see,' said Bones.

It was then that I saw Oscar, our Mum's younger brother, talking to the hookers lined up in the door-ways. Oscar was something else. He'd been living in England for over forty years but he still chatted like he was in Jam Down. Sometimes even we had trouble understanding him. The fact that he had no teeth in his mouth and refused to wear dentures didn't help matters. I pointed him out to Bones and we sneaked up behind him as he poked his bald, shiny head into a half-open doorway.

*Girls*
*Girls*
***Girls.***

'Watcha gut?' he asked a happy hooker.

'Wot d'ya want?' said the busty cockney female as she hid her lethal weapon behind the yellow door.

'Watcha gut?'

'Wot d'ya want?'

'Watcha gut?'

'Wot d'ya want?'

'Somting ot.'

'How hot?'

'Teamin.'

'Steaming?'

'Yes, dat's wha me seh, teamin.'

'Will Lucy do?'

'No, she tu juicy.'

'Jill?'

'She mek mi ill.'

'ME? Will I do?'

'Yu? Ah ave tu see.'

Uncle Oscar stretched out his hungry hand to sample the goods.

'No, no, no. No touching. Money first.'

'Ow much?'

'How long?' she asked seductively.

'Four hours,' replied Uncle Oscar eagerly.

*Girls*
*Girls*
*Girls.*

The lady's black fingernails beckoned him into her erotica. He was just about to cross the threshold when I tapped him lightly on the shoulder. Uncle Oscar raised his hands in a kung fu style.

'No threesomes, you know the rules, Elijah.'

The scarlet lady shut the door before I could get a good glimpse of her.

'I didn't know your name was Elijah,' said Bones with a cheeky smile.

When Uncle Oscar turned around and saw us he was not amused.

'Yu jus bus mi groove. Yu ave to ave ah code name if yu workin undacova, an Elijah is mine scene,' he said.

*Girls*
*Girls*
*Girls.*


Uncle Oscar moved away from the doorway and the street lamps caught his face. We were surprised to see his lip was badly swollen.

'What happened to you?' asked Bones.

'Can't an ol man relox imself henymore?'

Uncle Oscar quickly did up his donkey jacket.

'Ah did ave ah fight wid ah fella ah work,' said Uncle Oscar. 'Yesterday wuz mi firs day ah work, an ah ad ah fight,' he kissed his teeth. 'So mi jus cum down ere tu lek arf som ot steam, so mi could forget, cause dis is where ah get mi tings.' He pointed a fat finger in our faces. 'Ah don't want nobaddy tu noh bout dis yah place,' he pushed his lips in the direction of the yellow door where the happy hooker had disappeared, cos once dem Jancrows fine hout, deh start bringeen dem frien an fuck up di place. Den ah ave tu fine som where else tu relox. Yu noh ow dem dutti Jancrow stay, dem jus draw breaks an pull chair up tu di table an nah contribute nuttin, deh can't keep nuttin tu demselves. An dat dere place ah mi hideaway. Ah don't want nobaddy fi upset mi happle cart.'

*Girls*
*Girls*
**Girls.**

'Your secret is safe with us,' said Bones. 'So where are you working now, Uncle?'

'Jus down by Hackton Lane,'

'Acton Lane?' I said.

'Yes. Hackton, yu deaf or wha?'

'Mum was trying to get a hold of you yesterday. She was phoning all round town but no one knew where you were. You should give her a call.' said Bones.

'Ah go carl har lateah. Mi nah stay ah mi yard. No one don't noh where me deh. Ah got som serious problems.'

'So you got beaten up?' asked Bones. 'Somebody mash up your mouth.'

Bones wasn't going to let Uncle off the hook that easy.

'Everyting kick arf yestaday wen mi clock een ah eight een di mawin. Mi firs stop wuz di canteen. Yu noh ah don't joke wid mi food.'

Bones nodded.

'Dat's ow di problem start. Ah wuz starvin like Marvin. So ah ad miself tree sausages, two piece ah bacon, tree egg well-don, mushroom, bake bean, ah tomato, two roun ah toas, an ah cup ah tea.'

Uncle Oscar winked at me.

'Ah noh yu might tink ah wuz greedy, but ah grown man need im food. Wen di cashier ring up di till, she jus smile an tek mi moni. She is ah lovely gyal. Claudia Powell is har name, saaf brown eyes, an ah hourglass figure, coffee colour skin, an long, long legs.'

He smiled at Bones. 'Anywhey, so ah walk down aisle affta aisle ah look fi si down, everytime ah go fi si down, one ah di white workers seh, "Dere's somebody sittin dere might."'

Bones and I restrained ourselves from laughing. Uncle Oscar had a way with words. We nodded and made sounds of encouragement to keep him going.

'Now, fi di firs few minute it wuz hall right, but, wen me look pun mi plate an realise mi sausage ah get coal, an me ah walk roun like ah ediot, ah get vex man!' he said, passionately, cos, ah don't tek mi food fi granted. Ah tek it serious. So di firs free seat ah si, me jus si down an start nyam.'

He kissed his teeth and then he scratched his bald head. 'Bones.'

'Yes, Uncle.'

'Clarkie.'

'Yes, Uncle.'

'As di bacon an mushroom lick di back ah mi troat, ah did noh somting wuz rong cos hall ah di black worka dem jus get up an leave di canteen. Claudia jus look pun me an shake her ead, har eye dem look vacant, an dere wuz sweat pun har forrid. Yu noh Tony, don't it?' asked Uncle Oscar.

'The guy you play dominos with in the gambling club?' I said.

'Yes, yes, dat's im. Ah im get me di job,' said Uncle. 'Tony get up an run towad di door. Im wuz shakin like ah leaf an Claudia wuz lost fi words. She look ready tu bahl eye wata.'

Uncle Oscar touched his lip and winced. I could tell from the sour look in his eyes that his pride had been hurt. He looked down at the pavement and bounced the painful words off the cracked concrete.

'So ah wuz een di canteen an hall of ah sudden ah feel ah vice-like grip pun di back ah mi neck. Ah lowa mi fork from mi mout, an slam mi han down pun di table. Di ole canteen jus go quiet . . .

'Ah look down, an si mi breakfas dat ah pay mi big two pounds fah, scatta hall ova di table. Den ah ot burnin feelin ina mi groin mek mi bite mi lip, as di tea dash wey pun mi trousers. Ah gravelly cockney voice seh, "Ah tol yah dere was sombody sittin dere." Di voice wuz cumin from ah yellah, twist an chip up teet, liver-lipped, fish-face, renkin, rasclaatt, Eas-End rent-ah-bwoy. E wuz obviously di baas. E wuz younga dan me but me still hactive. Ah look pun mi bacon ah lie ina pool ah tea pun di floor, den pun im hugly face, ah jus get vex, an roll up mi lef fis an lick im cross im nose bridge.

BLAM!

'Im fly houtta im chair one time, an bounce hoffa di table like ah rubba ball. Blood start POUR from im face.

Im get up hoffa di floor, an as di fucka rush forwad, ah jus spin roun an gi im ah bitch kick.

DUFF!

'Followed by more tump: BIFF!! BOF! BIP, BIP, BOFFFFFF!!!

'Wen im frien si ow fas mi han wuz movin, dem jus dress back. As im ah groan pun di floor, ah dig ina im jeans an tek mi two dollar an buy back mi food. Yu noh dem wey de?' Uncle Oscar shrugged his shoulders proudly. 'Den as if nuttin appen, Tony an hall di black worka dem jus walk back een an start finish dem breakfas. Claudia jus look pun me an smile as ah orda. Tree sausage, two piece ah bacon, tree egg – well don, mushroom, bake bean, ah tomato, two roun ah toas, an TREE CUP ah tea. "Yu is somting else", dat wuz hall she seh tu mi.'

He looked at me and Bones. 'Henywey, ah tek up mi plate an go back ah di seat an start eat. Ah neva look up, but ah could ear im spar dem ah drag im houtta di canteen. Di cleana cum een an clear up di trail ah blood im leave, one lek hout ah bitch scream as she si two yellah teet glimmerin pun de floor. As ah finish mi food, an drink mi laas cup ah tea, di big han ah di canteen clock touch nine. Ah kiss mi teet, cause, it wuz time fi start work. An ol shifty black man walk pass an whispa, "Watch yu back, ah get ah new job ..." Ah'd only bin een di buildin fi arf an hour, an ah man ah tell me "WATCH YU BACK AH GET AH NEW JOB!" Ah mean, ah ad tool een mi bahg ah did want fi unpack. Ah neva bin given di key fi mi locka.

'Down di corridor ah could ear sombaddy ah carl mi name, "WILLIAMS!! WILLIAAAAAMS!!!"

'It wuz di foreman, im burs een di canteen, im red-rimmed swollen eyes magnify by di national ealth glasses im ave arn. Ah short fat man, bald, who obviously ave ah bad tempa. E lead me briskly im hoffice, slammin di door as we reach, im bellow "WILLIAMS, WHAT DO YOU THINK YOU'RE PLAYING AT?" im threatan, rant an shout at me. Ah try fi hexplain my side ah di story, but it wuz no good, ah get ah caution. If e ave fi speak tu mi hagain, fi HENY reason, ah sack.

'Ah fine hout lateah dat day from Claudia dat di man, ooh wuz now een ospital wid concussion, ah broken nose an two teet missin from im mout, wuz im younga breadda. Dat mek me undastan why im neva sack me. Im wuz embrass an shame, it woundna look good, an im couldn't live dat down, if ah lef affta mashin im breadda wid ah jumpin turnin kick tu di troat, so im did want mi fi stay ah Ford till im breadda cum hout. Ah jus tink tu miself, im wuz dyam lucky, ah neva gi im breadda di right han, cos dat woulda sen im clear ah Coventry.

'Lateah dat day ah wuz hinjoyin miself workin pun ah car which wuz passin ovahead pun di production line, wen Tony run up tu me an shout, "Im de ya, im de ya, im ah cum!"

'Now. Ah discova anada ting bout Tony, di man wuz slow een di ead, hall im seh wuz, "Im de ya." E NEVA SEH IM AVE *GUN*, ah im carryin gun, ah even RUN!!! De man jus look me bold een di face an seh "im ah cum".

'Henyhow, di nex ting ah noh, ah feel somting whistle pass mi ead, an buss up di tyre pun di car mi did ah work pun. Tony jus dissappear, ah neva si im hagain. Ah don't really blame im dough, cos hall ah could si, bout twenny yard away, wuz di roun, ollow nostril of ah double-barrel, sawn-arf shotgun ah point ina mi ches. Di foreman breadda return. Im nose wuz spread hout ova im face, im eyes dem black an blue, di gap ah im teet mek im look like ah vampire, an di bastard ah aim di silver bullet ah mi heart! Bwoy, ah run fi mi life, shot ring hout, workers curl up pun di shop floor, ah hide behin dem bench. Ah jump ova bodies an weave een an hout di bench like ah snake. As ah dive unda ah car ah hit mi mout arn di floor. Dat's ow it get like dis. Di car jus cum offa di production line, di ol shifty black man wind down di windough an seh, "AH TOL YU FI GET AH NEW JOB."

'What a time to tell you I told you so,' I said.

'Well that's black people for you,' said Bones.

'Henywey, quick as ah flash, im duck down ina di seat an ah bullet jus shatta di winscreen. Ah tell yu bwoy! Mi roll hout from unda di car, one time, an spring hout trew ah hopen windough, run cross di yard, into di street, trew di traffic, an jump pun ah bus. Dis ah di firs time ah stop run since yestaday. If ah door slam tu ard, ah sombaddy shout tu loud, ah up an awey. Dat's why mi cum down ere tu relox.'

'Come in the gambling club,' said Bones. 'I'll buy you a drink.'

Uncle Oscar thought about it for a second.

'Plus, there is something I want to talk to you about,' added Bones. 'It's private.'

I got the message and walked towards the Karmann Ghia.

'Where are you going?' asked Bones.

'I've got another appointment,' I replied.

'Clarkie, don't be gone all night. I've got to pick up some paintings from Mum's house later, then we're all going to my club.'

# S I D E  35

I got into the Karmann Ghia and sped off. I went home, held a fresh, towelled myself down and put on my yellow suit. The lining was blue silk. I felt like I was stepping into a Rolls Royce. I needed to be in an £80 an hour limo to bring it off, not in Froggy's £8 an hour Karmann Ghia.

I hit the street, posted a few more letters to myself and got back in the car.

*Hopelessly in love. I'm hopelessly in love.*

S I D E **36**

*Hopelessly in love. I'm hopelessly in love.*

Thunder rumbled. The courtroom light flickered. I glanced at my watch it was 8.46pm. Melanie put a file and some loose papers into a briefcase. She had an emblem of a rose pinned to her jacket, black stiletto heels. I was standing by the witness box.

Melanie sniffed hard and used a tissue to wipe her nose. 'I must go and see my allergy doctor. I'm sure I'm eating the wrong things. It affects my sinuses and gives me a headache,' she said, handing me a bottle of vodka.

'Are you sure you want me to open it?' I asked.

Her face was expressionless. 'That's what you're good at. It always eases my headaches.'

I unscrewed the lid. 'I've been given some info that says you wanted to see me go down. I trusted you too much.' I gave her the bottle.

'Whoever told you that is a barefaced liar. As far as I'm concerned there was no conflict of interest and I've won more cases than I've lost.'

'Did you have a drink beforehand?' I asked, feeling uneasy.

'Clarkie, just relax, you're irritating me. I got paid to do a job. I wasn't the judge. I wasn't the jury. The past is eating away at you.'

I suddenly felt short of breath. 'Yeah. Eighteen months in jail.'

She walked over to me and looked me straight in the eye. I could feel her breath. Her hair smelt of honey.

'Things could have been different. I met you first. But you couldn't trust your emotions,' she said.

'I wasn't ready.'

'You never are. You're a denial person.' She frowned. 'I remember the day I first saw you sitting in the police cell. You looked like a sick puppy stranded in a downpour of rain. So sexy. Then later that week I bumped into you shopping in Sainsbury's. I wasn't sure how I was going to feel after eighteen months, but now you're here I am. I'd still fuck you.'

'What did you say?' My voice sounded far away.

'You heard.'

*It's truuuuue, I love yoooooou.*

Melanie lifted up her skirt and seductively adjusted her knickers. They were sexy, playful, cute not trashy.

I could feel my body heat rising. She put a palm behind my neck and pulled me forward towards her warm trembling lips, her active tongue. I twisted, and was able to breathe properly. Her breasts were crushed against mine, my erection was immediate. I could sense the urgency in her body, that she wanted to profit from my months of abstinence. Her fingers slipped into her handbag and she pulled out a condom.

She looked at me sharply. 'Relax,' Melanie said, pulling me down to the ground. She had a butt like a pear. I ripped her knickers off. She gasped. Her skin had a tantalising, faint, indefinable aroma.

*Leaves flutter in the wind*
*Your scent it brings on angels' wings*

*I am yours love without a pause*
*I am yours our warmth shall open doors*
*Think of me*
*Be with me*
*Grow strong like an Oak tree*
*Free, jump, spring like the rolling sea*
*This fragrance is not by chance*
*The joy of love it is meant to enhance.*

S I D E

*Just a little bit*
*Just a little bit*
*Just a little bit of your love.*

I touched Melanie's shoulder. 'Did I hurt you?'

She had a contented smile on her face. 'That wasn't punishment. That was my reward. It was just like having an ice-cream. My headache has gone. Maybe this is the cure. It beats drink.'

'Your reward? I'm confused.'

She laughed, twisted around, sat up. 'Come on, Clarkie, we both know what's going on. It was just sex.' She stretched her hands above her head. 'I've got one set of emotions for you and another for Bones. So have you. You were just taking your revenge on me.' She started putting her clothes on. 'Seventy per cent of divorce cases happen because one partner did something silly, even though they cared about their husband or wife.'

'Well, if that's the way you feel, now we're equal,' I said.

She was confident in her sexuality. Our bodies were striped with light coming from the street lamp outside the window. Déjà vu, just like in my dream.

'You're not equal with me,' said Melanie, putting the vodka bottle to her lips. 'Maybe with Bones, but not with me. If you do things for revenge it doesn't always pay-off. Subliminally, you're getting back at him not me.' She put on her shoes. 'Has Froggy got anything against Bones?'

'Why?'

'I can just sense it. And I think it's rubbing off on you.'

S I D E

*Every time I see yooooooooooou.*
*Feel like I'm in looooooove.*

I drove the Karmann Ghia like a bat out of hell. I threw my fantasy list out of the window. I lit a cigarette and squinted through the smoke.

S I D E

**Caption: 9.34pm**

Police officers had a scrawny white youth up against a wall and were giving him a serious shake down as I entered the gambling club. In the corner, a young attractive woman was kissing an old sick-looking man – a classic example of money talking.

Bones was tapping away at his computer. A spreadsheet was on the screen, and he was inputting information. There were different columns: merchandising, books, films, TV, computer art, sculptures, music, fashion, web divisions, paintings, hammer code, photography, fragrance, licensing, games.

It was showing the amount of money that he anticipated making in the year ahead, based on his previous year's performance.

Bones nodded his head, jotted down some notes in his ideas book and glanced at his watch.

Willow was sitting next to him, his eager eyes scanning the facts and figures.

Froggy brought drinks over to the table. There was no sign of Uncle Oscar.

Willow took a sip of his beer, lowered his glass and scratched the side of his nose nervously.

'So basically you want to use my paintings as collateral? For your plug operation?' asked Bones.

Willow nodded. 'They're going up in value.'

'Why talk to me? Talk to the art dealer. Buy them from him.'

'I've tried, but he's not selling to everybody. It's just his friends he's dealing with, the people in his network.'

'So what you want to do is buy my paintings from me in drugs money. If you buy them from me everything is in cash,' said Bones, his voice now sounding impersonal and wooden. 'Under the table. You'll get the paintings or the works, sell them, get a cheque from some respectable New York society person and then the money is clean and you'll have a lot more than what you paid in cash.'

'So ah di same pattern as JUGS street style den?' said Froggy. He paused, then went on. 'Yu get DI JUGS from di manufactura, BROK it down een tu wholesale an retail.'

'Exactly,' said Willow. 'Plus you get a cut at both ends Bones, the cash and some of the clean profit.'

I sat down and took a sip of Bones' rum and blackcurrant.

Willow was in his element. It sounded like he'd lit a fuse in his voice and it was about to explode. 'I've got a lot of money parked off. Things are getting bigger for you, your career is taking off, all your work is selling above estimate. I know a couple of other men I could bring in to the operation. Form a consortium. And we use the Net to run things, no one will ever know. When Froggy starts doing his thing then we could branch out. You don't have to stay with that Sloaney who lives on Flood Street.'

Bones shut his computer and glanced at me. He was very controlled. 'How did your appointment go?'

That was his way of telling Willow that he was not interested in his scheme.

Willow shifted in his seat. 'Bones, I don't care how big you become. You're always going to be that little boy from Harvist Road to me.'

I leaned over and whispered in his ear. 'I've got something I want to tell you.'

'Pause, pause, pause,' said Bones, putting a finger to his lips.

S I D E 40

*This is for the players in the hood, making their*
*way earning their pay in an ordinary day.*

Lightning forked out in the night sky. It started to rain.
Bones and I got into the Karmann Ghia.

'I've got something I want to tell you,' said Bones,
tracing his forefinger idly along the computer casing.
'Then you can tell me what you've got to say.' He
switched on the stereo. 'I've downloaded some money.
I've sold the interactive rights to the computer game.
I'm getting involved in a lot of other avenues. The
rise of the Internet, cable and wireless industry has
created a massive vacuum and I'm feeding it,' he said,
as soft music oozed out of the speakers. 'I don't like you
working for Willow. You heard for yourself down there,
you heard what he was trying to get me caught up in.'
He handed me a thick roll of money. 'I hope that will

keep you on the straight and narrow. Jus take it. Take it. Take it. Take it. Take it. There's a lot more where that came from.' There was a sad note in his voice. He looked out on the street.

'It's open season out there, absolute crap is being shunted down cable by the TV providers and they're shipping it out to the market place. I'm fucking it all up in a radical style. Wait till you see my club,' said Bones, proudly. 'It's virtual reality. I'm pumping in other venues from across the globe, it's leading edge in terms of audio-visual, a sensory experience, it's not passive. TV is boring. That's the reason there's a vacuum. The real world is a better window, especially at night, that's when I come alive.'

As I held the money, images of Melanie flashed through my mind. Sprawled across the table, her face flushed, on the floor on her hands and knees.

I reached for the stereo and turned the music up. At the back of my mind I wanted to get away, but Bones' words were hypnotising me.

'They interviewed these kids in America and asked them "Who is Elvis?" Do you know what the kids said?' asked Bones. 'The kids said, "I don't know".' He chuckled. 'There's a whole new generation out there saying all this old stuff is irrelevant, where is the new stuff?' The tone of his voice got more serious. 'I've never voted in my life, I don't identify with any of the parties. You know, people on the underground have done more to change things and created better industries than some of those politicians.' He leaned back in his chair. 'My street credibility is my currency. Everything runs on credit. That's the only thing Melanie doesn't understand about me,' he said, staring at me.

Bones was a man on a mission, he was at the front end of it all. He was in the right place at the right time but he was deserving. There was something in his personality that people found uncomfortable, the only way I can describe it is like an earthquake, a fire or a tornado. They felt something bigger was threatening them. Technology was helping him do more complicated things quickly and he loved that. His work was intuitive not linear, it was serious but not sterile. The people who worked a regular 9 to 5 for corporate companies picked up their pay cheque at the end of the month. If Bones didn't sell paintings in the early days he didn't eat and he had to be original to survive.

'I've helped to make Arthur D Clarke jeans the

most stylish thing to wear. Do you know how I did that?'

I shook my head in the negative

'By putting together a web site that just smashed Levis and Diesel.' He showed his teeth in a loveable smile. 'Advertising companies are dropping like flies. What the corporates are competing for is the commodification of the digital youth culture, fashion and street. Is that above your head?'

'No.' I didn't really understand a word he was saying, but I was glad he was sounding off; it gave me more time, it made it easier to prepare myself for the ugly confession.

'I've got a big handle on that,' said Bones. I just get out of my bed and do my thing. Three worlds have collided. There was a bang and a smash, there's all this stuff taking place, fragments are flying off in different directions. I'm in the zone. I feel as if I can touch, kiss, caress the future.'

*I've got no time for your silly games.*

When he said that I suddenly saw another flash of Melanie and decided I had to tell him. It was going to be painful for both of us. I felt as if I was strapped into an electric chair. I shifted and got myself ready for the jolt of electricity. I was scared, wrestling with myself, the expression on my face was giving the game away, but he didn't see it. I opened my mouth, my stomach tightened, I was ready for the outcome.

Bones took an exquisite diamond ring out of his pocket and passed it to me. I stiffened.

'Tell me what you think of this. It's for Melanie. I'm going to ask her to marry me.'

A soft R 'n' B song pumped out of the speakers.

'It's real special,' I said, trying to keep my voice under control. I'd messed up big time. I felt guilty.

## What's it all about this crazy love?

'This is our favourite tune. It was playing on our first date.' He lifted his shoulders, like a bird ready to fly away. 'We were in this restaurant on a boat, talking about trust, loyalty, commitment.'

'What did you say about trust?'

We looked at each other. Bones had a warm glow on his face. I felt bad.

'I told her a South African proverb. Trust is a little

bird. You must treat it very carefully, because once it flies out of the window it never comes back. What were you going to tell me?'

### *What's it all about this crazy love?*

The rain swept across the street. I didn't say a word. How could I? When I'd walked into the gambling club and saw him sitting there with Willow, I was ready to blame the girl, yeah I was going to blame Melanie. He was my brother, Melanie meant nothing to me. I was sure I could persuade him to my way of thinking, he'd be hurt but he'd eventually forgive me because I was closer to him. But the ring changed things. It was different. I mean, if I told him, from that point on if I saw Bones in woe and worries, I'd be thinking that it was because of me.

### *What's it all about this crazy love?*

Bones' phone rang, he glanced at his digital watch. '... I'll be there in ten minutes,' he said, talking into the phone. '... Are the people I need to meet there? Yeah he's with me. A'right I'm out.' He smiled and put the phone away. 'Let's get Froggy and get outta here, we're running late. I've got to pick up a painting and some disks from Mum's new house.'

'I don't feel like going to Chameleon. I jus wanna get to my bed.'

Bones squeezed my arm affectionately. 'OK. Forget the rave, but you haven't even seen Mum yet, or her new gates.'

'I spoke to her on the phone this morning.'

'It's not the same.'

*Oh but I'm afraid I caught you in a lie.*

S I D E

### Caption: 9.53 pm

The big moon floated in the night sky, casting a brilliant white light on the trees and the detached houses. Froggy parked the Karmann Ghia. We all got out.

Bones pointed to a white house. Marble pillars

framed the front door, a light was on in an upstairs window. 'That's it, that's Mum's new place.'

'Nice pad,' I said, sauntering down the road. 'It's not too far from the old place. And not too upmarket to make everybody jealous.'

'It's perfect for them. It's got this great cellar.'

I wanted to get the incident with Melanie out of my head so I changed the subject. 'Bones, I want to set myself up training fighters, and maybe go on an evening course to learn how to repair cars. That way I'll have two businesses. Will you help me set it up, invest some money? I know you've given me some already, but if I could have a little more I could really stand on my feet.'

'Put it down on paper, get a plan. Then I'll look at it.'

He was so matter of fact in his delivery that it almost sounded rude.

Froggy cut his eye at me, nodded his head and walked up the path holding his SuperVHS camera. It was like he was telling me that it was my turn to deal with Bones' new attitude to life.

*You never know what you've got till it's gone.*
*You never know what you've got till it's gone.*

S I D E **42**

Bones pushed open the living room door. It was dark.
Froggy and I were a pace behind him.

A flashlight popped.

A loud cheer went up.

Bones flicked the light switch.

I turned to run.

Froggy grabbed my arm.

The room was packed with friends and family.

They all shouted 'Surprise!!'

A DJ put the needle on a record. A jazzy beat flowed.
Bones smiled. The guests clapped.

I looked at Bones. He'd set me up like a real
professional. 'I'm gonna kill you,' I said.

Froggy put his camcorder to his eyes and started
filming the proceedings.

My Mum and Dad hugged me. Their warm bodies felt
good against my cold heart. An oil painting of Bones

and me was hanging on the wall. A period when we were happy.

'Welcome home, son,' said Mum, wiping tears from her eyes. 'I feel like dancin arn top ah di table.'

Dad was dumb, so he used sign language to communicate his joy to me. As I watched Dad's sentences materialise in the air, there was a constriction in my chest that made breathing difficult.

Melanie looked splendid in a red crushed velvet dress. She kissed Bones on the lips and me on the cheeks. She was holding a glass of vodka in one hand and a bottle of beer in the other and she had a brooding expression in her eyes.

Froggy's camcorder was pointing at me as guests came over and greeted me. Uncle Oscar raised a glass. He was wearing the same clothes I'd seen him in earlier so I put two and two together – my surprise party was what Bones and he had been talking about privately. He was standing next to Mrs Birchfield, an obeah woman.

Bones gestured to the DJ to lower the music. He cleared his throat. 'I just want to say a couple of words. Clarkie, we all missed you and I want to thank you for stepping in when I was getting my butt kicked and taking the rap.'

I was touched, but deep down somewhere inside me I felt sick. I wanted to come clean but I would have been crazy to give myself up now. I had to wait and that was the most agonising part. When would the right time come?

'I know you had to pay the price for my mistake,' continued Bones. 'But I want you to know that I love you, even though you're mad at me for not coming to see you as much as I should have.'

Bones came over and hugged me. He loved me and he meant it. Everybody clapped.

Mum and Dad joined in the embrace.

'Stay in di neighbourhood fi ah while,' said Mum. 'Don't follow Bones an Froggy an travel tu far behin God's back.'

'OK, Mum. I've got the message. I won't go to South London.'

She placed a tender hand on my cheek. 'If dere is henyting yu want tu talk about, my door is hopen. Yu los ah likkle weight but ah soon get yu back een shape. Yu still smell good, dough.'

'I like your dress, the flowers are nice,' I said.

'I've ad it fi five years.'

'It's still working,' I said, praying that Mum wouldn't take this occasion to make a speech and let out all my baby secrets.

She held my hand softly and pulled me closer to her. 'Ah noh dere wuz ah time wen yu ah grow up wen yu thought ah didn't like yu much.'

'That's not true.'

'Gimme ah piece ah yu ears fi ah secon.'

'OK.'

'Yu thought Bones wuz my favourite an dat ah wuz halways down arn yu ead. But dat wuz because ah did want di bes fi yu. Do yu undastan dat?'

'Yes, Mum.'

'Gimme ah hug den.'

*Booty call, booty call, booty call.*
*It's a booty call.*

Bones tapped a champagne glass with a spoon to get attention. 'While everybody is here,' he took out the diamond-studded ring, which glinted in the light, 'Melanie, this is for you. For the lady I love.'

*I'm in need of love,*
*My baby's in need of love.*

Melanie's eyes lit up like a Christmas tree. It was fear. She was trapped. There was no way she could have run out of the room; that would have caused too much embarrassment. So she had to go along with it all. Bones slipped the ring onto her finger. I smiled, trying not to appear too stunned.

*I'm in need of love.*
*My baby's in need of love.*

'Oh, my God. 'It's beautiful,' said Melanie, nervously.

Bones handed her a bunch of red roses and kissed her. She showed everyone her ring.

Froggy leaned over to me and grinned ruefully. 'E LEK har lead im by di nose like Pinnochio.'

'Cos they jus lead you by the dick,' I said, turning hot then cold.

I noticed Pauline, the woman I'd met at Howard and Shirley's restaurant, standing in the room. She was wearing a divine ankle-length green dress, matching earrings and watch, her hair was shoulder length. She smiled at me. She was an oasis.

Froggy's eyes were on Melanie. 'She's one APPY BUNNY, looks so appy she could cry.'

Bones put his arm around Melanie's waist. 'We haven't decided the date for the wedding yet. There's food, drink, music so everybody jus let loose and be happy. And later the party continues at my club, Chameleon.'

Bones led Melanie to the middle of the floor and put his arms around her. The DJ played a slow R 'n' B tune. Bones pulled her close to him as they danced. He only had eyes for her, he was getting it on, the feeling was strong. I felt wrong, the lyrics in the song made things worse.

*Kiss me thrill me but don't misunderstand me.*

The rhythm was floating above their heads. My heart was carrying a heavy curse, it didn't belong in my body, it should have been buried in a dark, out of the way cemetery.

*Kiss me thrill me but don't misunderstand me.*

Couples began to fill the dance floor.

Vanessa, an ex-girlfriend of mine, asked me to dance. As I was wrapped up in her arms my mind drifted back to the good times Vanessa and I'd had. Sometimes she'd bell me in the morning and start talking dirty, that's how she got horny.

*... I just wanted to talk to you, Clarkie. Shall I come over? Or are you going to come by me? I want to see you, I'm moist thinking about you. Tell me what you're going to DO to ME? Are you going to kiss me all over? Bite my nipples? Cover me in honey? My nipples are so hard they look like bullets ... Clarkie, you should feel them.*

I shook off the memories and came to my senses. I felt eyes on me, they belonged to Melanie. I exchanged a nervous smile with her, her eyes couldn't hide how she felt. Bones slipped his hands a little tighter around her waist, he smiled too and looked over at me. I caught Froggy staring at me. He turned his head away quickly. And that's when the paranoia set in, it spread like cancer and I knew I had to bust the set.

*Tonight we'll video our love show,*
*we'll do it nice and slow till our juices flow.*

When the record finished Bones pecked Melanie on the lips, then approached me.

'Bro, can I talk to you in private?' He stared at me hard.

'Yeah, sure,' I said, letting Vanessa go. The relationship had been good while it lasted, but it wasn't one I wanted back.

Mum tapped me on the shoulder. Pauline was at her side. 'Pauline tells me yu've halready met.'

'Briefly,' I replied.

'Good, den yu'll be able tu help har.'

Mum turned to talk to another guest. Bones raised his eyebrows and spread out his arms, indicating that he was ready.

Pauline fiddled with her earring. 'I don't want to take up too much ...'

I cut her short. 'This is not the right time. I'll catch up with you later.'

I walked off with Bones. She looked dumbfounded. I overheard Froggy talking to her in my slipstream.

'Raw. Clarkie's R.A.W. Raw. Is like deh PEEL im

hoffa wall like ah fungus.' His tone was sly. 'DERE'S no controllin im.'

'I don't need you feeding me information,' replied Pauline.

'Well, EXCUUUUUUSE me,' said Froggy, taken aback.

S I D E  **43**

The cellar had been converted into a studio.

'How many paintings are down here?'

'Over three hundred,' said Bones. 'Plus hundreds of computer files on the hard disk. I've got my own Deadmeat web site, which is linked up to Chameleon. I'm making everything interactive. Hunter doesn't know this exists. I told you it's all about having multiple access points.'

I glanced at a bank of screens and a machine that looked real expensive. 'What's that?'

I was killing time. He was the one who wanted to speak to me, he was making my job easier. If he asked me the million dollar question, I only had to say yes, and accept the punishment. I didn't have to find my own words.

Bones went over and kissed the machine. 'An Avid, top of the range, it does standard editing as well as 3D effects including film, wipes, dissolves, textures, wraps, EDLs, reverse neg and colour correction. I can shoot my own film, cut it myself, sell it on the street or plonk it on my site and distribute it through the world-wide web. Multi-media is everything into everything. It's like having my own TV station or film studio. I can put in ads, anything.' He ran his fingers tenderly over the keyboard, his eyes alert. 'What did you wanna talk to me about? You went all quiet in the car. It must have been important or you wouldn't have brought it up. I know that much about you.'

'Women. Your woman. Melanie.'

I'd finally found the strength.

'You think I'm moving too fast, don't you?' His voice was sharp. 'Look at this, bro. This is it – my masterpiece. Close your eyes.'

'I hate surprises.' This was not the way I wanted the conversation to go.

'Each surprise is only once, it can only have an impact once. So shut your eyes. Come on.'

I did as I was told

'Open your eyes.'

Bones had unveiled a large object in the corner of the room. A nude marble statue of Melanie was standing in front of me. It was sexually frank. The face evoked a calm mood, the profile tremulous, it was a deep psychological study. A bunch of roses and a gold plaque were at her feet, the plaque read, 'Keep Off The Grass'. I felt a hostility to the statue in the rigid silence.

'How long did this take?'

'Over a year,' said Bones, sniffing the damp air. 'I didn't carve the marble. Well, I started it and then I got Froggy and a couple of my technicians to execute it. It is truly flesh. You would think I moulded it by kisses and caresses,' he said, placing his hand on the statue's cheek. 'I almost expect to find it warm. Clarkie, touch it. It's not the real thing.'

I touched the statue's shoulder. Bones smiled. I heard soft footsteps behind me. I turned. Melanie was standing at the top of the stairs. Her small eyes glittered. Bones had not heard her. He was too engrossed in his work of art.

'See? She's warm, Clarkie. I kept her inside of myself. I thought of Melanie, only of Melanie, and she just emerged from the stone, shaped by my passion.'

Bones sprinkled rose petals at her feet and began to recite a poem, his tone tender: 'Sunlight washes green meadows. Rising bread, the smell of sweet dough. Eagles wings spread apart, high above red mountains. Waterfalls, and there you are washing your body in a silver fountain. Heart a beating. Feeling. Mind a dreaming, reeling. In my secret garden. Love flies like a dove, in my hand it lands. Warm, red, hot, passionate, strong and definite. Keep Off The Grass. Let's touch the future and not live in the past. Keep off the grass. Let our love last.'

I looked over my shoulder Melanie was gone.

S I D E **44**

*Joy and pain*
*sunshine and rain*
*are not the same.*

Froggy was wiping his trousers with a handkerchief
and cussing bad words under his breath. I shut the
cellar door. The passage was ram up with people
talking, eating curry mutton and rice, Jamaican patties,
drinking, laughing.

*Joy and pain*
*sunshine and rain*
*are not the same.*

'Ah ATE dat gyal yu si. She so heggs up,' said Froggy,
sucking his teeth. 'She jus ran pas an BOX mi drink

houtta mi han. Look PUN me trousers. Ah SPEN good moni fi dem.'

Mum had the front door open, she looked out into the night and shouted, 'Melanie!'

'She nearly knock di tray AH food Mum ah carry pun di floor,' said Froggy, gaping at me. 'She cum houtta di cella, try fi hopen di bartroom door. SOMBADDY wuz een dere so she EDGE pas everybaddy an run een tu di dark like she si ah DUPPY.'

Uncle Oscar came out of the living room with a plate full of jerk chicken.

Pauline fanned herself with a piece of paper. 'It's really hot in here.'

'Is Froggy's breat,' said Uncle Oscar with a cheeky grin.

'Ah MI hormones,' said Froggy, pinching Pauline's butt as she walked by him.

'Hey!' Pauline spun around, quick as lighting. 'If you ever do that again,' she pushed him in the chest, 'I'm gonna slap you hard. You're too nasty.'

'Why yu NEVA tun di udder cheek?' said Froggy, with a frozen smile on his face. 'Yu is meant tu be ah Christian. Yu AVE DI cross pun yu ches but nuttin arn di hinside. Dat's why yu can't fine no ozband. Yu theifin bitch.'

Pauline stood her ground. I could hear her fight to control her voice. 'I've grown up with men all my life. I'm like a man. 'Your mouth is so loose and horrible. I don't need to listen to your rubbish.' She turned her back on him.

Mum shut the door and approached me. 'What's goin arn? What did Bones seh dis time?'

'I don't know what you're talking about, Mum.'

'Yu still ah protech im?'

'No. But, brothers don't always talk about brothers. Bones didn't . . .'

'Did e hit har?'

Uncle Oscar put his dentures into his mouth, his eyes on Pauline as he chewed a leg of chicken. 'Yu look good yu noh, Pauline. Yu so sexy, yu mek me hot unda mi colla. Yu gripe me belly.' He wiped his mouth with a napkin. 'If yu arks me,' he said, looking at Mum, 'Bones ave tu much moni, is as simple as dat. Im halways een an houtta di bank. Ah can't go near dem places.'

'This is not about money, Uncle. Mum, how many times have I got to tell you? I don't know what's going on.'

Froggy had to put his mouth in it. 'Dere like Romeo an Juliet, HALWAYS ah argue.'

'They were in love,' said Pauline, firmly.

'YU so XTRA,' said Froggy. 'Everybaddy noh wha Melanie like wen she AVE ah drink. She mek TINGS up.' Froggy's eyes met mine. The comment was directed at me.

'Dis is hall goin tu end een tears,' said Mum looking up to the heavens for salvation. 'Lord, wen Pastor James bless dis house ah did arks yu tu mek dis ah appy ome. Please don't forsake me.'

I made my way towards the front door

Mum held Froggy's hand 'Cum wid me son, Bones listens tu yu.'

Froggy took a few paces then stopped. 'Di doctor tell me TIDAE DAT me ave high blood pressure.'

'You're too young.'

'Serious, Mum. It wuz like God wuz talkin trew im. Believe me. Ah gotta WATCH mi diet, keep HOUTTA stressful situations. Ah don't want tu get hinvolved.' Froggy took a large bottle of pills out of his pocket. 'Ah gotta tek dese.'

Mum disappeared into the cellar.

*Joy and pain*
*sunshine and rain*
*are not the same.*

S I D E

## Caption: 11.10pm

A train hurtled over a bridge. Sheets of rain beat down as I ran along the street bawling, 'Melanie, Melanie.'

I stepped into the road. A horn blared, a Rolls Royce skidded to a halt. There was a loud thump as it knocked me to the ground. The driver got out and slammed the door. He had big feet.

I picked myself up. 'I'm alright. It's OK,' I said, brushing the dirt of my wet clothes. 'I'm alright.'

'Fuc you,' he said quickly. He was black and from his accent I could tell he was African. 'I ain't in-te-rest-ed in you, bullock head. If you have den-ted my car I'll kill you. I kill you. I kill you. I've heard a-bout people like you who jump in front of movin vehicles, but you ain't gettin no motherfuckin in-surance from me.'

He got back into the Rolls and drove away.

In the distance I saw Melanie crossing the road at a junction; her shoulders were heaving up and down, she was crying uncontrollably.

'Melanie!' I ran towards her, she started to sprint away from me.

'Go away!' she shouted, as her heels click-clacked on the concrete. 'Leave me alone! Just leave me alone,' she said, tensing up her fists.

I caught up with her. She screamed and pushed me away and continued running. She turned and took a swipe at me, the ring grazing my cheek.

'Just Fuck off! Fuck offff!' she yelled, looking at me out of the corner of her eyes. They were red. They couldn't hide the pain, they matched the darkness of the night.

'You're scaring me,' I said.

'I've got to stop it now.'

'Hold on. You're drunk.'

'To what?'

I pulled her towards me, she rested her head on my shoulder and sobbed. Her face was ashen, her breathing shallow, her hair dripping wet.

'A mess, a crazy mess,' she said, eyeing me. 'It's all wrong. I need a drink to blur everything out. What are we going to do?'

'We?'

The harsh headlights of a car swept around a corner. It was the Karmann Ghia. Melanie and I broke apart. The Karmann Ghia sped up the road and screeched to a halt, tyres smoking.

I gave Melanie a dark look. 'I'll take care of everything tonight. OK?'

'OK.'

Bones jumped out of the car.

Froggy was in the driver's seat.

Bones stretched out his hands in a fatherly manner. 'Baby, baby come here. Come here,' he said, cradling Melanie in his arms. 'Baby it's gonna be alright. Have the headaches come back? Is it a panic attack?' He nodded at me. 'Thanks, Clarkie.'

I paled.

'I feel like I'm breaking apart,' said Melanie. She had her eyes closed, her head dropped to one side, heavy, weak like the neck of a rag doll.

Bones tried to wipe the tears from her eyes. It was pointless because it was raining so hard. But that was the kind of guy he was, a quality person, nothing was too much for him.

'Don't worry I'm here now,' said Bones.

'I can't cope. I don't wanna go back. I. I. I . . .'

'Pause, pause. Then we won't. Come on let's go. It'll be alright, baby.'

'I left my bag with my keys at your house.'

'I've got your spare keys on my ring. Don't worry,' said Bones as he raised his hand and stopped a black cab. 'I'm right here. I wanna know, I gotta know. Am I giving you enough love?'

'Yes. It's got nothing to do with you, it's just me.'

Bones helped her into the cab. 'Kick off your shoes, it'll soothe you.' He was insistently loving. 'I'll massage them for you.'

S I D E **46**

When I got back to the house, Mum and her friends had taken over their own room, where they were playing dominoes and sitting and talking. Mum still had her old gramophone machine, she stacked up ten records:

*Nat King Cole*
*Jim Reeves*
*Kitty Lester*
*Mel Torme*
*Bobby Darren*
*Chubby Checker*
*Percy Sledge*
*Otis Redding*
*John Holt*
*Nina Simone*

That's all she had but that was all the old people needed. They sang and danced along to the music. There were not enough men in the room so Mum was dancing with Mrs Birchfield. Uncle Oscar was holding a bottle of rum; he was laughing and singing along with the song.

Mum shoved him in the back with her elbow. 'Shut up. Yu spoilin di record.'

When the track came to an end all the old people cheered and clapped. Uncle Oscar sat down on a sofa with a friend and the rum started talking.

The rain had stopped. Speakers were wired up in the garden. Food and drink was laid out. The weather wasn't going to get in the way of the party. Dad seasoned the chicken and put the slices on the barbecue. Froggy was in the garage, with some of the men, smoking herbs.

Pauline gave me a piece of paper with her telephone number.

'What are you doing tomorrow?' I asked, slipping her number into my back pocket.

'Going to church. Do you want to come?'

'Nah.'

'So will you help me? Will you talk to the kids at the community centre?'

A salsa beat pounded. I held Pauline's hand and led her to dance. 'Yeah, I don't see why not.'

I reeled her into my arms, froze and looked into her

eyes. She smiled. I squeezed her palm, she responded to my signal. Pauline dipped down elegantly and spun away from me. I confidently led her through some combinations.

Froggy came out of the garage and taped the moves on his camcorder.

Pauline and I were just getting warm when the music stopped abruptly. In the living room I saw Bones with his hand on the CD player. 'Everybody out!' he shouted. 'I said out!'

The guests mumbled amongst themselves. Bones picked up a bottle of whiskey and walked towards the garden. His face was stern.

'Clarkie!' he shouted, walking forcefully towards me.

Mum looked distraught, she was a few paces behind him. I quickly excused myself to Pauline. I felt threatened.

Bones swung around and confronted Mum. 'I want everybody to get out of the garden. The party's over. This is between me and Clarkie.'

Froggy and Mum hastily ushered Pauline and the guests into the house.

'How can a brotherhood dissolve into this?' asked Bones, as tears welled in his eyes.

'That's what I wanted to speak to you about,' I said, gently. 'I tried a couple of times but . . .'

'So you knew that Melanie was sleeping with her boss?'

I was speechless.

Bones took a large gulp of whiskey. 'I feel like I've got hell in my left hand, heaven in my right. The throne is in front of me and the angel of death is standing behind me trying to pull out my soul. If I can't trust you, who the fuck can I trust?'

'I saw them together yesterday.'

It was my get out clause and I went along with it.

'I need some drugs,' said Bones, as he slumped down into a chair, covered his face with his hand and started crying. 'I went back to her flat, why am I going through this? Why me? I was lying on the futon, naked. Melanie had just taken a shower, she came in with a towel wrapped around her.' He wiped the tears from his eyes. 'Clarkie I wish you had told me. I could have done something about it earlier.'

'I tried.'

I kept playing the middle ground. I wasn't sure if

Bones was trying to draw me out into the open. I felt as guilty as hell. I was watching him fall to pieces right in front of my eyes.

'I should have known there was something wrong when I kissed her and she didn't respond like she usually does.' He coughed and patted his pockets, looking for his inhaler. He couldn't find it. 'I asked her what was the matter and she said she didn't feel well. He held my hand tight. 'Clarkie, I need you to see me through this.'

'I'm here.'

'I caressed her breasts, then I slid my hand between her thighs. She said "Don't". She resisted me for a while, then she relaxed and put her hand on my back. She looked real surprised when I asked her if she was on her period.'

'Why did you ask that?'

I had to play like I didn't know a thing.

He whispered intensely in my ear. 'She said she wasn't so I said, "If it's not a Tampax what's this then?"'

'What are you talking about?'

Bones broke down in tears again. 'I . . . I . . . I . . .' he heaved, 'I pulled a condom out of her.'

I knelt down and hugged him. His voice kept breaking up. 'I threw it across the room. Melanie put her head in her hands. I asked who it was? I had a right to do that didn't I, Clarkie?'

'Yeah.'

Bones slowly began to regain his composure. 'I wanted the truth. That was when she told me about her boss. What kind of animal does that?' He drained what was left in the bottle. 'He must have known. He's either stupid or he done it on purpose. It was wedged up in her cervix all the time. It worked its way down when she got wet. I wrenched the ring off her finger and threw it out of the window.'

'Did you hit her?'

'No. I just kicked over the furniture. Mum was right. She said the more successful I got, the more I had to leave room in my heart for a traitor.'

> *Kill the night*
> *The blackness,*
> *The blackness*
> *Kill the night.*

The Karmann Ghia was parked outside Howard and Shirley's Crib. Bones was standing on the street. He opened a can of beer and took a large gulp. There was a six pack on the back seat. A police bird flew low over the buildings, its searchlight beamed down. The interior of the Karmann Ghia was bathed by the harsh light. I'd already been to my gates and changed into my other suit. It was clean and dry.

I was sitting in the passenger seat smoking a cigarette and speaking into Bones' mobile phone. '... I can't hear you! Mum ...' I said, as the deafening sound of the rotating blades echoed above my head. '... Is Pauline still there? I said, is Pauline! Pauline. Is Pauline still there? Tell her I will call her! No! I'll call her. I'll look after him! Bye!'

A man with a swollen face and a black eye walked

past. A woman with a scarf tied around her head leaned out of the window of a housing estate across the street.

'Next time it won't be a fucking tennis racket,' she shouted. 'I'll wait an drop a fucking fridge on your head!'

The police searchlight moved on and the car was thrown back into darkness and silence.

Froggy came out of the restaurant, Bones followed him and got into the car. Froggy slipped two plastic packets of weed into Bones' hand.

'Dat's ARN me,' said Froggy 'Careful wid it. Mine di skunk tweed don't LICK arf yu ead, Dufus.'

Bones picked a magazine off the back seat, tapped some of the weed onto it, took his time and picked out the seeds. 'Let's go to Chameleon,' he said, taking out some Rizlas. 'And Froggy don't chat my business too loud, we're living in the world of boom mikes.'

> *Kill the night*
> *The blackness,*
> *The blackness*
> *Kill the night.*

S I D E **49**

## Caption: 1.37am

There was a long, snaky queue outside the warehouse in South London. A blue neon light read **http.//www. deadmeat.com.chameleon**, shining above the venue like a beacon. Everything was digital, video surveillance cameras were mounted on walls.

The buff security guards wore puffer jackets with the logo Armshouse Inc. They used X-ray sticks to frisk the sea of bodies, their boots were polished. The women security guards looked liked they had the strength and determination to bring down any muthafuckers that got out of order.

A building across the road had scaffolding erected outside, big plastic sheets were hanging down. A twenty-foot Chameleon logo was projected onto it, just like the Batman sign. The funky logo was a vibrant expression of Bones' lifestyle. It stank of music. He'd obviously used a mood board to create it. It was extra raw and super real. Froggy was energised. 'Party people SEH YEAH!'

'Chameleon is a monolithic project,' said Bones, admiring his own work. 'It's backed by sharp-suited Japanese business men. Sony have given us all the latest games, we've even got prototypes to test. In Japan, Sony have bought a string of clubs. They've even set them up in the basement of some of their buildings.'

'Why?' I asked.

'They know what's going on, what the future holds. I'm meant to be going over there next week, because they want to buy British club culture. They want me to set up the same vibe, to encourage their youth to have style, to develop, to create. They know their time of copying is over. They're tired of American popstars and icons. So I'm getting backing from their business community because they're trying to understand us, mainly because we're not retro and we're pumping energy into the future.' He had a sombre look on his face. 'But now with all this Melanie business, I don't know if it's worth it. I'm going to cancel the trip,' he said, throwing a dead joint out of the window.

Cars were parked bumper to bumper.

Froggy began to sing, 'It's party time TUNITE, it's party time TUNITE.' He clicked his fingers and broke into another melody. 'War! What is it good for? Absolutely NUTTIN! Seh it hagain!'

The headlights of the Karmann Ghia framed twenty-four well toned legs. They glistened like golden saxophones, their heels, boots and sneakers playing a gentle tune on the concrete as they walked past us.

Froggy put the SuperVHS camera to his eye and captured the women's images. 'Dem look like dem ah HUNT man. Wow! Whata dress, she might as well be WEARIN scotch tape.'

> *Kill the night*
> *The blackness*
> *Kill the night*
> *The blackness.*

Goldie, a young man who had defiantly put some of his money where his mouth was by coating his teeth in gold, pulled up in a devious black Mercedes with fuck off fat chrome wheels. His tinted window came down and rugged beats boomed out. His brother was sitting next to him and Doc Scott was in the back drinking a can of Red Stripe beer, wearing a black puffer jacket with the Reinforced crew's logo. Doc Scott was a white youth, dark hair, kind face, shy looking. He was awesome behind the decks. He must have just finished playing his set. I felt sorry for the crowd, he must have hurt them real bad.

*Inner city life.*
*I'm jus feelin di pressure.*
*Inner city life.*
*I'm jus feelin di pressure.*
*Inner city life is gettin ah hold of me.*

Goldie was an ex-graffiti artist of the highest order, an intriguing character, originally from Wolverhampton. He was the closest thing the UK had to a US rap star. He'd lived a bit. If you saw him once you'd never forget him.

*Yu need ah likkle drum 'n' bass inya face.*

'Howyadoin' East London,' said Bones, taking a pull of his asthma inhaler.

The expression on Goldie's face was worth a gold bar. That was what he was into, in his mind he was a goldsmith and his job was alchemy. 'Don't fuck with me or me and the Reinforced will rush you,' said Goldie, laughing. His teeth sparkled, the inside of his mouth looked like a disco.

'I'm gonna make some new music. I've got a sound, a frequency that will sell. We should do something together again. I've some anonymatic codes and rides,' said Bones eagerly. 'I'm sick and tired of this Break Dance psychology that is going on with the drum 'n' bass scene,' said Bones, rolling up another big head. 'I'm going to do the music for my Deadmeat game. They're paying street man shit money for the music to computer games, a grand, while them others is getting fat Gs for games like Wipe Out!

'Dem BWOY dere is jokers,' said Froggy. 'Dem don't noh wha fi ARKS for. Wen dem seh ah G, dem seh yeah. Ah di right management dem need.'

'But they're getting bought out and the rest are getting royalties. That was what was happening in that Breakdance film. Did you know Jean Claude Van Damme was in that movie?'

'Don't worry WID im,' said Froggy. 'E's bin smokin ah lot tunite. Is ead is ROCKIN bout ah lot mo dan usual. So Goldie, you ain't stayin fi di competition?'

'No, Boss. Got things to do. I might pop back later.'

'Ah jus hope ah di Japanese version ah Tekkan. Di Henglish version tu slow. It will fuck up me combos. Di trophy AH CUM OME wid me,' said Froggy.

Goldie put his hand to his ear, which meant he would bell Bones later, then sped off. A convoy of cars followed him. He was keeping it real and rolling with the soldiers. Goldie and the Reinforced crew had everything screwed down tight. They dominated the drum 'n' bass scene. They were the forerunners, so if they wanted a jazzy flavour for the summer they kicked that off. If they wanted it dark in the winter everybody else had to follow.

*Inner city life.*
*I'm jus feelin di pressure.*
*Inner city life.*
*I'm jus feelin di pressure.*
*Inner city life is gettin ah hold of me.*

# S I D E  50

*Every star in the sky is so far but it tells
us about universal love.*

Froggy parked the Karmann Ghia and we were just
about to alight when Bones held my hand and said,
'Clarkie I want you to look after this for me.' He gave
me a disk.

'What is it?' I asked.

'It's got the details of the hammer code,' said Bones,
lighting his spliff.

Froggy looked disappointed. 'So wha APPEN? Yu nah
GI it tu me?'

Bones put a reassuring hand on his shoulder. 'Clarkie
is here now.' He glanced at me. 'Looking after that
is like looking after a spare key to the door of a
big mansion house. You got to have Bruce or some
Frederick to understand this, some people are just

dealing with Heinz and 57 varieties, you get me? I've always had Bruce.'

I was puzzled. 'Bruce and Frederick?'

'Foresight,' said Bones.

'It's Forsythe,' I stressed.

'Yeah but you know what I mean. I've got Frederick. Not Heinz, hindsight, some people just come up with 57 varieties after everything is done, and they carry on like they know everything. That's what that code is about, it's full of Frederick.' He sighed. 'The way I'm feeling I don't know what's gonna happen to me. The bottom has just fallen out of my world and I feel a great need to get away from all this.' He snapped his fingers. 'I've decided. I'm going to beat her boss up,' he said, his face clenched like a fist. 'No. Clarkie, I'll pay you to break his fucking legs, kneecap the shit-cunt.'

'The drugs are making your tongue confused,' I said. 'You can't blame the man.'

'Why the fuck not!' he yelled. 'Let's go to Melanie's flat. You can be my witness. I want you to hear everything.'

'Leave it till the morning, we'll do it tomorrow.'

'Promise?'

'Promise.'

Bones put his asthma inhaler to his lips and sucked on it, just the way a baby puts a feeding bottle to its mouth. He was satisfied.

I was petrified.

Froggy listened.

'Maybe the bad things that happen are necessary,' said Bones. 'I needed to taste it. To feel the bitterness. I've hurt people. I don't want to do that any more. The lower I go, everything gets more magnified and I ask myself, "What am I in all of this?" 'Bones coughed. 'My mouth is dry. Ganja mouth. I been smoking too much. Froggy, can I have some of your drink?'

Froggy passed Bones his bottle of Volvic water.

'Life goes ARN,' said Froggy. 'Dere's plenty mo fish een di sea. She's jus anada BRICK een di wall.'

'Just shut up,' said Bones. Shoving the drink back in Froggy's hard.

*Every star in the sky is so far but it tells us about universal love.*

The bald-headed woman with shaved eyebrows who I'd met in the kitchen in my house had been transformed. She was wearing an electric pink rubber suit, and was holding a hand mirror and a clipboard. 'All the people on Bones' guest list this side,' she shouted. 'Everyone else use your credits. There's no pulling rank. I don't care who you are.' She raised the hand mirror to a young man. 'Honey, if you were doing my job, I don't think you'd let anyone into this place looking like that.' From the way she chewed her words and spat them out real fast, I was sure she was into speed. Poor man's Charlie.

A police car drove past in slow motion, the officers' eyes freeze-framing the proceedings. Drug dealers selling plug merged into the shadows and crept behind a brick wall plastered with posters saying 'Wanted Cyber Vigilante. Calling card, a dead white rat. Phone police on (0208)01814503240, URL – http://www. cybervigilante. com Reward: £10,000 for information leading to arrest.'

*Police and thieves in the street.*

Plug was the latest designer drug. It came on small white pieces of paper that you slipped under your tongue so that it could easily be absorbed into the bloodstream. When the paper turned purple, you had the full hit and you were plugged in and your emotional euphoria was amplified. You could get weaker currents by buying papers that turned grey or blue, purple was the top buzz. Ravers hated to be unplugged. It was one of the easiest products to smuggle, so there was a good supply in prison. Plug also came in liquid form broken down with anaesthetic. That was more expensive, the hit was harder and the consequences could be more dangerous, so only the die-hards pursued that line.

*Kill the night.*

As we walked past the growing queue, I noticed Dillinja, a rudebwoy from Brixton, and his sidekick,

Lemon D, smirking to themselves as they watched the cop car. Froggy went over to Dillinja and touched fists with him, a sign of respect. The tunes he made were rough, Froggy liked the fact that he changed direction with every record and opened up new pathways. The super-confident boxer Prince Naseem Hamed and his entourage arrived in a stream of bullet-proof Benzs. I asked him what was the secret of his success.

Prince Naseem Hamed's response was quick and sure. 'Allah.'

*Police and thieves meet in the street.*

An A & R man wearing a Deadmeat/Chameleon bomber jacket left the queue and approached Bones. 'Have you listened to the Daniella track yet?'

'How old is she?' asked Bones.

'Thirty.'

'Thirty! At thirty she should be reminiscing not thinking of making a comeback. Who does she think she is, Tina Turner?'

'No. EARTHA Kitt,' said Froggy chuckling. 'Is bout time Daniella stood aside an lek ah NEX woman trew. Yu get me dough?'

'Will you do the video and album sleeve?' The A&R man looked worried. 'We've got a megabudget.' Froggy nudged Bones. 'Tink major halways TINK major. Look, at di end ah di day, if E'S payin, do it an tek di dollars.'

'That's dark. That means I'm doing one thing an thinking another.'

'Welcome tu di MUSIC business,' said Froggy.

The A & R man was a very determined fellow. 'You guys have heard her demo, what do you think?'

Bones paused for a second. 'Do you want the truth or the barefaced lie?'

The A & R man bit the bottom of his lip.

'You ain't got no Frederick. I could plug in my fax machine, go to the toilet, tape some splish-splash and I'd get a better sound,' said Bones. He turned on his heel and headed towards the club entrance.

The bald-headed woman smiled at Froggy. 'I've been working hard for Bones for a long time. How about talking to him on the downlow. He looks a bit stressed or I'd do it myself. I wanna rise.'

Froggy looked surprised. 'Rise? RISE?' he held his penis. 'DI HONLY rise yu ah go get is DIS.' A group of ravers formed around Froggy. 'Ah can't help YU hout tunite,' said Froggy, loving the attention. 'Di lis is

TIGHT,' he said, giggling foolishly. 'Dat's di wey Bones want it, talk tu im.'

We followed Bones into the club. The security guards parted to let me and Froggy through. Their beady eyes were alert as ravers slipped red vibrocards into machines and eighteen credits were wiped off.

*Police and thieves meet in the street.*

We stepped on the conveyor belt with a crowd of eager ravers.

*Hello this is your captain speaking, the mother ship connection is about to begin, rebirths are applauded. Get ready for take off. Thank you for travelling with Chameleon once again. The temperature on planet Chameleon is rising, the arenas are bursting with energy, the gladiators on the decks eagerly await your arrival, you know the rules, their job is to hurt you. If you have any trouble breathing there are yellow buttons on the walls, press any of these and oxygen masks will pop out, a video steward will then appear on the screen and talk you through the process. Thank you. Enjoy your trip.*

The ravers' faces were flushed with anticipation. Like Alice, they were going through the window into Wonderland. They smiled as they set foot on the orgasmic complex, they'd hit the dreadzone, a wall of sound, every nerve in their body twitched, muscles leapt with excitement. They were ready for the hallucinations, they were ready to escape the confusion and turmoil of their day to day lives. They resisted apathy. They were ready to replace it with drugs, sex and drum 'n' bass.

*It ain't over till it's ooooover.*
*It ain't over till it's ooooover.*

The venue was jam-packed with hot sweaty bods and liquor. Ravers blew whistles and horns. Dancehall wooden speaker boxes were integrated with the state of the art technology to give it a moody feel. A circular bar ran around the main room, with no staff serving, just machines; people tapped in their orders and used their cards to pay. Elevators took VIPs like Dillinja and Lemon D to the lower levels, where the underground vibes made them feel more at home with the Amen beats.

Bones had accomplished the amazing feat of creating a magically enchanting environment, sublime and beatific. The ravers never got old, they just partied like Peter Pan.

Bones shook people's hands and listened to what they had to say. That was the nice thing about him – even in a moment of personal pain, he still made time for everyone. I couldn't imagine him being single, for as long I could remember he'd always been in some sort of relationship.

*It ain't over.*
*It ain't over.*
*It ain't over till it's ooooover.*
*It ain't over.*
*It ain't over.*
*It ain't over till it's ooooover.*

Ibex, a three piece band with two vocalists, were tearing up the main stage like mad dogs; they were foaming at the mouth and delivering beats you could eat. The event was being filmed and relayed across the Net.

*Stormy weather, stormy weather.*

The drummer had a big smile on his face, his eyes were shut and he was rolling with bad intentions, wearing a ski hat sporting the word Pervert. His torso was bare, he had silver earrings in each ear, and pierced nipples. A broken drumstick soared into the air, he quickly plucked another one from a leather bag without losing the juicy speeded-up JB beat.

Ibex were tight. This was their big night.

*Stormy weather, stormy weather.*

The lead singer was bumrushin the show, he was an energetic charismatic performer, in a long Shoalin gown. He sky-dived into the ravers, he seemed to enjoy kicking a couple of them in the head as he screamed out the chorus.

*Stormy weather, stormy weather.*

The drummer shouted.
  There was silence on stage
  Red lights faded up.
  The party people clapped and cheered as Ibex took

their well deserved bows. A couple of vampires were hunched in a corner draining the NRG but Ibex were too strong. Television sets were rigged up around the stage, England versus the United States was being beamed in live from LA.

I pointed to the screen. 'What's all that about?'

'MG, the lead singer, is an England fan,' said Bones. 'He only agreed to do the gig if he could watch the match at the same time. If they don't make it I'm gonna bite pom-pom.'

*The album backwards tells you*
*how to close the gates.*

The Deadmeat/Chameleon merchandising store was buzzing with t-shirts, bags, mugs, water bottles, chains, baseball caps, jackets, postcards. The image was on a badge, pinned to the arm of a soul sister, it was printed on a t-shirt worn by middle-class geeks. It was growing legs, shedding its skin and getting ready to suffocate the world.

The comedy arena was slamming with the country's best stand-up comics and an audience of laughing ravers. There was a kitchen that served a delicious

Caribbean menu. A cinema room was set off to one side, ravers were sitting on big cushions doing plug as they watched a sci-fi Kung Fu movie.

The games room was packed with DJs, MCs and record producers, all limbering up for the Tekken competition or playing Red Alert.

There were computer rooms where ravers surfed the Net.

They logged on to machines around the world, typed in the letters DIR and checked what the machines had on them, they changed directories by typing CD or just got involved with various news groups.

*The computer world can be switched off with the flick of a switch.*

*You don't need a passport to enter countries on the Internet, but we've still got to crack China. They're afraid of it.*

*It has no soul.*

*It is fascist, Una Bomber was right.*

*It is not like you need health, shelter and the Internet.*

*It is a white geek thing.*

*It is controlled by corporates like IBM.*

*If you look at video and movies, what is Hollywood? What are they? Movie people are very creative, very smart, they understand business and they are flogging stuff for big dollars. If you look at voice people what are they? They tend to be white English engineers, doing boring telephone and mobile phone type services, plain old telephones, pots. If you look at the Internet what are they? All sorts, everybody else, the rest. The place they all seem to be colliding around at the moment is cable.*

*Who is in control?*

*Who is driving it?*

*Who's got it?*

A man with skin like polished ebony, wearing a Chicago Bulls baseball cap, John Lennon style glasses and t-shirt, was browsing through a directory. The words University of British Colombia, United States Of America came up on his screen.

*Free at last, thank God almighty free at last.*

'Ah log EEN tu one ah dem VIRTUAL chat news groups ah ome,' said Froggy, 'an no one TALK tu me.'

'That's not surprising,' said Bones

*The culture is in the dialogue.*

'Dem NEVA noh ooh ah wuz. Yu ad tu choose wha KINA person AH creature yu wanted tu be. So mi pick ah black man. An me ah walk roun an no one ah talk tu me. Hall di white people WUZ togetha, hall di aliens. Dere wuz mo aliens dan heny udder group.

'That may have been because there were no other black people, or they'd had the same experience and disguised themselves as white, or aliens.'

'So what did you do?' I asked.

'Mi log HOUT. AN cum back een as ah alien.

HALL di udder aliens cum ova ONE TIME an welcome me like ah breadda, LIKE AH BREDRIN, an we did ave ah serious reasonin session. Di vibes wuz strong. So wha dat tell yu? Dat shit really it ome.'

*The culture is in the dialogue.*

'But you should know that Froggy, that shouldn't surprise you,' said Bones, slurring his words. 'That is what part of the whole Chameleon vibe is about. As long as you are transparent, then it's fine, no one knows your colour. You could be fat, short, bald, a dog, a cat, a robot. If the end user doesn't know your age, sex, it's fine, they don't really want to know. But you stay real to the message you're communicating.'

'Right, right, RIGHT,' said Froggy, watching him carefully.

'A chameleon is still a chameleon whether it's green or brown, so in the twenty-first century it will all be down to your intellectual property and how you use it.'

'RIGHT, right, right.'

'If you ain't down with it you might as well become a broomologist.'

Bones logged onto a machine. 'Make room for the couch commando.'

Froggy watched eagerly as Bones did some naughty business and accessed a government FTP site. He knew the secret address of the machine, he cut through all the security checks and entered a password.

The tall ebony man wearing the Chicago Bulls baseball cap leaned over and glanced at Bones' computer screen.

Bones grinned and winked at Froggy and said, 'This is a government building in Washington, not all that pornography you're always locked into.'

Froggy pursed his lips. 'Bees go where di honey is.'

'It deals with UFO sightings. When I got to the password stage I had 30 secs. It's surprising, a lot of people just use their first names as passwords. How stupid can you get?'

'WHA yu recommend?' asked Froggy.

'A combination of alphanumerics. So you might do your middle name, followed by your birth date as a password. A combination is a bit harder to suss out.'

*Why should white guys have all the fun?*

The screen fired up, Bones clapped his hands together. 'Bingo, now we're in the UFO site-Hackers rule the Universe.'

Froggy put a finger on his lip and studied the information. He took out a notepad and pen.

Out of the corner of my eye I saw Hunter making his way through the crowd, with a well-heeled gentleman.

'I'm sure that guy has been morphed,' I said, looking at Hunter.

'Don't upset him. He is the A and the Z, he has access to all the collectors.'

Hunter had the same easy manner of an estate agent showing a client around a property as he gestured theatrically. 'Bones designed this place. Isn't it wonderful?'

'Yes,' said the well-heeled gent. 'But let's wait and see what he produces in the next show. I want to see continuity.'

'Yes, of course, of course,' said Hunter, putting his arms behind his back. 'My gallery took on his work, took on his future for that very reason. Bones, this is Lord Haversham. He collects your work.'

Bones tried his hardest to pull himself together and hide the effects of the drink and drugs.

*Why should white guys have all the fun?*

'It's nice to meet you in person,' said Lord Haversham. He was wearing a bow-tie, had balding sandy hair, his eyes were china-blue. 'I've seen you on TV couple of times and read about you in magazines. How does it feel to be legitimate, to be a success?'

'I was a success the day I sprayed my first piece on a wall.'

'But now you are bourgeois?' said the well-heeled gent as he adjusted his bow-tie.

'I'll never be bourgeois.'

'Hunter is, all his artists are.'

'Well, I suppose I'm giving him a little street cred then.'

'What do you see as the most important thing in contemporary art?'

Bones composed himself. I gave him a look which said 'You're on your own.'

Hunter was quick to the draw. 'That's a difficult one ... Well, I suppose.'

Lord Haversham did not care for the interruption. 'Let the young man answer.'

Bones paused for a long time before he spoke, then there was something strained and uneasy about the way he spoke. 'It has to be kept alive ...' said Bones, coughing and clearing his throat. His voice brightened up. 'Challenge people's perception ... of their environment ... but the ultimate key to the success is the quality of the work.'

Lord Haversham's thick eyebrows rose slightly. He was listening intently. I was surprised that Bones' train of thought was so coherent.

The music pumped and visuals of skate and snow-boarders jumped on the screens in the background.

Bones was up to speed. 'The only thing that sits on the wall of the collector is the painting. And if that ceases to speak to the collector the hype is over. Which in a way is a nice phenomenon.'

Hunter nodded approvingly.

'Why?' asked Lord Haversham.

Bones didn't hesitate. 'Because ultimately it means that you can't fake bad art into good art and I don't like conning people.'

Lord Haversham turned to Hunter. 'I'll take those pieces.'

He walked off. Hunter raised his thumb at Bones.

'How did you do that?' I asked.

Bones sighed with relief. 'I jus Bill Cosbyed his arse.' He rubbed his eyes. 'I'm going to digitise everything and put my library, the paintings on to computer, that's what that disk I gave you is about. I'm slowly going to stop using paint, that way I can control it more.'

'Why would a guy like that Lord Haversham want to buy your work? Is it because it's street?'

Froggy tapped away at a terminal.

'It might mean something to him,' said Bones, in a drugged voice. 'Or he's got a space on the wall. He thinks it's going to go up in value, he think it's important. He's seen as the sort of person who buys expensive art work.'

*Why should white guys have all the fun?*

Bones looked over at Hunter and Lord Haversham who

229

were sitting at a bank of computer screens, next to ravers wearing VR masks and sensor pads, fully fledged members of the digital community. Lord Haversham sat in front of a console grasping a joy stick.

'I've plonked a lot of paintings on the Deadmeat website,' said Bones, groggily. 'Hunter is showing him through them. You can actually move through the environment. Touch things. The hot links are various objects like walls, stones, cats, doors. You click on them and go into other pages and other domains. It's all in 3D.'

Lord Haversham and Hunter seemed to be having a good time.

*Why should white guys have all the fun?*

Bones' eyes were still on Lord Haversham. 'Look at him, he's very rich, but he still wants to meet interesting people. Buying my work is a way of getting in on a whole social scene and being valued. But whatever it is, collectors like him have all got one thing in common.'

'What?' I asked.

'They are always constantly wondering is this artist,

is Bones' work, going to go up in value? Or am I going to lose money? Is Bones going to be the new star of the future? And am I going to be recognised by having bought work early?'

'I get you.'

Bones' mouth tightened. 'Hunter is almost like a con man, doing deals over the telephone and the Net. It's all unspoken.'

'Behind the back?'

For a moment his face was still, then he began to talk slowly. 'If I go into a shop and say I wanna buy a pair of shoes.'

'You still on about shoes?'

'Hear me out. I go in, I take out my money and the deal is done. But with art you don't go into a big time gallery and say "I want that Picasso painting" and walk out with it. Some collectors are not interested in seeing the work. That's what's pissing me off with Hunter. I'll have an exhibition, and somebody will hear that I'm having a show in Germany, and people start calling up or Hunter sends out the catalogue and does the deal over the telephone.'

'That's business, rudebwoy. Supply and demand. He makes money and you make money.'

'Clarkie, it's not as easy as that. It gets very tricky. I mean it's all built, based on confidence. It's a world of image. It's almost perfect because it is very hard to say, you know, what the value of an art work is in the end. It only goes down to people's opinions.' His voice softened. 'With a company you can at least say, well things are looking very bad for cars this year, so I don't think that shares in Renault are going to go up. Whereas with art it's just a fleeting thing, and there are certain variables that a gallery or dealer like Hunter will try and influence.'

'Like?'

'I can't talk about them right now,' he said, twisting his mouth. 'But, when the time is right I'll show you everything and how the disk is going to run things.' His voice weakened. 'Come on, I need a drink. Melanie is fucking up my head, sawing away at my nerves.'

*The culture is in the dialogue.*

*Those that know know and those that
don't make silly mistakes.*

S I D E **52**

Bones put his arm around my shoulder and pulled me away from Froggy and the computers. He used his card and got a rum 'n' blackcurrant out of the machine.

'I didn't hit her. I wanted to crack her skull,' he said, sighing.

'Your eyes are flying.'

'I should have kicked her in the cunt,' snapped Bones. 'I'm gonna get him. Where's your gun?'

'I ain't going down that road with you.' I said. His voice was dim. 'I need something bigger than what you got.'

'It ain't the size of the gun. It's the effect of the bullet.'

'I need something bigger than what you got.'

'It ain't the size of the gun. It's the effect of the bullet.'

'I need something bigger than what you got.'

'It ain't the size of the gun. It's the effect of the bullet.'

'I just wanna scare him,' said Bones, taking a sip of his drink. 'Make him get on his knees and beg, watch him cry like a baby. I know where the gun is. It's taped under the sink in the kitchen.'

'One minute you're telling me to change and now you want me to go back.'

Bones stared at the floor and said in a tired voice, 'It's personal. Was I weak? Am I weak? Am I soft?'

'You did the right thing. You walked away.'

He blinked thoughtfully. 'Her boss must think I'm a fucking ediot.'

'We've all got shadows.'

'What the fuck do you know about love?' he said, staring directly at me. 'The only person you've ever loved is yourself. From the age of five it's been me, me, me. I should talk to Froggy, he'll understand, he knows more about love and relationships than you,' said Bones, walking off. I saw the tall black man with the Chicago Bulls cap approach him.

S I D E

*Rinse out!*
*It's time to get physical.*
*Rinse out!*
*It's time to get moody.*

*Bleep ... Bleep.*

*Those that know know and those that don't make*
*silly mistakes.*

*You've got to find a way of getting us back, bring us*
*down with a round from the laser cannon.*

*Ask for what you really want, ask for what you*
*really want.*
*Ask for what you really want, ask for what you*
*really want.*

The selector flipped some wax onto the turntables and

the intestines of Chameleon began to bubble to the drum 'n' bass fever. The fact that Bones was in the house made everything more intense.

> *Oh my God, oh my God!*
> *What?*
> *Terry this is a record album.*

> *The album backwards tells you*
> *how to close the gates.*

> *The fever.*
> *The fever.*

A fit-looking female wearing Arthur D Clarke shorts and a fluorescent t-shirt fanned herself with a flyer. She was dancing, sweating like she was going to lose two pounds, clothes squelching against her skin. Her feet were moving like crazy, like they were on fire. Her body was running, it had more bends than a Porsche. She had large black pupils, her mouth was generous, her teeth were white and even. She finished dancing, sat down at a glass table and took off her gloves. Her hands were brown, slim, finely boned, French manicured nails, a large silver ring on her right hand. She took out a small clipper, snipped off the tip of a cigar, and lit it with a gold lighter. She was an ultracool babe with a classic profile. She sat back in a chair, blew the smoke out and tapped the ash into a glass tray.

*The fever.*

A devilish grin spread across Bones' long, chiselled face as he eyeballed the women. 'Yeah man, there's woman like sand in here.' He put his inhaler in his back pocket. 'Forget Melanie. There's nough pom-pom for everybody tonight. It's going to be raining sex I can smell it.'

And that was it. He dived straight into the bubbling crowd, pulled out his Rizlas, wiggled his tiny waist to the dope beats and started chirping to some red-skinned fly-girl in a tight micro-mini.

*Rinse out!*
*It's time to get physical.*
*Rinse out!*
*It's time to get moody.*

S I D E

*There's a vibe goin on, goin on.*
*There's a vibe goin on.*

The music was as dark as a minute to midnight.

*There's a vibe goin on, goin on.*
*There's a vibe goin.*

Strange lights flickered above my head like a magnificent meteor shower. It was breathtaking. The tension was rising to the surface. The sound effects were right on the brink. There were bods taking plug, E, speed, crack, weed, opium.

*There's a vibe goin on.*
*There's a vibe goin on.*

It wasn't a tight cosy rinse, but an intense trau- matic soak that ripped through the senses. You couldn't tell when one record was starting and when another was coming to an end. My legs were numb, they were gone, the selector was putting us through a hybrid of dance-hall drum 'n' bass and abstract sounds that kicked at over 160 beats per minute on a transglobal vibe.

*Rinse out!*

The music wasn't about detail, it was about atti-tude, anything that could make the party people strike a pose.

*Rinse out!*
*It's time to get physical.*
*Rinse out!*
*It's time to get moody.*

It was a different place from the one I had left eighteen months ago; it wasn't any better or any worse it just had lots of different strands. The music had grown out of about four pods and now it was cross-fertilising and multiplying at a furious rate. 3D animated images were shooting across backdrops. Fluorescent paintings, were hanging on the walls. Robots of varying shapes and sizes were moving to the subsonic beats. The ultra deep bass vibrated through my body.

Cleveland Watkiss, a tall Nubian man with a sweet set of pipes was the MC; he was rinsing the mic, narrating the cosmic journey for the ravers. He flicked a lighter rapidly in front of his face. The golden flame lit up his stoic features. His flow was spiritual, musical, he was giving a sermon and baptising the congregation with the sound.

*21st century sounds of the underground.*

The clothing the ravers wore was all about symbols, a language of its own, put together to make sentences. Mixed and matched to shock. Flesh was the subtext. The psychology was in the flow of the garments. The flavour was acquired from Dalston, Brixton, Portobello and Shepherds Bush markets.

You could tell the American bods by the way they

dressed; they were obviously influenced by different drugs. They looked like walking videos, their TV culture informed their garments.

It was a melting pot in there.

Everybody was shocking out.

There were black people, white people, red people, yellow people, wearing black leather, yellow leather Lords, dons, donettes, jodhpurs, redhats, hot pants, Afros, flares, beehives, crewcuts, platforms, winkle-pickers, bobs, loafers, kangols, applejack hats, argyll socks, suede Fila, Adidas, Nike, Converse, Air Jordan, Michiko sneakers, YSL, D&G, DKNY, Stone Island, C.P. Company, Prada, Ralph Lauren, Polo Sport, Mecca, Hilfiger, Fabu, Posse, Carhartt, Nautica, Versace, CK, Phat Farm, Artwear, Tony Phillips, Jessica Odgen, Alexander Miguel, Roger Grant, Issey Miyake, ski caps, Stussy t-shirts, Touch t-shirts, t-shirts with no brand names, t-shirts with corporate logos or bastardised versions made especially for clubbing, Moschino mish mash print shirts and jeans, R flight jackets, lumberjack shirts, baggy cords, jeans with pin tucks worn low on the waist, pit caps, combat gear, smart suits and trousers with attention to detail, Edwardian double-breasted jackets with big pockets, skate little sister gear, hipsters, tight striped trousers, Gothic long sleeves, pre-Raphaelite massive skirts, ruffles, over the top collars, expensive cloths, no polka dots, no accessories, K9 gloves, silver and gold FX specs, lowrider tights, Q shades, crushed velvet knickers, Minister Farrakhan ties and badges, fluorescent rings, alien zips, ribbed rubber underwear, suspenders and lace, see-through fabric, sports bras, speedo swimtops, cod pieces, pouches, hand-bags, exotic perfumes, long-nailed young stars, aromatic cologne, rebel belts, Eric Redd belts, crotch huggers, zero max scarfs, slacks, high heels, low heels, Doc Marten boots, CG braces, Gwen Like earrings, Reebok, WERE ALL IN THE HOUSE. Everyone and everything was mixed up getting down and feeling hot, HOT, HOT.

*Finda space, finda space.*
*To feel the bass, to feel the bass.*
*Finda space, finda space.*
*To taste the bass, to taste the bass.*

The Japanese were a crew unto their own, they were taking photographs of everything. Bones had a theory that they couldn't understand music loaded with bass, that they preferred higher frequencies. They mumbled amongst themselves and exchanged notes, they seemed to respect the music coming out of the speakers. Hell, ninety per cent of it was made on their equipment. They knew every sound, but every now and then they bowed their heads and paid homage when they were pleasantly surprised by the noise.

The Japanese crew flicked their lighters in the air and shouted, 'Rewind, rewind, rewind.'

*Stop it!*
*You're hurting us!*
*Stop it!*

*Abstract sounds.*
*Oh my god, he's coming into land, oh my*
*god he's coming into land.*

The selector was controlling the ravers, he was a dynamo of energy, the whole club revolved around him, he had his own individual style and mixing technique. He was standing in a fuzzy blue light. His image was beamed onto a backdrop, he was being filmed live. I recognised him, it was Mark, a member of 4 Hero. He was wearing police sunglasses, a lilac shirt, a yellow tie with a Chameleon tie pin, a well-cut suit made out of army fatigues, cuff links with encrusted blue stones.

*It's all over.*
*It's all over.*
*It's all over.*

A mellow groove was on one turntable. Mark slammed the fader across and cut up the other piece of vinyl like a madman, he was hard-edged. The rinse was solid. He wasn't into no dishwash tunes. He was just flavouring the area with moody sounds.

## Stop it!

*Check, check, check, check, check, check,*
*check ... check the sounds of the underground,*
*touchdown to the sounds of the underground.*

The Japanese crew waited with bated breath, they didn't know what Mark was going to play next. He had a reputation for playing just 30 secs of a tune, and as the crowd began to say 'Ohhhh' or 'Ahhhhh' he would switch turntables and lick in another groove.

*Respect to man like Grooverider 'n' Dego, Ian,*
*Gus, the Reinforced crew in the house.*

Mark fast forwarded the motion and brought in a beat that made the warehouse erupt.

*Stop it!*
*I'm havin' a heart attack.*
*Stop it!*

*Solar feelings.*
*Solar feelings.*

Ravers, DJs and producers crowded around Mark's turntables, they wanted to learn, to see the master at work, they sipped their drinks and watched the moves.

*Rinse out!*
*It's time to get physical,*
*Rinse out!*
*It's time to get moody.*

The drum 'n' bass fever Mark was spreading was raw, British and personal. He was smashing it.

I nodded my head to the brutal groove. Cold droplets of water hit my forehead. Condensation had formed on the pipes and the air vent above my head. It was just a flexing night.

*Reload. Time to reload. Reload,*
*Reload. Time to reload. Reload.*

S I D E  55

*I'm going back to country living.*

Froggy was watching Bones and the fly-girl working it in the darkly lit eclectic room. She was giving it a juicy one. He leaned over to me. 'E tink im goin ave dat gyal fi BREAKFAS, I don't tink im stan AH chance IN h . . .'

The fly-girl looked young, she must have been

over eighteen or couldn't have got a card to get in Chameleon. She had schoolgirl legs, her breasts were small, but her movements were all grown up, she pushed her hair away from her face and smiled. The smile made her look about thirteen years old.

A fat rastaman poked his natty head between us, smiled politely and said. 'Yu ave heny Rizla?' We both shook our heads in the negative.

Froggy looked at him scrounging then turned to me with an arrogant smirk on his face. 'Ah ATE DAT. E noh E WUZ cumin tu ah rave an shoulda bring nough tings wid im. True or lie?' He paused, leaving a gap for my reply.

'True,' I said, as I eased my back against the wall.

'I mean MATCHES or ah LIGHT is different.'

His big eyes scanned the large space then homed in on Bones, who was now in a dark corner slow dancing with the sexy fly. She moved her fit limbs seductively, stopping every now and then to flick her long hair back and to pull down her yellow micro mini, which was riding up her thick, coffee coloured thighs.

*Sha la la la sha la la laah sha la la la laah*
*sha la la la.*

Bones was locked in heaven. He had everything he wanted in his arms. He rubbed his eager groin gently against the fly's crotch.

> *I need my girl, but she's so so so so far away.*
> *There's nothing like this.*
> *There's nothing like this.*

The music was trapped in their bodies, the fly's upper body was solid, but she pushed her pelvis forward, like a warm tide running up a hot sandy beach. Bones had his eyes shut, they were head to head.

> *Telephone line, telephone line, the telephone*
> *line will make you mine, telephone line brings me*
> *sunshine.*

> *Bleep ...        Bleep ...*
> *    ... Bleep        ... Bleep*

S I D E **56**

A female security guard tapped Bones on the shoulder to get his attention. He reluctantly moved away from the fly-girl. Bones beckoned me over and we went to the CCTV office. It was plush, his paintings hung on the wall, a smoked glass window overlooked one of the packed dance floors. Different areas of the club were highlighted on the bank of close circuit television screens.

The female security guard yawned as she sat down. Bones' eyes focused on the box containing the image of the bald-headed woman outside the club.

There was still a long queue. She adjusted her radio microphone. An American man was coating her.

'I gotta son who's older than your arse,' said the American, drawling his words. 'I don't need you disrepectin me, talkin to me like you're eatin dick.'

The bald-headed woman looked at the clip board.

'You've got to pay. I can't see your name on the list. Normally, I shouldn't even be allowed to let you in because you haven't got any credits, but we'll take your money. Even though cash money is for poor people.'

'I ain't being schooled by you. Get Bones.'

The security guard glanced at Bones. He leaned forward pressed a button and spoke into a microphone.

'Fuck him. He's got the wrong attitude.' Bones turned away from screen and shook his head. 'The plughead wasn't even dressed right.'

The guard asked Bones if he wanted any personal security. He shook his head and said he was fine. He could handle people coming up and talking to him tonight, he didn't need security to tell them when the time was up.

We went back into the arena. A 3-D image of a space ship floated above the ravers. Bones moved through the bodies until he reached the fly-girl; he tapped her digits into his Psion organiser and pulled out his vibrocard, wiped it through a machine. The fly-girl pressed the button for Cinzano and lemonade. She slipped a long arm around Bones' waist and pointed to her friends. Bones wiped the card through the machine again, she ordered six drinks and took them over to her thirsty crew.

The music slowed down into a lovers' rock rinse.

*Natural wooooooman. Natural wooooooman.*

The lyrics and the bass combined perfectly. They vibrated my body and brought a smile to my face. I'd just positioned myself to pull a beautiful Nubian princess with a smile like sunshine, when Froggy bust my set by putting a Malibu and pineapple juice in my hand.

He turned and asked the princess' younger sister to dance, she said, 'No.'

And he said, 'A'right STAN up dere an bleed tu death.'

Then, as if that wasn't enough he slurped his Canei, licked his lips and started talking about his car.

'Yu NOH Clarkie ... Mi Karmann Ghia ah go mek ah REAL difference. Every gyal yu deal wid is ARN ah bus ticket, but wid me tings is different, yu get me?'

That was it. It was car talk at every available opportunity.

'It's GOOD value for money yu noh? Dem base di shape ah di Porsche arn it.'

*Sweet lady I don't want to cry over you.*
*Sweet lady I don't want to cry over you.*

Bones came over to Froggy and in a drunken haze told him that he wanted Froggy to give him and the fly-girl a lift to her home in East London. The friends she had come with wanted to stay and rave. Froggy wasn't very happy about the idea, and he suggested that Bones take her back in a cab, but Bones wasn't listening. He beckoned the fly-girl over and pointed to Froggy and said that he'd drop them off. She took one look at Froggy and decided that she'd rather walk than get in a car with him, and to make matters worse she got turned off Bones as well.

*I'm moving grooving in love.*

'Is that the sort of company you keep?' she asked in a condescending manner. Her Cleopatra-like eyes fluttered disapprovingly at Froggy as they examined him from head to toe.

'Yes,' said Bones proudly, in his defence.

'Well, if you walk with dogs you will lie down

with dogs,' she said arrogantly. And full of her own self-importance, she turned her little toffee nose up in the air and briskly carried her firm buttocks towards the kitchen, where she calmly picked up a steaming plate of curry goat and rice. She was carrying on like her DO-DO don't stink.

Froggy wanted to box her in the face there and then, but we restrained him.

*You did wrong your heart went out to play*
*you lost me what a price to pay.*

'She RENK an HOUTTA horda,' he hissed.

'This is Bones' club. Take it easy,' I said, as the fly swung around and stared at him. Her eyes sparkled like raw diamonds, she ran her delicate fingers through her shiny black hair and turned her back on us and started laughing with her friends.

'AH don't GIVE AH SHIT!' wailed Froggy. 'Di SMELLY ole mus feel seh she nice. Bones! Yu bettah TELL har tu hapologise ah it's ME an YU tunite.'

Bones knew there was trouble in the air. Froggy wasn't shaping. He would throw licks first and ask questions later. He had no control over his emotions,

how he talked was how he felt, there was no middle ground.

'Har face FEAVA fart,' said Froggy. 'Clarkie. Did yu
SEE ow much mek-up SHE ave arn?'

'Yeah,' I replied softly, trying hard to diffuse the
situation.

'AH wouldn't TEK ah gyal like dat tu ah DOG race
EVEN if she wuz FAVOURITE tu win. Yu si di size ah
har feet?' he growled.

I sent Bones to look for the fly. He came back saying
she wasn't coming. A group of her friends hovered past
us and shot quick glances at Froggy. We overheard one
of them passing comment.

'Yes, she's right, di bwoy hugly. Een hall my days ah
neva si ah bwoy so hugly. Yu noh wen two eyes mek
four? Dat's ow hugly e is. An did yu si di size ah dem
jerry curls unda im arm-pits?'

'He's a chief,' said another.

So that was it.

Froggy shouted, 'YU FUCKIN BITCH! Yu ain't dark an
lovely, yu dark an hugly!'

S I D E **57**

Froggy marched over and physically confronted the fly. Bones pushed the security guards back and pointed to himself, indicating that he would handle it. He moved a group of photographers towards an exit.

Everybody gathered round to watch, they pushed and shoved to get a ring side view.

Bones urged, then begged, the fly to back down.

Eventually, when she had got all the attention she wanted, she blurted out a squeaky, half muted, 'Sorry.' And continued to shovel large spoonfuls of hot rice into her ruby-lined mouth.

Froggy looked at her menacingly and said, 'Dat's A'RIGHT DEN ... Dat's a'right den. Dat's a'right ... den.'

S I D E **58**

*Bleep ... Bleep.*

The fly went off with a high-stepping home-boy.

The people started dancing and the rave was in full flow again, as if nothing had happened.

Froggy was upset, he wanted to get out of Chameleon, but he knew he couldn't just walk out as that would lose him points. His eyes were like big satellite dishes as they circled over the talking heads, picking up the good the bad and the ugly vibes. The south-side was a die hard area, where many a man had lost an ear or a finger and gained a scar in return. Of all the places in London, I couldn't understand why Bones had to choose that as a location.

*Your love's in my system.*
*Rock the Rhythm.*

Bones floated around the rave, pulling on his inhaler, smoking spliff after spliff and drinking cup after cup of rum 'n' black. He was pretending not to care, because he could see his razor-tongued fly getting sexually intimate with the home-boy. I thought he was going to have an asthma attack any minute. He knew he wasn't meant to smoke. Nothing was going right for him tonight.

The fly was kissing the home-boy's neck and rubbing his spine. She was just doing it to get Bones jealous, and Bones, like a big jackass, retreated behind his rum 'n' black and got more and more out of it.

*Met you it was the way nature planned it.*
*I was looking for love now I've found it,*
*I couldn't stand to be without it.*

Froggy gave me the signal and we were out of there. We didn't want Bones to make a fool of himself and get some bad publicity.

# S I D E  59

Bones was gone, I lifted him up in my arms like a baby and carried him out of Chameleon by the back exit. He was mumbling about Melanie and how he wanted to kill her and her boss, then he started on about the fly-girl, how she had embarrassed him and how Froggy had put him in a difficult situation. Then, he went on about how he wanted to get back to Mum's house to meet somebody. His sentences and thoughts were all jumbled up; one minute he sounded like he was crying the next he was laughing. I decided to agree with what he said until we were over the water. In the morning, when he sobered up, I would sit him down and tell him the whole truth. I'd accept the consequences.

A crowd of guys from the south-side were sitting in their low rider Jeeps, watching us. I noticed the fly-girl talking to them.

Froggy pulled the chair of the Ghia forward and

I pushed Bones' alcohol-ridden body into the back seat.

'Fuck DEM pussy 'oles,' said Froggy, looking at the cowboys. 'Deh neva TEK mi alive. If deh touch mi deh bettah kill me FIRS, cos if deh don't ah goin cum back fi hall ah dem.'

The guys from the south-side were fat, gold chain wearing backstabbers, who liked to hang their names around their necks and put their big sovereign rings in your face. Living in the city had never been pretty, but in the south they always seemed to overstep the mark. There was no reverse gear on those motherfuckers. They loved to play at being cowboys and thought nothing of putting a bullet through your head, throwing you off the rugged map of life and making you brown bread. They weren't fronting. They were short guys with inferiority complexes, a thing that would stay with them for the rest of their lives. Their half cocked ganja-filled eyes were red and ready to attack, their pouting lips were harder than rocks as they kept an eye on the security guards, their sound systems were thumping dark beats as they gave us the evil blackman's eye.

*Oh Jah, Oh Jah, Oh Jah,*
*what a natural mystic.*

One of them left the growing pack, bounced past me growled and said, 'Di laas ting yu ah go si is Silva. Watch yu back, cause dere won't be no kickin. No punchin. No fightin. Jus Silva. An ah go clean mi gun ina yu nose ole.'

The security guards looked on from a distance. They moved forward as the little fucker shaped his hand into a pistol and aimed it at my forehead.

'We ah go tun dis yah rave een tu ah lick shot party,' he said coldly. 'An guess who ah go get di firs lick?' He had a half a cigarette behind his ear. As he talked I could see the paper in his mouth had turned purple. He was plugged in. His eyes froze on me. 'Yes, yu. Yu ah go bite di dus firs,' said the cowboy through a broken grin.

*Oh Jah, Oh Jah, Oh Jah,*
*what a natural mystic.*

I ignored the cowboy. I didn't want it all to go off. I

was in no mood for a hard fight, the cowboys most probably had guns, machetes and cutlasses concealed in their rides and they were just looking for an excuse to use them. If firearms were discharged that would mean Chameleon would get a bad name, but I prepared my mind because, if it came to it and the shit did go off, I was ready to dark them out.

S I D E  60

## Caption: 3.21am

Froggy fired the car up and pulled off. 'Ah neva even get ah chance tu get hinvolved een di TEKKEN competition. Ah bin practicin fi two weeks. Ah WOULDA beat HALL dem.'

I breathed a big sigh of relief as I saw the lonely cowboys driving in the opposite direction.

Froggy slipped in a Doc Scott tape. 'Dis BABY only cost mi two G. Mi buy it OVA di HINTERNET an regista it hellectronically.'

'Is that all you got in your head? You know some men live in their cars. That is all they've got, one nice car and they've invested their whole life savings in it.'

'So WHA?'

'I mean, they've got their clothes in the boot, they haven't even got a roof over their head. They're living from place to place.'

The Karmann Ghia roared past the Brixton front-line like a bat out of hell. Streetlights flashed, buildings flipped past the windscreen like the dots on a rifled deck of cards. It was then I noticed a white mini in the wing mirror, a few hundred yards behind us. I couldn't make out who was in it because it had tinted windows, but it made all the turns we did. I saw part of the registration, 2029. I thought about telling Froggy, but decided against it until I was sure. We stopped at a set of traffic lights, the mini turned off into a side street.

*The blackness.*
*The blackness.*

'Ah goin FIX har up so SWEET. Yeah ah goin fix har up, so dat wen MAN an MAN si har pun di street, dem goin ave fi gi har TOTAL rispek,' chuckled Froggy as he put on his Deadmeat ski cap and glided over Westminster Bridge. 'AH noh she blue now, but ah goin RESPRAY HAR BLACK. Jet BLACK. Watch di speedo nuh, ah ton twenty an she NUH feel it. Nobaddy can touch dis.'

*Kill the night.*
*The blackness.*

As we hit the Harrow Road, the Karmann Ghia lost power. The moon was high. The sky was full of weird shapes. A dead cat was stretched out in the shadows. Steam rose through the grilles of a gutter. A corrugated iron fence was smeared with graffiti and a line of posters saying 'Wanted Cyber Vigilante. Calling card, a dead white rat. Phone police on 01814503240. URL – http://www.cybervigilante.com Reward: £10,000 for information leading to arrest.'

*Kill the night.*
*The blackness.*
*The blacrrrrrrrrrrrrrrrrrrrrrrrrrrrrh.*

The eclectic Doc Scott CD blatantly came to an abrupt

stop and the Karmann Ghia conked-out, right in the middle of the road. Froggy looked at me nervously. He rested his egg-shaped head on the small steering wheel and started cussing. An endless stream of profanities flavoured with obscene remarks rolled off his long sticky tongue before he took a deep breath, counted to ten and shook his head in disgust. I could tell Froggy was embarrassed, because he had this habit of biting his bottom lip when he was ashamed or felt exposed.

S I D E  61

## Caption: 3.45am

Music boomed out of a block of council flats, the drum 'n' bass of dance hall reggae bounced off the Ghia.

*Movement of jah people.*

I sat in the passenger seat, dumb-struck.

*Movement of jah people.*

Bones was curled up in the back, spaced out.

*I'll never ever ever fall in love again.*

My nerves began to tighten. I felt my jacket pocket, the hammer code diskette Bones had given me earlier on in the night was still there.

Froggy glanced over his shoulder at Bones. He was in slumberland, counting sheep or feeling women. He lay there clutching his NOKIA 2110, which his life revolved around. He was a virtual corporation.

Bones was snoring, totally unaware of our predicament. His skinny spider like legs suddenly splayed out to the sides and his wiry mouth dropped wide open.

'WHAT ah HUGLY bastard,' said Froggy. 'JUS look PUN im.'

I was going to pull Froggy up about the way he was referring to my brother but I decided to let it go.

There was no point making the situation worse than it already was.

*No man is an Island you can't make*
*it on your own.*

Froggy was beginning to get irritated, 'Yu can SI is BRAINS trew im NOSE ... We goin ave fi wake im up yu noh.'

'Yeah I suppose you're right,' I said softly.

Froggy sucked his teeth and scratched his forehead. With his free hand he drummed the dashboard impatiently.

'AH unda, unda. Ah jus WANNA get back tu di yard an lock miself een ah room FI four days, wid ah couple ah buckkles ah fizz. AN jus get arn di Sony playstation. Yu get me? Mi nah ANSAH di phone tu heny one.' He winced in pain and rubbed his lower back. The blinding rays from passing cars bounced sharply off the rear view mirror and into Froggy's misery-lined eyes. 'We might as WELL get hout AN push,' he eventually said, reluctantly.

We waited until the coast was clear, dragged Bones out of the back seat, stumbled onto the pavement with his dead awkward weight and left him sitting in the doorway of a Kentucky.

*You broke my heart, tore it apart.*

He looked a picture of innocence with his head resting against the glass shop front and his hands clutching his balls.

It took all the strength we had but we pushed the Karmann Ghia towards the pavement. It hit, then hugged the kerb like a worn-out turtle that had reached the beach and was taking a breather before it once again braved the cruel sea.

*You're sweeter than honey to me,*
*when you kiss me my mind feels so free.*

Froggy massaged his lower back and looked at its empty shell for a second then raised his hands to the star-spangled sky and began to laugh. 'Ah SPEAK tu soon blood, Ah SPEAK tu soon. Wha we goin do WID yu breadda?' he asked, pointing his crooked finger at

Bones. Who was now lying flat out on his back with his head tilted sideways to the kerb, using the hard, cold, concrete paving slab as a pillow.

I opened the bonnet and had a look at the engine; the light was bad, I couldn't see all the connections. I knew a little bit about car maintenance but Froggy didn't have any tools.

A black cab came down the road, its yellow hire sign was on, I put my hand out. The light went off and the driver roared by.

'You stay with him, while I go and get a mini cab,' I said.

'Di nearest cab station is bout AH mile up DI road. Ah cumin wid yu.'

'What?'

'Put im EEN di car. We can cum back an get im. Unless yu ah go CARRY im?'

# S I D E 62

The Harrow Road was deserted. By the time we reached halfway tree all the drunks and weird creatures of the night had already rolled past us. So, with just our footsteps for company, we made our way towards the mini cab office. Froggy was a big guy who walked funny. If he stretched his spine and straightened up he could have added an inch or two to his height, easy. But you couldn't tell him that, because he had all the answers. Talking to Froggy about his back was a real touchy subject.

He was thirteen when he suddenly started to suffer from scoliosis, a crippling condition. He reckoned it was because of a clash in a football match. He had to spend the best part of that year in agony being stretched on what his mother, Shirley, called 'a medieval torture rack'. Bones and I went around every day to play with him, we brought him things to cheer him up. Bones told him what was happening at school and did some of his homework for him. Froggy lost interest in art, which was his best subject, he just spent most of his time on his back watching TV. He had an operation on his back when he was fourteen. He stopped wearing body casts and a male corset when he was nineteen, and that was when I started to train him. I made him do aerobic exercises, and wrote down a program which he had to keep to. I took him down to the boxing gym and worked on his abdominals and started getting him to hit the bag. But underneath it all he felt that he had missed out on the best part of his youth. There was nothing anyone could say to change his mind on that. Maybe that was the real reason why he was so loud and up front now – he was just making up for lost time.

So I just watched him as he lazily kicked a tin can into the air. It picked up speed, buzzed and echoed for a while before it landed with a loud clunk in a slimy gutter. Two cats arched their backs and slowly turned their demonic eyes towards us. They hissed in delight as they copulated, on a broken, graffiti-smeared wall.

Froggy and I were stopped abruptly in our tracks by a loud wailing.

'Yu EAR dat?' asked Froggy.

'It sounds like someone's getting killed.'

Our ears located the sound as coming from the black-coated cemetery across the road. I wanted to carry on walking but Froggy wasn't having it.

'Yu SCARED?' he asked mockingly. He loved to play chicken and this was a perfect opportunity for him to test my nerve. I wasn't going to admit that I was thinking it could be the Cyber Vigilante.

'Nah, I just want to go and get the cab, get Bones home and give my bed a snore.

'Cum arn it won't TEK ah sec,' he said.

And before I knew it we had our noses pressed against the cemetery's iron rails. The night air smelt sweet, the smell of death was like no other smell on earth. Froggy strained his eyes to see into the distance. He had a mischievous smile on his face. The yellow street lamps helped to show us that the wailing was coming from a woman. My pupils refocussed and adjusted to the darkness, and as they did so, the woman's sleek contours became familiar to me. She had her dress hitched up around her waist and was squatting over a grave. I was surprised because she didn't have any knickers on, and her naked backside jutted out like a soft, ripe peach as she pissed on the grave and shouted.

'Bastard, you bastard. Bastard you bastard.'

Froggy squinted as he placed his camcorder to his eye.

'What'ja doing?' I asked, curious.

'Yu can't be an artist by jus LOOKIN hout ah di corna ah yu eye.'

'You're sick.'

'Hall great artists steal from life. Yu grew up arn di rong side ah DI cash till. Yu should be able tu relate tu dat.'

'That's Mad Mary,' I whispered.

I knew it was her. She lived a few streets away from me in the Rise. And she was the kind of woman you don't forget. Froggy didn't respond, he was in a different world as he kept on repeating, 'What ah STROKE AH LUCK eh?' over and over again to himself. He didn't blink. He just kept his eye on the prize.

Anyway, Mad Mary pissed till she couldn't piss no more, then she opened a Tennant's Super licked it back one time and bawled out, 'Bastard, bastard.'

Froggy shifted his lips in my direction, I heard him

draw in his breath sharply as Mad Mary moved her wet peach to get a better angle.

'It wuz HALL ah BLESSIN een disguise. Dat FEISTY gyal ah di rave, di car brokin down. Us si een Mary. Ah pure magic.'

'I'm missing. You coming?'

'Nah. Ah goin wait ROUN fi ah while,' said Froggy, reloading the video cassette.

'I'm going to find a cab.'

S I D E **63**

A black dude was arguing with a white guy who was restraining an Alsatian on a leash.

'If that dog bites me, I'm going to bite you and the dog,' said the black dude. 'You should keep it under control.'

'Are you threatening me?' asked the white guy.

'It nearly bit me.'

'I said sorry.'

'What am I going to do with that? If it sunk its teeth into me, it's there for life. Sorry ain't going to help it heal.'

I entered the mini cab office. It was a run down establishment which needed more than a splash of paint. The wiry female controller brushed cigarette fumes from her sour eyes and informed me that there would be no cars available for another hour. She was listening to a tired looking transistor radio. An update on the Cyber Vigilante story held her attention.

I stepped out onto the badly lit street. A couple were alighting from a black cab, I ran over to it, the driver was black, so I figured my luck was in. I told him where I wanted to go and he turned the cab around and drove back to the Karmann Ghia.

A white mini with tinted windows roared off as we pulled up. I turned to check the number plates, but once again all I saw was 2029.

I asked the driver to help me lift Bones into the cab, but when he realised that Bones was drunk, he didn't want him anywhere near his cab. He told me to forget about the fare and drove off. I decided to leave Bones and go home, phone around and try and borrow a car.

S I D E **64**

## Caption: 4.30 am

The phone bleated as I shut the front door. I thought it might be Bones.

'... Is Bones there?' asked a female voice. It was Melanie.

'... No.'

'... Clarkie, how could you have done that?'

'... What?'

'... It was irresponsible. You were irresponsible. You did it on purpose. So the condom was your idea of revenge. You're putting me through hell. Are you happy?'

'... It was a genuine accident.'

'... You expect me to believe that? That's a lie. A mind fuck.'

'... I didn't think it would turn out this way.'

'... Did you tell Bones?'

'... I went along with what you said.'

'... So where is he?'

'... In the car.'

'... What's he doing there?'

'... Sleeping. He's just down the road. What are you doing?'

'... Taking my clothes off.'

'... And now?'

'... Walking around the room.'

'... Naked?'

'... Well I haven't got anything on.'

'... Listen, Melanie. I want to see you.'

'... What for?'

'... To talk?'

'... That's what we're doing now.'

'... I hate that attitude of yours.'

'... Where is the car?'

'... On the Harrow Road near Ken Fuckries.'

'... So it's by the Kentucky?'

'... You drinking?'

'... How can you tell?'

'... I heard the ice falling into the glass.'

'... Yeah, a little nightcap. I was waiting up for Bones.'

'. . . Vodka and coke.'

'. . . That's right. It helps my allergy pills go down real smooth.'

'. . . Can you pick him up in your car?'

'. . . I'm drinking, you're giving me bad advice. Hold on, I'll get dressed. I'll be around in five minutes.'

'. . . It's amazing how everything works out when you follow your instinct.'

S I D E **65**

The doors of the Karmann Ghia were open. Bones was gone.

'That's strange,' said Melanie as she pulled her Citroen alongside the Karmann Ghia. 'I thought you said he was drunk.'

'Well obviously he wasn't that drunk,' I said. 'Why can't he stay in one place? Where the fuck is he? Let's drive around for a while, see if we can find him.'

Two drunks were slouched on the ground with their backs against a wall. They were knocking back bottles of Thunderbird. One was male, the other female. Melanie and I walked past.

'I haven't had any pussy for six months,' said the male.

'Why don't you go to the toilet and jerk off?' said the female.

'That's cold.'

'Like you haven't gone to the toilet and done that before. If I was a man it wouldn't bother me.'

'Why? What do you mean?'

'I'd just go and grease it up with Brylcreem.'

Melanie tapped in the code. The iron gates opened. We walked into the cobbled, U-shaped courtyard. We entered a stony building, walked up four flights of winding stairs until we reached her flat. It was a converted loft. Spacious, the same shape as the enclosure.

There were two suitcases in Melanie's corridor.

'Well we've done the best we could under the circumstances. Don't look so worried, Clarkie, I'm sure he'll turn up eventually.'

'What's with the cases?' I asked

'I'm going to Paris on Monday afternoon,' she said, looking at me. 'We've checked your house, he's not there, he's your responsibility.'

'Well somebody has been there in the time I've been away, they've pulled out drawers in the kitchen.'

'Where's Froggy? He wasn't at home either.'

'He's on another mission. It could have been him but I can't think what he was looking for.'

'Like I said, Bones is your responsibility now. You can borrow my car to look for him.'

We walked into Melanie's front room. She flicked the light switch. Nothing happened.

'Shit. That's the last thing I need.'

Melanie made her way to a table lamp. A harsh light hit her face. I clenched my fists. I thought it was an intruder, the Vigilante.

'Hi, honey ... I'm home,' said Bones, sitting in a

chair. He was holding a torch in one hand and a gun in another. The beam punched me in the face.

'What does she mean I'm your responsibility?' asked Bones, sucking in his breath disgustedly.

'Give me the gun,' I said.

Bones tightened his grip around the trigger, his eyes half closed, glazed by the drugs. His face was drawn, pinched with pain.

Melanie took a step backwards. I heard her breath hiss in slowly, like a snake. I was as scared as hell, but there was no way I was going to let Bones see the fear in my eyes. I relaxed my hands, they were the only weapons I had. My guts were all knotted up and beginning to hurt. Bones' stare was lifeless, it was hiding things that I would have given an arm to know.

'It's not the size of the gun, it's the effect of the bullet, the trigger, don't pull it. Don't push me I'm close to the edge,' said Bones, in slow drawl, still soggy from too much alcohol. 'You can wear my love, you can wear, you can wear, you can wear my love. You can wear, you can wear.'

His eyes were red. He was high. He levelled the gun at Melanie. Bullets littered the wooden floor. There were empty bottles of spirits. I couldn't think, so I simply looked at him wondering what was going to happen next. He was just humming.

Bones aimed the gun at me. 'How about a little slap and tickle?' His eyes searching, serious. 'If you looked at my life you'd see what I see.' He slowly put the gun to his head and started to hum a classical composition. 'It's not the size of the gun it's the effect of the bullet, the trigger, don't pull it.' His face relaxed, preparing for death. 'Headline news, headline news. Read it in the headlines, read it in the headlines.' His voice strained. 'Single men raise their hands. Both take off your shoes.' Melanie was shaking uncontrollably. I was fighting hard now to keep a grip on myself. I only had seconds left.

Bones jerked the gun at me. 'Single men raise their fucking hands!'

I raised my hands slowly, trying hard to keep my composure.

Bones pressed the remote control of the CD player. The classical arrangement he was humming floated out of the speakers, it was a tune by Bobby McFerran.

Bones closed his eyes and opened them again. He stared at me with a peculiar expression. 'It's not the size of the gun it is the effect of the bullet.' His voice hollow. 'I said all the ladies in the house say yo! All the ladies say fuckin yo!'

His whole character seemed to have changed. More mean, dangerous, callous.

'Yo!' shouted Melanie.

'All the ladies say yoooo!' said Bones, leaning forward in his chair.

Melanie trembled. 'Yoooo!' She urinated. A pool formed on the floor.

I felt numb, there was moisture in my eyes. A frozen feeling restricted my thoughts and movement.

Bones laughed and waved the gun in the air. 'Everybody say yo!'

'Yo!' Melanie and I said in unison.

Bones snarled, showing his teeth. 'Yo! Yo! Yo!' He pointed the gun at Melanie, then at me, then back at himself. A triangle of death. 'Yo! Yo! Yo!'

'Yo! Yo! Yo!'
'Yo! Yo! Yo!'
'Yo! Yo! Yo!'
'Yo! Yo! Yo!'
'Yo! Yo! Yo!'

'Louder!' yelled Bones. 'Yo! Yo! Yo!'

'Yo! Yo! Yo!'

Bones tilted his chin at an aggressive angle and pulled the trigger rapidly, there were six loud clicks, no bullets were discharged ...

S I D E

### Caption: Sunday 10am

The house was quiet. I'd slept well. No nightmares just good quality Zs. I found Pauline's digits in my yellow suit and gave her a call. A deep male voice answered.

'Is Pauline in?' I asked politely.

'... Yes, thanks.'

'... Can I speak to her?'

'... What's your name?'

'... Clarkie.'

'... Clarkie?'

'... Yes.'

'... Clarkie Yes? Or just Clarkie?'

'... Clarkie.'

I finally got past the deep voice and Pauline came on line. My heart began to jump excitedly and she quickly put it back in its place. She told me that I'd been abrupt and rude the previous night at my party and I needed to brush up on my interpersonal skills. I apologised profusely, she softened a little and gave me her address and invited me over to her house that afternoon, to talk about what she wanted me to do at the community centre in more detail.

I put down the receiver and dialled the digits of Mrs Birchfield, the Obeah woman.

'... Ello. Ooh dat?'

'... Clarkie.'

'... Ooh?'

'... Clarkie.'

'... Yes. Wha yu want. Mek it quick, ah ave tu feed Queenie.'

'... I want to confess.'

'... Go tu di police.'

'... I can't.'

'... Wha yu hexpect from me?'

'... Something to ease the pain.'

There was silence ... Then she hung up. If Mrs

Birchfield moved in next door to you, your lawn would die, she was that type of lady. Dangerous! But I thought I'd risk phoning her, it was a long shot and I'd obviously miscalculated. She was not my greatest fan. I remembered a time when I was about thirteen and I got caught stealing some crates of soft drinks from the garden of the local corner shop. The owner called the police and Mrs Birchfield's lips circulated the rumours.

'Dem ketch Sister Clark's bwoy yu noh. Ah halways knew e would cum tu no good, from di time wen e wuz gettin Christen an e hit Pastor James een di face wid im heavy han. Ah knew e would cum tu no good. E cum hout by is legs, dat's why. If e ad cum een tu di worl ead firs, it would be ah different matta, but im legs cum firs an e's bin arn di run ever since dat day. Now ah days deh carl it ah breech birth, but dat bwoy is somting else. E wuz born wid im eyes hopen. Is madda tell me dat, so dat tells yu somting bout di bwoy. Knowin im, ah bet im eyes wuz hopen di hole nine months e wuz een im madda belly. E wuz mos probably sittin een dere een di fluid wid im legs cross an im big finga een im mout, workin hout som devious skism. Ow many babies do yu noh born wid dem eye hopen?'

When I got a little bit older she still never had a good word to say about me.

'Hall e do is eat, sleep an shit. Den draw welfare from har Majesty's Good Government, e can neva old down ah job, no sah one day e tell yu e want tu be ah haccountant, di nex ah hengineer or ah computa hexpert.'

Her mouth was a lethal weapon, she had sent an innocent man to jail and destroyed a perfectly happy marriage with her brand of chit-chat. She rarely stepped outside her door but she knew everybody's business. That was because a lot of people came to her house to get her potions or advice. Before my trial a lot of guys from the area said that I should go and see her, pay her some money and that I would get off, or get a lighter sentence. They had all been round to see her for various reasons. One day, when I was about seventeen, I even saw my Uncle Oscar going into her house. I jumped over the back fence and put my nose to the window. I could see my Uncle Oscar sitting talking to her, she was rubbing some ointment on his bare chest, chewing some herbs and sliding the juice down his back. Later on that night Uncle Oscar visited our house, so I got him round to the subject of

Mrs Birchfield. He was evasive for the first few minutes until I said, 'I saw you.'

His eyes hardened. 'Where?'

'In her house. She was rubbing stuff on your chest.'

Uncle Oscar picked me up by the scruff of my neck and took me out outside and threw me into his Ford Zephyr.

'Wha else yu see?'

'That's all.'

'Yu sure? Wha yu ah do dere?'

'I wanted to see what she does.'

'Why?'

'Every day when I come back from the gym I see people going in there, different people. I didn't know you were going to be in there.'

'Shit.'

'I didn't mean to do anything wrong.'

'Ooh else yu tell?'

'No one.'

'Bones? Mum? Yu tell Mum?'

'No, like I said, I told no one.'

'Good. Good. A'right yu is ah big man. Keep awhey from Mrs Birchfield, yu ear?'

'So what were you doing there?'

'Dere will cum ah time, yu will noh di time wen yu will need har, den an honly den go si har, she's an Obeah woman. Yu noh wha dat is?'

'Kinda witchcraft.'

'No dat ah white man bullshit. Wha she deal een is di real stuff. Back ome style.'

'So why do you need it? Do you want to be stronger? Win the pools?'

'Nah, a'right, yu noh Donna, di woman ah bin movin wid ah while?'

'Yes.'

'Nuh tell nobaddy dis. Well ah tink she put ah hex arn me. Dat's strickly between yu an me, rememba?'

'A what?'

'Ah spell, ah dyam spell. Every woman ah look at now look so hugly. Is honly Donna ooh look good tu mi.'

'Maybe you are in love?'

'She put an hex pun me, mek mi forrid sweat, so ah went tu see Mrs Birchfield, tu undo it. She tell me, ah right, Donna do it from back ome. She wile. She bring somting wid har wen she cum back, she mus ah boil it, dash har knickers een wid it, an gi it tu me tu drink, but Mrs Birchfield sort everyting hout. Ah si Donna dis evenin before ah cum tu di ouse an she look like har old self, not dat she no beautiful fah har age, but she look like har self, so now ah don't eat ah drink from har ouse. Me treat har like everybaddy else.'

I realised it was a mistake to have dialled Mrs Birchfield. I wanted some guidance, but I couldn't risk telling her all the finer details. I'd committed a sin and that was all I was prepared to say. I didn't want her to chat it and I wasn't going to take her advice. The police were the last people on earth I would go to.

S I D E **68**

Grey, everything about the maze of interlocking build-ings was dull and dreary. The council estate where Pauline lived was just the same as all the other con-crete jungles. Cold, harsh, desolate, the only warmth came from the heartbeats of the souls that inhabited them. In the distance, a section of the estate was being knocked down by builders with heavy, tall machinery.

There was a solid iron gate with a letter box in front

289

of the door. I rang the bell, holding a bunch of flowers behind my back. I figured I'd been a little bit off at the party, I hadn't really had much time for her. So I was trying to win some points.

A young boy who looked about ten years of age opened the door. He cut his eye at me.

'Er, my name's Clarkie. Is Pauline in please?'

'You're the face to the voice?' the boy said, standing in the doorway.

Pauline's voice drifted down the stairs. 'Darren who is it?' She came down. 'Clarkie, come in. Darren go and finish your homework. And make sure you tidy up the living room.'

Darren reluctantly unlocked the gate, stepped back and let me in. His eyes were suspicious.

'I'm glad you phoned,' said Pauline, locking the gate and shutting the door behind her.

'I'm sorry about last night.' I handed her the flowers. 'I want to explain . . .'

She smiled. 'They're lovely.'

Pauline led me into the front room. She went into the kitchen, got a nice vase, filled it with water, cut the stems off with a sharp knife and put the flowers into the vase. She sat down on the sofa next to me

'So how is everything going?' she asked nervously.

'Fine. And you?'

'Fine.'

'What do you think about the state of the economy?'

'A bit like the weather, it could be better.' Pauline smiled, awkwardly.

'Yeah. Yeah. I suppose you're right,' I said, clearing my throat.

Darren was sitting between us reading an Anansi story.

'I'm just going to the kitchen to get a glass of water,' Darren said, his face set in hard lines.

He got up, placed the book where he had been sitting, marking his territory. He looked at both of us, took a few paces, then turned around quickly. Pauline and I smiled at him.

Darren ran his fingers lazily along the keys of a piano. His computer games cases were scattered over the floor. Pauline glanced at a chess board. 'Do you play?'

SIDE **69**

Later on that afternoon I left Pauline's flat. She walked me down the passage. There was yellow tape on her neighbour's door and more on the ground, outlining the shape of a human body.

I stopped at the markings. 'What happened?'

Pauline's reply was straight to the point. 'He got stabbed last night. It's such a shame, he was a real nice guy. I wasn't in at the time. I came back and people told me what had happened. Mr Jackson, was his name. A timid, frail man. He got picked on a lot by the kids on the estate.'

We walked on.

Darren popped his head out of Pauline's door.

'He's a nice kid,' I said.

'I've sacrificed everything for him.'

Darren had his coat on and was tailing us.

'Protective.'

'Yeah, in a sweet kind of way. When I go out he tells me what time to come back in. He vets all my dates.'

'He made his voice sound so deep I thought it was your husband.'

'He's the only man in my house. When I get back inside, he's going tell me what he thinks of you.'

Pauline decided not to use the urine-soaked lift. We took the stairs.

I decided to take my opportunity. 'Can I ask you a personal question?'

'Within reason.'

'How did your husband die?'

Pauline paused for a second or two. 'He was shot at a blues party. He was one of the guys in the sound system. He stepped on someone's shoes. That's how it started, and things just escalated.'

We got to the bottom of the stairs and walked through the underground car park. Darren was still behind us. Pauline continued. 'I wasn't going to go to your surprise party. Your mother persuaded me.' A faint light glinted on her high cheekbones.

'How long have you and Froggy known each other?'

The high road was busy.

'About eight months. He leaves me feeling ...

scared.' Her voice was chilly. 'It's just clicked,' She snapped her fingers. 'You know what he reminds me of? A duck. On the surface it looks like it's doing nothing, but underneath the water its feet are paddling away furiously. He acts like he's eighteen.'

The local residents were holding up placards and protesting about the prostitutes on the estate.

Pauline breathed out heavily. 'This is no place for a growing boy. I can't wait for them to start knocking down the block I live in. I'll get rehoused on a normal street or get some money and buy my own.' She glanced over her shoulder. She raised her eyes to the sky as Darren hid behind a post box.

'The last straw was when Darren and I went on holiday. When I came back I'd been burgled. They'd bent the gate back, crawled under it, kicked in the door and taken my things. CD player, TV, video, things like that. Anything they could get under the gate. I can't wait to move.' She pointed into the distance. 'That's my school over there, the grey building, and over there is the community centre.'

'Looks like a crack house. Can I see your school?'

S I D E **70**

Pauline opened the classroom door, there were colour-ful paintings on the wall. They had the power, freedom and innocence that only children could conjure up.

'I had to get my teaching degree.' Pauline sat on the edge of the desk touching her hair, focusing on me. 'I lived in a tower block and when I looked out of my window I saw another tower block. The only way I could escape was to shut my eyes and use my imagination.'

'I heard that.'

'But for these kids it's like a dead end.' Her voice softened. 'Your Mother said you were the sort of person who would be good to talk to the kids in the centre. But ... one thing doesn't fit in ... where did you learn to dance?' Her eyes were steady as she looked at me.

'Howard, Froggy's father taught me. So how about you?'

'A friend at work found the restaurant and said it did really good food and she started doing the classes. I was doing ballroom dancing at the time. I used to take Darren with me and was looking for a change.'

'Darren?'

'He used to sit at a table and do his drawings. That's what you have to do sometimes when you're a single mother. Darren and I have spent many a Saturday night in a café drinking orange juice. We have a great time.' Her eyebrows went up. 'And before you say anything, there is nothing in the Bible that says thou shalt not dance.' A faint smile played across her mouth.

'I'll come and speak to the kids and in exchange you go out with me for a meal.'

'No, I don't think so,' she said, bowing her head slightly. 'I've been let down by men too many times. They always expect more.'

'The wrong men. I'll call you.'

I turned to leave and bumped into Darren, who was standing in the doorway with the caretaker. He made just enough room to let me squeeze past. Then he moved over to his mother and put an arm around her waist.

S I D E  **71**

When I got back to the house, Froggy was standing on the pavement looking at the Karmann Ghia. 'Ah get it back from DI garage. Jus ah faulty battery DAT'S hall.' He had a frown on his face. 'Look wha DEM bastards do TU MI paint work,' he said, pointing to the wing of the car. 'DEH key it. Scratch mi baby. Yu can't leave heny ting heny where heny mo. DAT'S goin tu cost me moni.'

He got into the Karmann Ghia, picked up his SuperVHS camcorder and started watching some film footage.

'WHERE Bones de?' he asked.

'I don't know. I'm a little worried about him. So what happened to you last night?'

'Jus ah LIKKLE runnins. Mi ah hopen up me own club. SO ah ad wuz tu meet som people,' he said, giving me some drawings.

'Where is it?' I asked, unfolding the papers.

'North-side. Camden Town. EVERYTING deh-deh, yu get me? Bones will mos probably go mad wen e FINE out cos e is bout loyalty an me is bout MONI, yu get me? Ah don't skin up BOUT DAT. Dat's wha it is tu me, moni. Tell me bout Mary,' he said, getting into the car.

'What do you wanna know?'

'Wha yu noh? Get een LEKS go fi ah drive.'

I moved over to the passenger seat and gave him back the sketches.

Froggy shook his head. 'Yu DRIVE. Me tired. Ah NEVA sleep much laas nite, tes drive it fi me.'

S I D E  72

I drove the Karmann Ghia hard and fast, like I was chasing my enemy. 'She used to be married to this guy, Cornell was his name, he cut hair in Jack's barber shop on the Harrow Road,' I said. 'Across the road above the butcher's shop they had a flat.'

Froggy was all ears. 'RIGHT, right.'

My knees crowded the wheel. 'I didn't really know Cornell to talk to, but I used to say, "Yo", if we bucked up in the street, or in the bookies. He was the one who turned her mad. She was alright, then he started fucking around with obeah, voodoo, ju-ju and all that kind of stuff. He came from a small island in the West Indies where that type of thing was common. The only person he got on with was Mrs Birchfield.'

I moved down the gears, hunched over the wheel and took a tight corner.

A smile faded from his face. 'GWAAN rudebwoy, me ah lissen,' he said, serious, intense.

'Anyway he started predicting future events. Jack fired him from the shop, and things got worse. It got to a stage where people would jokingly ask, "Ay, Cornell, what's going to happen today?" One soft grey day in March he turned round and said, "I'm going to die", and started laughing. He did, just like he said, that night after making love to Mary.'

The laughter came back to Froggy's eyes. 'RAAAA-AAAAH.'

'The story goes that, he came, rolled over and died one time, and he never left Mary a red cent. The flat, the money he had in the bank, the car, he gave everything to his sister, Mary never got a nickel. So it was rumoured that she used to go and pay regular visits to his grave, just to see how he was doing even though he was dead and buried. I didn't believe the gossip until I saw her in the cemetery with my own eyes.'

I took a short cut and shot down a bus-only lane. Sirens blared. Froggy smiled and looked in the wing mirror. 'Ah tink we might be een luck. Ah hope dat's ah nex fire hengine.'

A police car tailed us and pulled us over. The officers got out of the car. A black officer was having a conversation over his walkie-talkie.

Froggy nudged my elbow. 'Clarkie, AH NEVA really ad time tu tell yu. But ah regista di car een YU name an haddress.'

'What?'

'Well yu noh. Ah brok up WID Tina AH did ave no where tu stay.' He added quickly, 'Ah didn't TINK yu wuz cumin hout so soon. AH wuz goin tu change hall di details nex week, yu get me? Jus old it down, yeah?'

I wound down my window and contained my anger.

'Can you get out of the car please?' The black officer listened to a message coming over his walkie-talkie. 'Have you got your documents, sir?'

'No not on me,' I said, getting out of the car. 'I've just bought it.'

'When?'

My smile was bitter. 'Yesterday,' I said, looking at Froggy.

He nodded. His eyes were full on my face, there was a worried look in them as if he was asking me to explain everything away.

'Can you open the bonnet please?' asked the black officer.

'Where have you come from?' asked the white officer.

I stared at Froggy for a few seconds before I spoke. 'Home.'

The white officer lifted the bonnet and inspected the engine, while the black officer opened the glove compartment and checked the inside of the car.

'Where are you going?' asked the black officer, dryly.

'Tu check hout mi venue,' said Froggy, his eyes shining.

The white officer shut the bonnet and came over to me. 'The registration number of the engine and the chassis number don't match. According to this,' he pointed to his walkie-talkie, 'the engine is stolen. You're under arrest.'

I wanted the ground to open up and swallow me. There I was pretending the car was mine, not grassing on Froggy, and now I was in the shit.

'You take his car and I'll follow,' said the black officer to his partner. He flicked a glance at Froggy. 'You're lucky that the car wasn't stolen or you would be under arrest too.'

Froggy got out of the car. 'Ah go CARL Melanie an tell har WHA appen.'

'She's a barrister not a solicitor,' I said, scowling.

'Yeah but she noh wha TU do. Mek HAR deal wid it.'

I got into the police car and watched Froggy running towards a phone box. Things were never straight when you were dealing with him; there was always a catch somewhere down the line.

# S I D E  73

'I bought it early yesterday,' I said sipping my coffee. 'From a friend, in good faith. I haven't seen the guy for ten years, I bumped into him and he was selling the car.'

A pretty female detective, with soft dark-blond hair that fell to her shoulders and an overworked look about her, was conducting the interview. Her name was Clayderman, she looked about thirty-five and had large dark green eyes, glowing skin, she was wearing no lipstick, her lips were light pink.

'So soon after coming out of prison?' she asked, her eyes searching my face, looking for a reaction.

'I wanted to be mobile.'

That's all I said to begin with, because in my experience police officers were excellent scriptwriters; you said one thing to them and they made up a whole story. If it was grass they could make it sound and look like plants, they were good at sensationalising everything.

Clayderman yawned. 'Where does your friend live?' She was wearing blue jeans, not too close fitting, a cream jumper and well-polished shoes, good leather, expensive. She had an air of confidence about her that made me feel that she was the kind of woman who would get served immediately in a restaurant.

'I dunno. It was the first time I'd seen him in years.'

She gestured to a tall, black plainclothes officer, who was sitting in the corner drinking tea and looking at me over the rim of his cup. He put his hands together and made a time out sign.

Clayderman sighed and spread her hands helplessly. 'You haven't been here more than five minutes and you're off already? Come on, stay and help me out, we're a little short of staff, I shouldn't be doing this, I should be working on the Cyber Vigilante case. Help me out?'

The black officer shook his head in the negative.

'Alright. Hold on, are you mobile yet? Have you got a car?'

The black officer was not one for words, he shook his head in the negative and took me back to my cell. His steps were firm. There was something vaguely familiar about the officer but I couldn't place it.

S I D E **74**

I fell asleep in the police cell and woke up dripping with sweat. My mind was delirious.

'Wayne? Wayne?' My voice was thin, I looked around the cell. I got up and started to walk around, it was an automatic reaction. I picked up speed and started to run, like a hamster in a cage.

S I D E **75**

Melanie arrived and took notes from me. Then we were ushered into the interview room by the black officer. I was visibly nervous as Melanie laid out the facts.

Clayderman listened carefully and said, 'OK. Fine. He's got seven days to produce his documents and give us the address of the person he bought the car from.'

'Can I have the car?' I asked

'Yes, of course,' said Clayderman. 'You can take the body, but you'll have to leave the engine.'

S I D E  76

Froggy was waiting for me outside the police station. When he saw me and Melanie he raised his arms joyously in the air, like a victorious boxer.

'Ah WUZ rong, Clarkie. Me een di rong,' he said. 'Ah should AVE told yu.'

I ignored him and got into Melanie's Citroen. She dropped me off outside the boxing club. I used the pay phone in the hall to bell Pauline's house. I wanted to find out if she was going to let me take her out for dinner. As I waited to be connected I glanced at a poster of Joey Blade. He was black, had a square jaw,

hard muscles, piercing eyes, a washboard stomach. He
was standing in the classical pose of a boxer, fists up,
gloves below the jaw, shoulders hunched.

'Hello. Hello. Darren, this is Clarkie. Can I speak to
your mum please?'

'. . . Not you again. Hold a sec,' his voice softer now.

Pauline picked up the phone. '. . . Are you at your
Mum's house?' Her voice trembling. '. . . I was just
getting ready to come over there. It's such a waste,
it's terrible. Tragic.'

I was confused. '. . . House? What's a waste? '. . .
Haven't you heard about Bones? He's dead.' Pauline
cleared her throat. '. . . I'm sorry, I'm really sorry . . .'

S I D E **77**

The cellar in my mother's house felt cold. A computer screen was divided into twenty-four individual
windows. It was an audio visual mosaic. The central
window contained video footage of children playing.

A droplet of saliva hit the screen. A pair of feet dangled above it. Nike trainers. Bones was hanging from a rope. He was wearing an electronic glove and a virtual reality mask which was connected to the computer.

Flies buzzed. A police woman covered her nose with a handkerchief and opened the cellar door, holding it ajar with her foot.

Mum was wailing uncontrollably. Dad's face was filled with grief as he tried to comfort her. He used sign language to express how much he was hurting on the inside. My throat was choked up, tears trickled down my cheek. I felt sick, sweat lined my brow and I was shaking. It wasn't the first time I'd seen a dead body but it was the first time I'd seen my brother like this. My stomach was heaving, I could feel the vomit rising. I had to look away. I wanted to hug him but I was frightened. Bones had been so full of life, now the breath was gone. The Scorpion had stung itself.

It was my fault, I was the cause and now I was looking at the effect. Bones had taken his own life. Did he die knowing that I'd slept with Melanie? Was the knowledge too much for him to handle? Did he think I had some sort of macabre control over him? I felt guilty and that I'd been robbed of the chance to redeem myself. Yes, robbed. Now it was my curse to live for the rest of my days knowing that I had indirectly killed my only brother. I'd been dishonest, the tentacles had spread out, and now the lie, the crime, was personified before my very eyes.

A flash popped as a police photographer took stills of Bones. A female forensic officer put on a pair of plastic gloves. She looked at the photographer, he nodded, she stood on a chair and took off Bones' virtual reality mask.

The officers helped her to get him down and they placed him in a black bag and zipped it up. I walked over to the bag, unzipped it and looked at his face. I mustered up all the courage I had in me and placed a gentle kiss on his cheek. His skin was cold.

S I D E **78**

Later that night, candles were burning, family and friends were gathered in Mum's living room. Some of Bones' personal belongings were laid out on a table. I picked up Bones' diamond earring and slipped it into my pocket. Pauline came up to me and gave me a big tender hug. Her timing was perfect, it was just what I needed.

I walked out into the night to get some fresh air.

Froggy was sitting in a black lowrider Lexus Jeep, he was wearing a dollar bill head wrap. He was talking on his mobile phone.

'Where did you get that?' I asked, looking at the Jeep.

'A'RIGHT Mary.' Froggy moved the phone to his other ear. 'A'right Mary. Ah si yu LATEAH. Bye, babe.'

He slipped the phone into his pocket and answered my question. 'Willow LEN it tu me.'

Melanie parked her car. She stepped out, she was all in black.

'Clarkie, I think we need to talk. I know this is not the Right time,' said Melanie.

'About what?' I asked.

'Last night.'

'Where's YU ring?' asked Froggy, running his finger along the steering wheel. 'Bones' body NAH coal an yu TEK it arf,' he said, glancing at the vacant spot on her finger.

'I've had enough of your nasty lip,' said Melanie, her eyes hard.

He gave her a cold-blooded grin. 'It ain't NUTTIN but ah ring, right?'

'What do you mean by that?'

'Ah leas now yu noh where E is ah nite.'

Melanie moved towards the Jeep. I blocked her path.

'Have some respect, Froggy,' I said, sourly shaking my head.

Melanie shrugged me off. She pointed her finger at Froggy.

'You better back off. Don't go there. Don't go there. This is all your fucking fault, you and your fucking mouth, telling Clarkie that I'd set him up on purpose.' She clenched her fist and thought about hitting him. 'You ain't worth it,' she said, walking briskly up the path. 'You want to do something about those burn marks you've got on your hand from smoking rock cocaine.' She rang the doorbell.

'Don't try an DISRISPEK me. Fish mout,' said Froggy.

Melanie put her hands on her hips, her head rocked from side to side as she talked. 'Who are you calling fish mouth?'

'Yu hoochie mama. Dis is di FIRS time mi si yu wear SOMTING dat ain't si trew. Paradin man EEN an houtta yu yard. Why don't yu jus go an sell yu frowsey pussy fi moni?'

'You want to smell yourself. When was the last time water touched your body? Just hold a fresh.'

'You're not a rock kid are you?' I asked Froggy. 'I don't know which is worse, the rock or AIDS.'

'I'm telling the truth,' said Melanie. 'The fingers never lie. Once crack addiction gets a hold of you, it keeps a hold of you. And Froggy, I'm going to personally make sure that your wife takes you to the cleaners.' She entered my parents' house and shut the door.

'There was no need for that comment about the ring,' I said, taking in the cool air, looking at his fingers. He curled them up into a tight fist.

'OW yu feel?' asked Froggy, picking up his video camera.

'Full of regret.'

'Don't YU FEEL guilty?'

'About what?'

'Di tings yu wanted tu SEH, could ave said but now yu can't. DOZE KINA tings.'

'Guilt is cheap.' I lit a cigarette. 'It's like something

to do with a crime. Regret is about love. You can't buy time.'

'Is true yu can't WALLOW een self-pity.'

Mrs Birchfield came up the road with Queenie, her dog.

I waved the smoke away from my eyes.

Froggy got out of the Jeep. 'Ah don't wanna get caught UNDA dat WITCHS foot.' He disappeared into the house.

Mrs Birchfield sprinkled water from a bottle onto the ground in front of her. She was wearing a hat and shaking her head from side to side. She slipped the bottle into her bag and folded her flabby arms under her teapot breasts. She made the sign of the cross as she walked past me and said a quiet 'Evenin'.

Queenie sniffed me and her tail stopped wagging, she glanced up at Mrs Birchfield, who shrugged. Queenie gave a low moan as they entered the house.

# S I D E 79

Melanie parked outside my house. We sat in her car for a few moments and talked about the last time we both saw Bones, alive. What he said. What he didn't say. The look in his eyes. She was grieving big time. Heartbroken. She felt Bones was getting his own back on her, that he wanted her to feel the pain he'd felt. The thought of him wandering through the streets after he left her flat brought tears to her eyes.

As I shut my front door I heard sweet soul music and soft voices, they mixed together ecstatically. I walked towards Bones' bedroom, which was where the noise was coming from.

On the carpet I saw a white G-string and blue silk suspenders, the sound of a woman breathing heavily hit my ears. A deep male voice said, 'Tun roun, tun yuself roun.'

Bed springs squeaked.

'Yeah! Dat's it,' said the eager male voice. The sexy voice belonged to Froggy. It was full of passion.

'Ooooooooooooooh! Yes, Uh, mmmm, yes, this my favourite position, rock the spot,' gasped the female, 'deeper, deep! deep! deep!' she cried.

'Yu a'right?' panted Froggy.

'Yeah ... It's swee ... swee ... swee ... the pain is sweet, uhh! God! It hurts so good inside ... I'm coming so much I want to piss.'

Then I heard the clapping sound of hot steaming flesh hitting warm wet skin. I stepped on a light blue dress as I pushed the bedroom door. Soft candle lights flickered, the orange flames danced like wild flamingos, throwing distorted shadows onto the walls and ceiling. The bank of computers jumped with ultra smooooooooooth graphics.

I could see Froggy and his mate making hardcore love in Bones' bedroom. His batti was pumping like a piston as he held the woman's slippery brown body. I still couldn't make out who she was, she was on all fours and giving Froggy precise instructions. I was annoyed with Froggy because Bones had just passed away and he was busy digging some woman in his bed.

'Ahhhh! That's it, you've hit the spot . . . Harder! . . . Yes, faster!' She threw her head back and said, 'Fuck me you bastard.'

Froggy did as he was told.

When she said, 'squeeeeze me', he did.

When she said, 'lick me', he did.

I went into the kitchen and opened the fridge. I was about to take out a tub of ice-cream, I always ate ice-cream when I was vexed, but as the interior light came on, I saw six cans of Tennant's Super in the lower compartment tray. I listened to the loud bawling coming from the bedroom, he was making her body sing a sweet melody. I looked back at the Tennant's.

There was only one lady I knew who drank Tennant's and owned razor sharp vocal chords like the ones coming from the bedroom. Mad Mary. Froggy was making love to MAD MARY. The thought of it put me off my ice-cream, not because she was nasty or anything. But I never imagined I'd find her in my house, having sex with a friend of mine.

I shut the fridge door and hoped that he didn't do anything to make her mad and piss on his grave.

When Froggy eventually came out of the bedroom,

he was beaming. He was visibly shocked to see me sitting in the front room with my foot cocked up on a chair watching the late night gangster movie. He obviously hadn't expected me back so soon. My ears picked up the sound of running water, so I knew Mad Mary was in the bathroom.

I didn't say a word to him, I was so mad. Froggy wanted to say something, I held up my hand and he knew I didn't want to hear it. But he didn't know why. I just couldn't believe he was so unconcerned about Bones.'

Mad Mary eventually came into the front room. She was wearing the light blue dress and flesh-coloured stockings. Her black hair had a golden brown tint, it had been cut in a short punk style which suited her round face. She walked over to me, and as bold as brass she offered me her hand. I wanted to decline but didn't want to seem impolite so I took it. Her flesh was soft, her grip firm. Her finger-nails were painted red, like her lips, and she smelt of sex, not a bad smell, kind of spicy and nice. Close up, I could see why Froggy had fallen under her spell.

'I've seen you about but I don't know your name,'

she said, her fresh lime green eyes sucking me into her erotic world.

'Clarkie,' I replied.

Then she turned away from me to find a seat. She moved like dynamite but gave me enough time to see her samba. She melted into an easy chair and crossed her long, slim legs over her soft centre.

I was shaking with rage but I didn't want to start an argument in Mary's presence. I noticed the telephone was not only off the hook, the plug had also been pulled out of the wall socket. Mary had a guilty look on her face. Froggy could tell I was upset, he could tell I wanted to be alone.

'I'm DUSTIN hout,' he said.

He rounded up his belongings, picked up a bunch of disks, handed me the spare set of keys, collected the cold cans of Tennant's, and put his arm around Mary.

'Ah CHECK yu tomorrow,' he said warmly.

'It was really nice meeting you,' said Mary politely.

I heard the Jeep fire up, a ballistic bassline thumped and it roared off.

*SUPERFLY! SUPERFLY! SUPERFLY!*

S I D E

*IT'S A DARK WORLD*
*IT'S A DARK WORLD*
*IT'S A DARK WORLD*
*BUT DON'T WORRY.*

### Caption: Monday

I was awakened by the ring of the telephone. It was Melanie. She was just leaving her flat but she said she would drop in later that day with some good news.

I couldn't get back to sleep. There'd been no nocturnal visits from Wayne so things were looking up. I took a cold shower, towelled myself down, rubbed coconut oil into my skin, and got dressed. Jeans, t-shirt, sneakers, no underwear or socks. I was going to use some Joop cologne, but decided against it. The scent was Bones' favourite. The Bottle was nearly empty. I couldn't even touch it.

For breakfast, I had four Weetabix with soya milk and honey, a bowl of fruit salad, fresh orange juice, a ginseng tablet, and three teaspoons of premiere royal jelly.

I'd just finished cleaning the house and Hoovering the carpets when there was a knock on my front door. I opened it and was surprised to see Pauline.

'Why aren't you at school?' My voice sounded hoarse.

'I've taken a day off to help your mum. Are you going to talk to me on the doorstep?'

'I'm sorry, come in.'

Over her shoulder, I noticed the white mini with blacked out windows pulling away. What was it doing outside my house? I was being watched by somebody, I was certain of that, and was going to find out who and why.

Pauline wouldn't let me do a thing. She told me to sit down and relax while she washed up the plates and put on the kettle. She placed a cup of steaming black coffee in front of me. 'You look like you should get some sleep.'

'I'm too frightened to close my eyes. I didn't sleep a wink last night.'

'What are you scared of?'

'It's a long story.'

'Well, whatever it is you've got no need to be afraid. Get some sleep now,' she said, giving me a friendly tap on the shoulder. 'It will do you good. Recharge your batteries. I'll be here. I've got a good book.'

'I don't want Wayne to sell me a dream as a nightmare. Not today. I can't deal with it today.'

Pauline sat down at the table with a cup of tea and looked at me anxiously. 'Wayne? Nightmare? What are you talking about?'

'Have you ever been sold a dream as a nightmare?'

She dropped a couple of sweeteners into her tea, sipped and said, 'Yes. I suppose in the past a couple of men have tricked their way into my life.'

'Wayne's good at that. She always comes, looks the same, blue jeans, white t-shirt with the words I love my attitude, bandana, gold tooth, bare feet, no make-up but the story she tells is always different.'

I lit a cigarette and started walking around the kitchen.

'Are you feeling OK? Are sure you don't want me to call a doctor. You might be suffering from shock.'

'Wayne comes to me in my dreams. The last time she called was when I was in the police cell. The only way I can shake her off is by walking in a circle, sometimes by running.'

The telephone bleated. I froze.

'Have you seen anyone?' asked Pauline, softly. 'I mean a professional, who can talk you through it?'

The telephone continued to ring. Pauline looked at me and I gestured that it was OK for her to answer it.

'Hello. It's Pauline,' she said, speaking into the receiver '... He's occupied at the moment. Yes. I'll make sure he gets the message.' She replaced the receiver. 'It was Froggy. He wants to arrange a time to download his files from the computer. He doesn't think you should sleep in the house until the nine nights have passed.'

'I can't go to sleep. The minute I close my eyes Wayne will be here. I know she's waiting for me.'

S I D E **81**

Shoes were lined up against a wall. Bones' bed was still unmade from Froggy and Mary's activities the previous night. The computers, telephones, terminal adaptors and other state of the art equipment were still connected. I took off my shoes and picked up one of Bones' t-shirts and smelt it. Joop.

'What are you going to do with his clothes?' asked Pauline, concerned.

'I'm going to leave everything for a month or so as it is, then I'll burn them. Take off your shoes.'

'I'm sorry,' said Pauline, as she slipped off her sandals. 'If you don't mind, I'll ask your mother for permission. Maybe we can bag them up and give them to Oxfam or a charity. I'll see how she feels.'

'I'll decide. I'll decide what happens in this house.' I could feel my lips pulling back in anger.

323

'OK, I'm sorry. I understand. It was just an idea,' said Pauline.

I stripped the bed and got fresh sheets. Pauline was standing in front of the computers. I'd noticed one of them had twenty-four images on the screen, the same ones that had been on the computers in Mum's cellar where Bones was found. There was a buzzing and a humming sound as the terminal adaptors found the right protocol to communicate with other modems somewhere in the globe.

'What's this on the screen?' asked Pauline.

'The computers are linked to the ones in Mum's house the ones in the cellar. Bones liked to have multiple access points. I said as I made up the bed.

'He didn't leave a note. Do you think this might be it? That these images together mean something? Is it some sort of code?'

I turned my head. Pauline was looking at film footage of children playing in various locations. The frames changed, she gasped, stumbled backwards away from the screen, quickly put on her shoes and walked out of the room. I moved over to the computers and focused on one that had just finished downloading. Child pornography files were on the screen.

'What the hell?' I said under my breath.

I clicked on the mouse and entered a file.

'Damn.'

I was shocked and sickened by what I saw, but before I could think, digest it, I heard the front door slam shut.

'She looks like a bitch on wheels. No, half bitch half cow.'

I spun around in the direction of the voice. It belonged to Melanie.

'There's a bell, you should try using it,' I said, as I switched off the computer.

Melanie put her handbag on the bed. 'I thought you had more style,' she said, turning her face up at the stained sheets on the floor. 'Sex already? So soon?'

'You jealous?'

'Just look at her. You think I'd be jealous over her?'

'The mistake I made was sleeping with you.'

'No, the biggest mistake you made was enjoying it.'

'I betrayed my brother's trust. Did you ever love him?'

'Yes in my kind of way.'

'How many of your other clients have you gone

to bed with? That's how you get your kicks, isn't it?'

'It's nice to see you actually using your brain to ask constructive questions but I wouldn't flatter yourself. I didn't even come when I slept with you. I hope she did.'

'Keep it in the family, first my brother then me.'

'I can't take rejection. That's why I'm the way I am.'

'Was Bones into children?'

'Yes, he wanted kids.'

'That's not what I mean. Sexually?'

'What kind of sick question is that? I was the only child he needed.'

I decided to change the subject. 'What's the good news? Let's talk about that. I need to relax.'

'Two things. The engine in the Karmann Ghia, I've spoken to officer Clayderman. They've found the car that it belonged to, it's a wreck. The insurance company say that it's not economically viable to repair the car and put the engine back in. The owner has already claimed his money. The police are dropping the case. It will cost you round about fifty pounds for the paperwork and you can have it back.'

'What's the second thing?'

'Bones made you an executor to his will.'

'My family's in mourning. Let's do it tomorrow.'

'I won't be around, I've told you I'm booked on a flight to Paris. I respect your feelings but business is business. You're in charge. His estate. Everything he owns. The game, nightclub, shop. His paintings. The computer art. Everything. You can do what Bones has said in his will, within certain limitations.'

'I don't want to think about money. I've got to make plans to bury my brother. Your fiancé.'

'I drew up the papers. Bones split it down the middle between you and your parents. You're going to need a will.'

'I ain't planning on dying yet. How come you're so cold? You could at least pretend you care. Doesn't Bones' death mean anything to you?'

'What does it mean to you?'

'It means I won't hear his laugh again.'

'Well you weren't worrying about that last night. When we were driving back from the West End.'

'I feel guilty enough as it is. I don't need you to remind me. You know what really gets to me? The image of Bones walking through the streets of London on his own. After pulling the gun on us. What was going through his head? He must have hated us.'

'Clarkie, listen to me. The bottom line is you've got a slight problem. And I've been busy working it out for you. I can solve it for you for a percentage, not a fee.'

'What problem? A percentage? You sure that's alright? You could be struck off.'

'I've covered my back. Let me break it down for you. Bones is dead and he can't take the money with him. So I've got to look after me.'

'Hang on a minute, you're not supposed to have an interest in this, aren't you supposed to be independent?'

'Normally my advice is always two steps away from the client. This is different. Now, do you wanna hear the deal or not?'

'That's cold.'

'I know Bones did a lot of computer art that he didn't tell anyone about. And that he was planning to move to another gallery and take it with him and say they were new works. Hunter signed a contract with him.'

'I don't want Hunter to get the money. He's his

dealer, he doesn't have to know about the new pieces. Out of sight, out of mind. His contract with Bones doesn't extend to me.'

'That's what I think, so we have to find someone else and say that they did the work in the same style. How does that sound? I've already got somebody in mind. I'll arrange it.'

Melanie picked up her handbag and made a move towards the door.

'Hold on, hold on, not so fast.'

'What's the problem?' asked Melanie, opening her bag and taking out a plastic container. 'I was only going to get a glass of water to take my allergy pills.'

'If you're doing the deal for the work, if you set yourself up as the dealer, what's stopping you and the front man or woman from doing a runner?'

'You don't trust me?'

'That's fucking right.'

'Let's change the game. We'll sign a deal. I'll make sure it's not null and void. It will be enforceable.'

'So who is the third person.'

'Froggy.'

'You guys will be at each other's throats.'

The telephone bleated. I answered it.

'Hello.'

It was Mum.

'... Ave yu seen ah eard from Melanie?' she asked nervously.

I gave Melanie a sharp look. I didn't say a word.

'... Di police ave bin roun ere lookin fi har.' Mum's voice sounded drained of energy. '... Deh seh Bones' death wuzn't ah suicide.'

'... What?' I lit a cigarette.

'... E wuz dead before e wuz hung. It is now ah murda hinvestigation.'

'... Are you sure? Murder?'

'... Deh want tu talk tu Melanie.'

Melanie had her ear pressed to the phone. She heard every single word Mum said, she backed away slowly. I felt my fingers tightening around the receiver.

'... OK,' I said calmly. '... If she gets in contact, I'll get her to get in touch with the police. A'right, bye, Mum.' I replaced the receiver and spun around to face Melanie. 'Shit! Shit! Shit!' I yelled. 'I can't fucking believe it. They're coming after us.'

# S I D E  82

Melanie and I ran down the path. My heart was beating hard. Her lower lip went between her teeth and she stared at me.

'Did you clean the blood off the back seat?' I asked.

'Yeah,' she said, taking a deep breath.

I opened the door of her Citroen and inspected the seats. 'Good, this is good. There's no trace. What about the boot?'

Melanie was rooted to the spot.

'What about the boot? Did you clean out the boot?'

I opened the boot. There were traces of blood.

'FUCKING hell. I leave you to do one simple thing and you couldn't do it?'

Melanie trembled nervously. 'I've been busy.'

'Busy?'

'I've been so busy I haven't had time to change my tampon. I'm going to be dribbling all over the place soon. Can't we do it now?'

For a moment, I almost lost my composure. I glanced at my next door neighbour, who was watching us as he fixed his fence.

'No. Give me the keys,' I said, firmly 'They're gonna be looking for this. Willow's got a lock-up I can put this in.'

S I D E **83**

Police officers searched the cupboards in the kitchen. Lady Luck was on my side. I'd left my gun in a different hiding place in the city. I acted real calm but I was feeling uncomfortable. I consciously stopped my hand from shaking as I lit another cigarette from the butt of an old one.

Clayderman gave her team of officers orders, they went up the stairs and into different rooms. She turned her attention to me. The black plainclothes officer was at her side, chewing gum. He watched me out of the corner of his eye.

'We found your fingerprints in Melanie's flat,' said Clayderman, picking up a small plastic container from the table.

'She's a friend of mine, my brother's girlfriend,' I replied.

'Have you seen her today?' asked the black officer. He had an American accent. Something seemed to be irritating him. 'Do you know how specks of your brother's blood got onto her bathroom wall? Spots in the living room?'

'No.'

'Her neighbours said they heard shouting coming from her flat,' he said. 'And they saw you three arguing outside her premises on the night he was murdered.'

'Yeah, I was at her place. So what?' I said, taking a pull of the cigarette.

'Your brother was dead before he was put in the cellar,' said Clayderman, looking at the label on the plastic container.

'What's that got to do with me?'

'You go into prison because of a case concerning

Bones. ABH, actual bodily harm. You come out. The next thing he's found dead,' said Clayderman, sharply.

'Are you going to arrest me?

'You've got an allergy?'

'What?'

'An allergy. The pills.' Clayderman held the bottle up. 'One tablet to be taken four times a day.'

'Yeah.'

'My sister takes some similar to these. What are your symptoms?'

The telephone purred softly. I glanced at it nervously. I moved towards it but the American officer blocked my path with his body. He was strong and well built. Cardboard-shaped shoulders. He had a lot of strength in reserve.

Clayderman picked up the receiver. '... Hello, who is that? ... Melanie? Melanie?'

The cigarette stopped halfway to my mouth.

Clayderman looked in my direction, she frowned, turned her back to me and said, '... Oh. No, no, I'm not Melanie. I thought you were. Who? OK. Hold on a second.'

Clayderman put her hand over the receiver. I took a deep drag and held the smoke down.

She placed the plastic container on the table and handed me a card with her telephone number. 'Give me a call if you remember anything else.'

I breathed out a thin cloud and took the receiver from her. She walked into the passage with the American and rounded up the other officers.

'Hello,' I said, speaking into the phone.

'... What's going on?' asked Pauline, her voice thin on the other end of the line. '... Who was that?'

I took another drag on the cigarette and coughed. Through the kitchen window, I watched Clayderman and the American get into a car loaded with floppy disks and hardware.

'... Are you at Mum's?'

'... No. I'm at home, I've been in about fifteen minutes. Who's there with you?'

'... The police. Can we meet? I'm in trouble,' I asked nervously.

'... I don't want to get involved. But I want to know what you're going to do about that pornography on the machine. That's what I was calling about. Your mother is going through enough as it is. Are you going to tell the police?'

'... I don't know yet.'

'... You seem to have found out more about Bones since he hit the autopsy table.'

'... Please. I want to see you. There's no one else I can talk to.'

'... I don't want to be drawn into anything. And it's a bit difficult because of Darren. Plus I've got to do school reports.'

'... Damn.'

'... Why me?'

'... You're the only person that has ever listened to me.'

'... Oh I don't know.'

'... Please.'

'... I' She sighed. '... I can't stay long. Tell me over the phone. Tell me now.'

'... Face to face. I don't know who's listening.'

'... Well ...'

'... Fifteen minutes. Can you spare that?'

'... I'll try and get my next door neighbour to look after Darren. I need a couple of hours.'

'... You got it.'

'... Where shall I meet you?'

I reached for my pack of cigarettes and shook

out another. I scratched a match, had trouble holding the flame steady. I sucked in the smoke and
coughed hard.

S I D E  **84**

*Don't make a grown man crrrrrrrrrrry!*

Bright lights beam down. The boxing club was empty.
'So is that the whole truth?' asked Pauline.
The ropes around the ring were blue and red. Pauline
and I stood in opposite corners. I looked at her from
head to toe, she smelt like a summer meadow fresh
from the dew. A dream come true. She was wearing
black shoes, leather, low heels.
She rested her back against the ropes. 'That's the
confession you wanted to talk to Mrs Birchfield about,
I suppose. So you only slept with Melanie once?'
'I ain't proud of it.'
Pauline left her corner and walked slowly around the

337

ring. 'You must have felt something for her, maybe you still do. What's her motive?' she asked wearily.

'Money. The will.'

'I'm not talking about that,' said Pauline, a blank expression on her face. 'Who did she really want?'

'The drink might have made her indecisive. She's an habitual drinker. She doesn't know what she wants.'

I could feel sweat forming on my brow.

Pauline shook her head in dismay. 'It's like she's come from the past with an agenda.'

I left my corner and walked round in the opposite direction to Pauline.

'Go over that bit again,' said Pauline, shivering slightly. 'When Bones had a gun and he was pistol-whipping you and Melanie.'

'The gun was empty. It was mine, I kept it under the kitchen sink. He attacked Melanie. A fight broke out. He hit me so I hit him back. He went into the bathroom and when he saw what I'd done to him he went crazy, started kicking things over. I pulled him out of the flat, dragged him down the stairs, and shoved him in the back seat of Melanie's car. We drove off, but he started getting out of control again. He was cussing about this and cussing about that. It was pure noise in the car. So I decided to play a joke on him. We parked the car. I got out, opened the boot. He was drunk and I'm stronger than him, so, I was able to pick him up and put him in the boot.'

'You lead such complicated lives. So that's why you defended her when your mother called, when the police were looking for her? It was to save yourself as well. That's what you want me to think.'

'He had pulled a gun on me. It was the only way of keeping him quiet. But it didn't work. There was all this loud banging and muffled shouts coming from the boot. I told Melanie we couldn't take him back to his house because I didn't know what he would do when we got there either. So we drove to the West End, and pulled up in a busy street. I opened the boot and quickly got back into the car. Bones was furious. He jumped out and in the rear view mirror I saw him kicking out at the car. He stumbled and fell down. It was like letting a wild cat out of a cage. He was fuming mad. So we drove off. I just wanted him to cool down.'

Pauline and I looked into each other's eyes. There was an emotional current flowing.

She looked away. 'That was the last time you saw him alive?'

'Yes. There, there is one thing that I haven't told you ...'

'What? Say it now.'

There was a moment's silence but it felt like an hour.

Pauline's eyes softened. I felt warm on the inside.

'I ... I ... I wanted to say that ...'

I chickened out, I was shy I couldn't really bring myself to tell her how I felt about her.

S I D E **85**

The bagel shop in the West End was packed. Pauline and I emerged holding cheese bagels.

'That was Bones' favourite place,' I said, as we walked past a female clipper talking to a punter in an alleyway. The punter pulled out some money and the clipper gave him a key.

'The clipper's just given him the key to his dreams,' said Pauline, her expression uneasy. 'Sold him a promise. People pay a lot for attention.'

'How come you know so much about all that?'

'I've never been a prostitute, if that is what you mean. I don't have to be one to know about it.'

'Point taken.'

'Some girls on my estate work the West End. I'm not perfect, I haven't always walked the straight line, there was a time when I used to steal to survive.'

'I thought you were as pure as the driven snow.'

'I know what it's like to open your fridge and see just half a bottle of milk and a screaming child waiting to be fed.'

'So what kind of thief were you?'

'Small time.'

'Maybe that's why I like talking to you. A crook that has never been caught is the best person to get an opinion or honest advice from. I know it sounds back to front but I know what I mean.'

'I got caught in the local supermarket. Darren's dad died leaving a lot of debts, they took the house. It was just me and my son against the world. I finally got caught by a shop detective. I had food down my jumper and I'd crotched a chicken under my dress.'

'You did that? Damn.'

'She took me into a room at the back of the store.

I was in tears. The shop detective's daughter was in my class at school.'

'Shit.'

'She knew my headmistress would sack me. And then I would be in an even worse situation, and do you know what she did? I'll never forget it.'

'Called the Feds.'

'She took twenty pounds out of her purse, got a basket, told me to pay for the goods and get anything else I needed with the money and never to come back into the store again.'

'That's true compassion.'

'And you know, when she came to the school to pick up her daughter, she never mentioned a word. She didn't talk or look at me again. Never. Never looked me in the eye. So, that doesn't mean Bones was bad or wicked.'

'I can't accept it.'

'Bones was sick and needed help. It could have been compulsion.'

'I can't believe he was into child pomography and I never knew. I went inside for him, I took the rap, we were brothers. Why would Bones encrypt and zip up certain files and leave something like that on his computer? Somebody either didn't want him to talk or they set him up.'

'Who? Who would be so manipulative and why?'

'Froggy? He was the only one close enough. The only one who knew the passwords to his website and his computers.'

'But why would he do that?'

'Maybe he wants to create a lie. The police are sure it's murder. The Cyber Vigilante could be the killer. I'm so confused. I can't believe Bones was a paedophile.'

'Was Froggy jealous of Bones?'

'I'm not sure. I've got to find out for myself.'

'That's what the police are there for. If it is the Vigilante's work, its best to let the police sort it out. That's what they're paid for.'

'I can't get my life started until I sort this murder out. The only thing we own are our memories. When I came out of prison I wanted my brother as he really was, but now I don't know what that means. What's eating me up is not what Bones was or what he did, but the deception.'

'You're feeling betrayed?'

I avoided eye contact with Pauline.

'Maybe, he did the right thing,' said Pauline, she

paused. 'If Bones had told the truth you wouldn't have loved him so much. The good thing is that you are still prepared to love him despite what he became.' Pauline stopped a cab. 'Clarkie, what is this really all about?'

'I'm frightened of being alone.'

As the cab pulled away Pauline lowered the window. 'Take care.'

'Oh, by the way, I forgot to tell you. I like your shoes, they're cute. Get a pair in brown,' I said, trying to make light of the situation.

'You get me a pair.'

I waited for the cab to disappear from sight, then continued walking. I turned into an alleyway, high with rubbish. I picked up an empty beer bottle. I was being tailed. I'd noticed the tall figure when I came out of the bagel shop. I didn't say anything to Pauline, there was no need to frighten her. It was a man, a black man. I couldn't make out his features, but he was wearing a long coat.

I waited for about five minutes but no one came. Whoever it was must have made other tracks. I put the bottle down and was about to light a cigarette, when I had second thoughts and threw the packet away. Enough was enough. I took Bones' diamond earring out of my pocket. I decided to find somewhere to get my ears pierced; there had to be a tattoo parlour open somewhere in the West End. Then it suddenly hit me. What if the person that had been on my tail had got into a cab and followed Pauline home? How could I have been so stupid? If it wasn't the police and it was somebody who had something against me they could take their revenge out on Pauline. On somebody they thought was close to me. Shit!

S I D E **86**

My reflexes pounced into action as a white hand crash-landed on my shoulder.

'I'm sorry, Clarkie, I didn't mean to frighten yah.'

The soft chirpy voice and warm hand belonged to MC Yello Jacket, a white Negro from The East who had made good.

With some of his dollars he'd bought an old disco in Westbourne Park just around the corner from the underground. He gutted it out, redecorated, called it THE DEPTH, made it a private members club, and charged one pound to get in. Bones was a silent partner in the business.

'D'ya want anyfink else ta drink?' he asked in a breezy manner.

I placed a hand over the mouth of the glass.

'Jus shout if yah want anyfink else,' said Yello, with a smile.

It was my fourth glass of brandy and it was chilling me out big time. I was so confused by everything I just wanted to inoculate myself with booze. I thought about going to buy some drugs, but decided that I wasn't going to start going down that road again.

I walked over to the payphone and called Pauline's flat again. It rang. I was just about to put it down when she picked it up. I was relieved. I told her about the stalker. Her advice to me was to get in contact with Clayderman and come clean, because it could have been the Cyber Vigilante. I told her to make sure she locked her front door and windows before she went to bed. She told me that she always did that anyway.

I took the card Clayderman had given me out of my pocket. I wasn't ready to call her yet, I had too much on my mind. I needed the brandy to level things out before I was ready to communicate with her.

I went back to my table and watched Yello cruise over to the other tables, making sure everybody was cool. Then he went back to work behind the bar, which was a converted white stretch limo. I fiddled with the diamond stud in my ear and savoured the taste of my brandy. I moved over to a jukebox and checked the tunes on offer; I didn't want anything that would remind me of Bones or make me feel depressed. I slipped a coin in and selected a tune that always made me laugh. I wanted it to heal my despairing heart.

> *Yah! Yah! Yah! Yah! Yah!*
> *Yah! Yah! Yah! Yah! Yah!*
> *Wooha! Wooha!*

There were demons in my head that needed to be exorcised. I was frightened that they would take hold and make me do something stupid. My brother was dead and I felt I was to blame for more than one reason. He'd left a distasteful legacy behind him and I could only redeem myself by finding out if it was true. I was emotionally strung out. I needed to get the tears out, I was tired and heavy from keeping everything in for so long. I mean, what else did I really have left? Like everybody else I had my own insecurities, I lacked confidence in certain areas. Froggy had played on that. He knew I was vulnerable when I came out of prison, and he used that to plant a seed in my mind, just like the way Iago fucked with Othello. The silly thing about it was, just like the Moor, I acted on it, I believed him, put his word before Bones' – which led me to sleep with Melanie.

How I wished I could turn back the hands of time and crush the crime. Before all the shit happened I had a stable family and anything outside didn't really matter to me, but now that was all falling apart. If my Mum and Dad found out about my fling with Melanie that would be it. I mean, family were the people you really depended on when things got rough, they had your back covered. Now, I was on my own. It was just me against the world. I thought about ending it all, jumping in front of a train, who would care? I didn't know if I had the courage to pass the test. I wanted to curl up in bed and use my pillow to soak up my tears. I felt so so cold inside.

There was Froggy. I still had to get to him, then I

could sleep the long sleep. We'll maybe there was one person who would be in my corner, Pauline, but I could tell she was still wary of me. And I couldn't blame her for that.

*Yah! Yah! Yah! Yah! Yah!*
*Yah! Yah! Yah! Yah! Yah!*
*Wooha! Wooha!*

I felt my eyes shutting, sleep was calling me.

A violent image of Wayne flashed in my mind. She was smiling, holding her hands open, beckoning me towards her.

*Wayne's body started to decay at a rapid rate. Her clothes began to rip and chunks of her flesh fell onto the floor. It began to bubble and spit as if it was being fried in hot cooking oil. One of her legs hopped up the wall and dripped red blood from the ceiling. The other one began to kick me hard in the shins. Bits and pieces of her limbs flew around the room, gaining speed then slowing down. I screamed out loud as the particles joined back together. Different coloured gases were emitted, then a contorted female apparition stood in*

349

*front of me. Wayne's jowls were long and her red eyes sunk deep into her big head. The skin was loose and patchy on her face. She took a step towards me and opened her mouth. Her thin slimy tongue transformed itself into a furious snake. I screamed hysterically as it curled its scaly body around me and began to squeeze the breath out of my quivering lungs.*

I jerked out of the dream and shook my head. Yello was standing behind the bar, dancing to the beats as he served customers. I pushed my brandy glass to one side. I knew I had to fight sleep, I couldn't fall into that dreadful chamber, horrors were lurking in the land of Zs.

S I D E  87

A couple were kissing in a car.

I approached Mrs Birchfield's house. I looked over my shoulder – there was no figure in a long coat behind me. I had second thoughts about going to Mrs Birchfields and wanted to turn back. But a tinny voice in my head urged me to keep going forward, so I rang her doorbell.

She was not surprised to see me. 'Wha tek yu so long? Ah bin waitin up fi yu.' Her eyes narrowed.

The gravel crunched under her tiny feet as she walked down her garden path. She held her hat as she leaned her big frame over the broken iron gate and looked up and down the street. Her wrinkled neck turned right, left, then right again. She told me to turn around three times and walk into the house backwards.

'Get hinside, get hinside. Quick. Ah don't want mi neighbours tu si yu. Dem tu nosey.'

I sat down on a old wooden settee which she'd covered with a thick coat of plastic. It creaked and moaned as I made myself comfortable.

'Tek arf yu shoes, ah don't want no dirt een mi yard.'

Queenie was fast asleep in her basket. Her tail flicked now and again as she dreamed.

The furniture in the room echoed of the past. The lamp shades, the drinks cabinet, the finely crocheted mats, the little ostrich that dipped its head continually into a glass attached to its feet. Every object had a story to tell. Some had come by sea in a big container when she emigrated to the land of hope and glory. But no matter what their shape or size, they were all cherished and cared for. The plastic on the settee was there to stop the wear and tear. My wandering eyes were drawn to a rocking chair which was placed in the centre of the room. An old clay pipe and a multi-coloured tobacco tin rested on top of a flowery cushion.

Mrs Birchfield picked them up and eased herself into the chair.

'So yu cum tu confess?' She loaded her pipe, struck a match on the coarse wooden arm and puffed the smoke out of both sides of her mouth.

'I've already done that, I found someone else.'

'But somting ah trouble yu.' She got up from her rocking chair, lit some incense and began to sprinkle water around the room. She held her chest, shivered from head to toe and talked in different tongues. She rubbed my temples, bit into a kola nut and listened as I told her about my dreams and the constant presence of Wayne.

'So dis gyal Wayne, she ever cum tu yu een di form of ah bull. Did yu ear chains rattlin?'

'No, Mrs Birchfield,' I replied.

'What about gruntin? Did yu ear gruntin?'

'No.'

'Di soun ah hoofs?'

'No.'

'Yu lucky. Yes. Yes. Yu spirit good. Yu spirit good.' She relit her pipe. 'Wayne did not happear een di form of ah Rollin Calf, so dat mean yu safe.'

'Rolling calf?' I asked inquisitively.

'Arf ghos arf bull,' she said, breathing in deeply. 'Back ome wen ah wuz ah young gyal, one chase me fi ova ah mile. It wuz goin tu kill me but me run like lightin an neva look back.'

This was the most serious I had ever seen Mrs Birchfield. She wasn't adding any sweeteners to the story, she was telling it like it was.

'If ah did look back ah wouldn't be ere now.'

She rocked in her chair, put out the pipe, made the sign of the cross and sprinkled herself with water. She mixed a cup of herbs and gave it to me, saying the drink would quieten Wayne down. It tasted bitter. I thought anything that tasted that bad must do some good.

She pulled her hat tight on her head. 'Tell me, wha yu noh bout di devil?' she asked.

The question caught me off guard but the look in Mrs Birchfield's eyes told me that there was a reason lurking behind it.

'He was an angel and he got booted out, kicked down to earth.'

Mrs Birchfield lowered her head towards the ground, rubbed her lap gently with both hands and gathered her thoughts. 'Een di Caribbean dere wuz dis story, ah eard it wen ah wuz ah likkle gyal, but ah neva forgot it, it wuz bout di devil's chariot.' Her voiced softened as she began to paint pictures with her words. 'Di devil's chariot ... It wuz gleamin white wid precious stones from hall di different galaxies. E clean an polish it everyday, an wen e wuz an angel een heaven it wuz fasta dan di west win. It could beat heny chariot dat di udder angels own, but di honly ting wuz it wuz pull by bulls. Six trong bulls. Di finest hanimals heny body ad ever seen. Deh wuz mo beautiful dan di udder pale horses deh race against ...'

Her voiced dropped an octave and she began to whisper. '... Wen e wuz banish tu Earth deh grew sick an frail. Deh los so much weight deh could ardly walk. Di angels try tu feed dem but deh refuse tu eat hout ah dem han. So tu stop dem from dyin deh wuz sent down tu Earth tu join dem masta. On Earth dem grow strong hagain, an wen e wuz leavin Earth tu set up is kingdom een ell e lef dem ere.'

'Why?'

'Cos it wuz trew dem dat e could ketch is followers.'

'His disciples?'

Mrs Birchfield nodded her head. 'Di rollin calf? Arf ghos arf bull?' She had me eating out of the palm of her hand. 'Dat's why ah did arks yu if Wayne cum tu yu een di form of ah bull, an if yu eard chains rattlin.' She directed her gaze at me. 'One ah tree witches ah try weave ah spell pun yu. If e ah she stan tu di right, di middle, ah di lef, right now ah can't tell.' She scratched the back of her head and beckoned me to lean forward. 'Yu ave tu play fool tu ketch wise. Ah did ave ah dream laas night an ah mek dis.' She produced a wooden effigy of Bones from behind her back. 'Laas nite wuz ah full moon, an een me sleep, ah si dis effigy pun di table, pun mi kitchen table. Its legs move slightly, den it jump arf di table, climb up di stairs an enta mi bedroom. Queenie wuz alseep een har basket, wen she si it she run hout. Ah wuz lyin een me bed, an di effigy jump arn it an stretch hout its ands, deh grew longa an longa, deh wuz hall cova wid wasps. As it put its han roun mi troat, ah jerk forwad an hopen me eyes, ah brok di dream. Ah look roun mi bedroom. Queenie wuz fas alseep een har basket. But ah noh wha di dream mean. Tek dis.' She handed me the effigy. 'Put it een yu ouse, unda yu bed, it will protech yu. It will stop di vampires from suckin yu blood an spittin it hout hinfected. One ah dem is Machiavellian, yu noh is characta, yu can predick is moves.'

'How do you know all these things?'

'Ah noh nuttin. But yu mus undastan certain fax. Yu is twenny-seven. Two an seven mek nine. So ah lot ah tings will appen tu yu dis year.'

'Good things?'

'Dat depend arn yu. Nine is ah good number. Dere are people arn dis planet dat ave bin sent wid numbers an dem ah do tings.'

'Numerology.'

'Carl it wha yu like. Wha me ah seh is dat. Di pass an di present is jus as concrete as di future. Dere are tings hout dere now dat want tu be born an dem jus ah look fi di right channel.'

'Meaning?'

'Murder wanted tu appen so Fred Wes', Jeffrey Dahmer, dem wuz channel fi it. Dat ting dat ah go roun an ah kill hall ah dem people. Di Cyber somting.'

'Vigilante.'

'Yes. Ah di channel fi dat. An now it time fi yu fi fine hout wha yu meant tu do. Yu ave tu fine di vampire before it fine yu. Das why ah gi yu di effigy, it will gi yu ah ead start. It mek ah wood, so jus be ah tree.'

'A tree?'

Mrs Birchfield stood up. 'Tink bout it,' she said, opening the living room door. 'An don't be afraid. Di devil can't arm yu til yu lek im een yu yard. E could be hout side yu windough oldin hall ah di jewels an moni een di worl but yu safe. Once yu lek im een. Den it is ah different ting. E'll tell yu where im waan si down an what im want yu tu do.'

Mrs Birchfield's words echoed in my ears as I walked down the dark streets.

S I D E **88**

I shut the front door of my house and was just about to brave the night in search of Froggy when I heard the tinkle of breaking glass. Under any other circumstances I would have carried on with my business, it could have been the kids in my neighbourhood, ripping the stereo out of a car. But the sound was closer to me than that. It was coming from inside my house.

I leaned against the door thinking, then opened it quietly, listening like a wild animal in the dark. I heard the sound of footsteps, they squealed on the lino in the kitchen. That meant whoever it was was wearing sneakers. I took a few paces forward, I stood still as I saw a dark figure in a long coat running up my staircase. I waited a few seconds then walked up the stairs real slow, I knew where they creaked so I avoided those spots.

I heard the sound of cupboards opening.

The figure was in my bedroom, looking through my things. The effigy was under my pillow.

My mind flicked back in the past. I remembered the afternoon when I first got out of prison, Bones had asked Froggy if he'd moved things around in his room. Froggy had joked that it was a poltergeist. Bones' suspicions were right. It must have been the same character who tailed me in the street, now they were in my room. They knew who I was, which gave them the advantage. But I wanted to find out who they were, what they wanted and who'd sent them. I was nervous, felt threatened, but I closed in on the person real slow. I clenched my fist, I looked left and right to see if there was a baseball bat or a heavy object in reach. There was nothing. I didn't really approve of taking a man out from behind, but it had to be done. The figure turned around and ducked as my fist cut through the air. It punched me hard in the solar plexus. I reeled back. SHIT! The guy was a fighter. Trained in some martial art. I WASN'T EXPECTING THAT! In the dark, I couldn't make out its features. It was wearing a black head mask, tight on its face, it looked sadomasochistic; all I could see was its lips and eyes, it was wearing gloves, I couldn't tell if the man inside the mask was black or white. He was a crazy criminal.

The figure ran out of the room and bolted down the stairs. I gave chase. He fell. I was nearly on top of him, he scrabbled to his feet, flung the kitchen door open, ran into the garden and, in an agile movement, swung over the wall. I slipped, clambered over the wall and ran down the little alleyway. I turned into the street. I saw a white mini roaring away, swerving to miss an oncoming car.

I was so frustrated I kicked out at the nearest object, it happened to be a van, the metal dented.

What was going on? What was that figure doing in my house? Looking through my things? Who was the guy? He was fit and strong. Fast. Was he the Cyber Vigilante? Whatever it was I was going to get to the bottom of it. I never backed away when someone came into my territory; if they wanted a war they would get one. Next time I'd be ready.

I held my stomach, it still hurt. I couldn't help thinking how lucky I was. This was the real world, I could have ended up with a knife in my stomach, but whoever it was obviously didn't need it, he fought fair. He was either a fool or very confident.

S I D E 89

'Give me twenty pounds,' said a hooker.

'Sit on my lap,' said a man in a parked car.

'I ain't wearing any knickers.'

The man opened the door. 'Sit on my lap.'

'You won't be able to handle it. Give me twenty pounds. Men have kicked me around like a football for years. I want the money upfront,' said the hooker as she got into the car. I watched the car pull away and walked into the gambling club.

I thanked Willow for letting me use his lock-up and asked him if he had seen Froggy. He told me that

Froggy was at his new club, checking on the final arrangements before it opened.

S I D E  90

A sign read **http://www.softwarehouse.com**, it was locked so I went around to the back. I was just about to step into the car park when I saw Froggy getting out of Hunter's Porsche. I slipped back behind the wall. Hunter shut the door. 'How come you're so quiet tonight?'

'I'm RECITIN what I'm goin tu SEH tu Clarkie,' said Froggy, refining his speech pattern.

'The police came to the gallery today.'

'Did DEH mention my name?'

'No. They wanted to question me because I was Bones' agent. Don't worry, everything is alright.'

'What di fuck did yu SEH? Everybaddy has somthing tu lose apart from yu. DAT'S why yu nah sweat.'

'I sweat on the inside but I still change my shirt

twice a day. Why would I kill the golden calf? That's what I said to the police. You don't kill high revenue, you don't kill your own magic.'

'Nice, NICE.'

'You fit the matrix of qualities I'm looking for right now. I've kept all the works that you have sent me in the last six months. Now's the time to let the collectors see them.'

'Get ready FI DI dawn.'

'Were there any new works? Do you know what Bones was doing before he died?'

'I've got access TU HIS web site. I've got some computer files dat reveal is true identity. Dere WUZ ah statue but it wuz shit. I'll si what AH can fine. My stuff is mo dynamic.'

'Yes, I'm sure. But I'd still like to si the statue and his last pieces so that I have something to compare yours against. You've finally stepped out of Bones' shadow. He's no longer there to make you feel like a failure.'

'Dere ain't no SHAME een di game.'

'What about Clarkie? How are you going to deal with him?'

'Di same way Kasparov deals. I'll FINE someting tu make im angry. Den di game's ova. When we get hinside di club, I'll boot up di computa an show yu what I've downloaded from dis Russian contact. It's called Deep Throat ah someting like dat. It's ah copy of Kasparov's database. E'S got hall dese moves programmed een dere. Di computa can beat hall di udder players. But it can't beat im. Yu noh why? Because DERE is ah time wen yu are PLAYIN an yu are playin by gut. An di computa can't do dat. It has no knowledge of reason. Kasparov can do somting an it becomes apparent LATEAH.'

'I've had enough of this airy-fairy stuff. Is Clarkie worth it?'

'It gives me pleasure. I hinjoy mental combat.'

I'd heard enough, I turned the corner. Froggy froze when he saw me, Hunter looked nervous. They weren't sure if I had heard them or not so they didn't know how to react. I decided to play fool to catch wise.

'Do I owe you some money?' I asked Froggy.

He shook his head in the negative.

'So why the fuck are your faces twisted up like that?'

'Ah can HEXPLAIN everyting. It's not wha yu tink,' said Froggy.

'All the time you were laughing and joking with

Bones, you were planning this? Taking money from his till.'

Froggy glanced at Hunter. 'Lek's talk EEN private.'

Hunter moved towards the door of the club.

'I'm sorry to piss on your fireworks,' I said, cutting my eye at Hunter.

He shut the door behind him.

Froggy approached me boldly. 'Ah AD tu get mine. Di structure ah mi life cum houtta ah NEED. Ah needed tu break wey from Bones.'

'Twenty years we've known each other. You must have hated Bones. To take money from the shop, the club, to invest in this?'

'E halways wanted people tu fit een tu im agenda. Treat me like ah bwoy. Ah thought ah wuz IS lieutenant. Is right han man. But e leave everyting tu yu. Yu LEAP een mi seat. Melanie tell me BOUT di will. Ah want my share.'

'That's a fucked up attitude ... you're screwing about that. So you know that she wants to cut a deal between us? Keep Hunter out of the frame?'

'Yu down WID dat?' asked Froggy.

'It's money.'

'Yu can't mek plans fi me. Ah got mi own plans.

Ah can't work wid di BOAT ah yu togetha. Bones knew yu wuz fuckin Melanie. NOH di hole fuckin time!'

I punched Froggy in the face. He crashed against a pipe. He held his back and grimaced. 'E pay me MONI tu watch yu an DAT alley cat. She's bin arn DI phone tu Hunta HALL day. She's tryin tu do ah DEAL wid im.'

'She wouldn't do that. You're a liar.'

'Ow can yu do business wid ah woman OOH fiancé's body no lay tu res, tu groun, an she halready TEK arf im ring? Ah'd shit een har mout.' I was about to hit him again.

'Yu Mum an Dad want tu si yu,' he said, backing away. 'Deh seh it don't matta wha time. Deh want tu talk tu yu.'

'About what?'

'OW di fuck should ah noh?'

I turned and walked away. 'I haven't finished with you yet. You broomologist.'

'Di problem WID yu, Clarkie, is dat yu lek down EVERYBADDY dat LUV yu. HOUTCAST!' shouted Froggy.

The words rang in my ears.

The interior of my mother's house was dark. I shut the front door and made my way to the kitchen. The room was lit by candles. Mum took a sip of coffee, picked up the remote control turned on the TV and pressed *play*.

Video footage of Willow's lock-up fizzled onto the screen. Melanie's Citroen drove up. I got out and unlocked the garage. Melanie was in the driver's seat. I went into the garage, got a bucket, filled it up with water. I began to wash the boot.

'Is the blood going?' asked Melanie.

'Yes, no one will know that Bones was in here by the time I'm finished.'

'Good. I'm sorry I didn't do it earlier,' said Melanie. 'If they ask me any questions I'll say the car was stolen. How long can we keep it here?'

'As long as we want. There's no problem.'

Mum switched off the TV. She got up from her seat and walked over to me. She looked into my eyes. I could feel her breath. She placed her hand on my heart. She took it off, wiped it on her dress and turned her back.

'You're not my son. Leave di key arn di table.'

My worst fear had been realised. My life was being ripped apart like a piece of paper.

S I D E **92**

The back door of the softwarehouse was shut. I kicked it hard, then moved around to the front and hammered on the metallic door. I wanted to get my hands on Froggy. He'd shot the video, I knew that the moment I saw it. Willow must have told him that I'd taken the key to the lock-up, Froggy had taken the opportunity. His undercover work had severely damaged my relationship with my mother, and he'd done it for his own gain.

The Lexus Jeep and Hunter's Porsche were in the carpark. I picked up a discarded metal bar and smashed all the windows of both vehicles.

S I D E

### Caption: Same day

The black American cop stuck a piece of gum in his mouth and put on his Chicago Bulls baseball cap. He led me down the corridor. I glanced at him out of the corner of my eye, still trying to place his face. I knew I'd seen him before. Or maybe he just resembled someone in my past, an old school friend. A work mate, a sparring partner. I longed to ask him his name but something told me not to rush matters.

I'd decided to turn myself in. I was going to come clean about Melanie's car, the blood in the boot. I just wanted to set the record straight.

Clayderman was already in the interview room, her eyes looked me up and down. 'I'm glad you've come in of your own accord, it saves us time looking for you. We thought you might be on your way to the airport.' She leaned back in her chair and placed her hands behind her head. 'We understand Bones left a will that could make you a very wealthy man. Melanie drew it up.'

'Grab a seat,' said the American cop, placing his chair next to Clayderman.

I sat down.

'We picked up Melanie earlier on in the day at the airport,' said Clayderman, grinning.

'She was dressed up like a cowgirl from Alabama,' said the American cop. 'I hope it was some sort of disguise. Because it would be real sad if it wasn't.'

'She's shown us the lock-up, the car, told us about the fight, you taking Bones to the West End, dropping him off. She's saying you did it, you killed him for the money,' said Clayderman.

I felt my mouth drying up. A cold chill ran down my spine.

The American cop yawned. 'I think you're both involved and money is your motive.' He looked bored. 'Right from the get go she was giving his wallet a work out. You're an ex-con, just been released, no work and Melanie knew the details of her boy-friend's will.'

'You're sleeping with her,' said Clayderman.

I was surprised by the statement.

'Who said that?' I asked.

'Melanie. She's been quiet straightforward about the whole matter,' said Clayderman. 'You want the money, you've got a stake in the will. It's cut and dried. You kill him, hang him up and make it look like suicide.'

I was in a state of shock, I was furious. 'So you're trying to pin it on me? I just came in here to say that I had lied about not seeing Melanie when you came around to my house. I came here to tell you the truth.'

Clayderman got up. 'You really expect us to believe that?' she said nastily. 'Why don't you stop wasting our time and just admit the crime.' She switched on the tape recorder. 'Take us through it step by step.'

'What do you want me to say? That I hung him?'

'We can start there,' said Clayderman firmly. 'Clarkie, make it easy on yourself.'

'I'm innocent.'

'That's what they all say. You didn't want to sit on the money, you wanted to spend. But right now a whole barrel of crabs has been let loose,' said the American cop with a smile on his face.

I buried my head in my hands. I couldn't believe what I was hearing. For the first time in my life, I had decided to co-operate with the police and now I was about to have a murder charge thrown at me. I knew my actions would make me look suspicious. You know, the frantic cleaning up of the blood. Hiding the car. But, I thought I could easily show them that I wasn't the murderer. I'd fucked up again. Now I was a prime suspect.

'So what happened?' asked Clayderman, standing behind me.

'Bones phoned me later that night. He said he wasn't going to come back to my house, that he was going to Mum's house, that he was going to sleep there. He was real upset about everything,' I said.

'That you were sleeping with Melanie?' she asked, moving in front of me.

'He never said that. He was just cussing the whole world; he sounded like he'd done more drugs. He sounded as if he was with someone.'

'How do you know?' asked the American cop.

I felt like having a cigarette, the pressure was

getting to me. My eyes felt tired. 'Because he kept cutting away from the call and talking to someone else, telling the person he won't be a second, you know, stuff like that.'

Clayderman wasn't letting up. 'So you expect us to believe whoever he was with might have killed him?'

'Yes.'

'Did you know anything about his compulsion for child porn?' asked the American cop.

'No, and that's one of the reasons I came in here. I wanted to tell you about that. It all doesn't hang right for me. There was no way that Bones would be involved in such a thing.'

'What people say and what they do are two different things. He kept it well hidden,' said Clayderman.

'Is that why you killed him?' asked the American cop, a wicked grin on his face. 'I think you were involved in the ring and he was going to expose you. That's the bottom line, why you knocked him.'

I was half-scared, half surprised. Things were going from bad to worse. I could picture myself standing in a crowded court room, going down for murder. The murder of my brother. My mother would be crying, for both of us.

There was a knock at the door. An officer came in and handed Clayderman a piece of paper. She read it and passed it over to the American cop. His eyes flashed with anger. 'He could have put it there himself,' he said, firmly.

Clayderman sat down. 'You are free to go.'

I wasn't sure I'd heard her right.

Clayderman focused on the cop. 'The officers have checked the URL. It's positive.' Her eyes met mine. 'You can go,' she turned off the tape recorder, 'but we would like to talk to you further about the pornography that was found on Bones' machine.'

I got up, my legs trembling like shock absorbers. I was confused. I didn't know whether to shout or cry. Maybe this is a trick, I thought. Maybe they are just playing with me, making me feel happy before they came up with their next line of questioning, and that would break me into a thousand pieces.

'We are sorry to have put you through this ordeal, but I am sure you understand. It was a tough call. We didn't want to mess up,' said the American cop, offering me his hand. 'I am sure you would like us to catch your brother's killer.'

I refused to take his hand. A few seconds ago he'd

been trying to get me to confess to murder. My heart still felt dark, the clouds had not lifted yet. I couldn't believe that I'd been so close to hell. I wondered what had saved me?

'Have you found the killer?' I asked

Clayderman rubbed her temples. 'No, but we know it wasn't you.'

My brain clicked into gear, and I remembered where I'd seen the American cop. He'd been at Chameleon. Bones' club. Yeah. He was sitting on a computer terminal. It was him, it was dark. He was looking through the University of British Columbia's directory. Then Bones and him had got talking.

'What's your name?' I asked him.

He raised his eyebrows, surprised.

'Scotto. NYPD 63rd precinct,' he said.

'What's a cop from New York doing in London?'

'Have you heard about the Cyber Vigilante?' asked Clayderman.

'I've seen the poster,' I replied.

'Well that's why I'm over here from the States. I'm here in an advisory role to help the British police.'

Clayderman cleared her throat. 'The reason we now know you are not the murderer is because your mother has just phoned us to say she found a white rat with a URL branded into its skin, under a bush in her garden. But there's still no reason why we should believe that you're not connected to the ring.'

'I've just got out of prison. I haven't had time to get involved in any organisation.' I said.

'We've found lots of files on Bones' computer, contacts to bulletin boards in various countries, that linked him to a paedophile ring,' said Scotto. 'We thought you were connected to it all. Something happened between the both of you and you broke his neck and hung him and tried to make it look like suicide. Melanie could have been your Lady Macbeth and then you were gonna make a break with the money. You would have got the money. But now you're innocent until proven guilty.'

'I think you can still help us by co-operating,' said Clayderman.

'How? I don't know anything about that stuff.'

'Step up to your responsibilities. It will help us to believe that you've got nothing to do with the paedophile ring. We need to create a picture of the lifestyle Bones led. It could lead us to other people,' said Scotto.

'There is no way Bones was into any of that. Neither am I. I grew up with him, I've known all his girlfriends.'

'You can think that if you want. You might even convince me if you can prove it. But anything you can tell us could help find Bones' killer and stop anyone else being killed. We want to find the person who is killing the paedophiles. To find the Cyber Vigilante,' said Scotto, earnestly.

'I still don't understand what that has to do with me.'

'Follow me,' said Clayderman.

S I D E **94**

Scotto sat in front of a terminal that was connected to a Hayes ISDN terminal adaptor. We were in an office in the Computer Crime Unit. Clayderman pulled up a chair and watched Scotto type in an URL. The window opened into the Cyber Vigilante web site.

# EVIL EVIL EVIL

*And I Looked And Behold A Pale Horse*
*And His Name That Sat Upon Him Was Death,*
*And Hell Followed With Him*
*And Power Was Given Unto Them*
*Over The Fourth Part Of The Earth,*
*To Kill With The Sword And With Hunger*
*And With The Beast Of The Earth*
Book Of Revelations
Chapter 6
Verse 8.

'OK, Buddy. This is its web site. It has pictures of the victims and various other components,' explained Scotto.

Clayderman turned to me. She smiled in a friendly fashion. 'All the people who have been killed so far have been paedophiles.'

'I was tracing the person in the States,' said Scotto. 'I don't know if it's a man or a woman. The Cyber Vigilante uses the Internet to home in on victims. Infiltrates their system, sets up meetings with other members, maybe to exchange files, contact magazines and addresses in person. After he or she has got all that information, they kill the victim by lynching them.'

Clayderman massaged the back of her neck. 'In Bones' case we didn't find the rat straight away, which threw us off the scent.'

'This is where you can help us,' said Scotto, clicking on a hot spot on the web site. 'Did you see or hear Bones arranging to meet any kids?'

'No,' I replied firmly. I thought hard. 'Well, there were a couple of times when I heard him saying he had to send email to some kids because they were asking him for advice, or that he wanted to swap games with them over the Net.'

'That fits the pattern,' said Clayderman, shooting a glance at Scotto.

'What pattern?' I asked.

'Kids being lured to various locations over the Net. Cyber solicitation,' said Scotto.

'What's that?'

Scotto and Clayderman exchanged looks. She nodded and Scotto spoke. 'OK, you get a lot of kids surfing the Net. It's a pastime, getting more popular by the day. For the cost of a local call millions of users can be reached.'

Clayderman took over. 'Do you have any children yourself?'

'No. Do you?'

'Yes, I have a daughter. Nowadays it's easy for a pervert to enter a child's bedroom. You know, a girl logs on to a machine in her bedroom, her parents are in the living room watching a soap, thinking she's playing a computer game or doing her homework. She clicks into a chat room, gets talking to various people, she strikes up a friendship with someone, they move into a private room, and that person persuades the kid to meet them.'

Scotto sounded grim. 'In America, there have been cases where a child has been sent money to buy a bus ticket by someone they have met on the Net, and then they've vanished without a trace, lured away from their home by a stranger.'

'So you think this is what Bones was doing?' I asked.

Clayderman's mouth twisted eloquently. 'It's every parent's nightmare, it's frightening to think that people are using the Net for these kinds of sexual rendezvous.'

'Everything is transparent so you can disguise your

age, sex, so what's happening is that children are making contacts, making friends with what they think are other children but who are adults,' said Scotto. 'Paedophiles, who are good at getting a child's confidence.'

Clayderman could see my chest heaving and she asked me if I wanted a glass of water but I told her that I was fine.

'Bones could have been building up relationships with the kids over the games, swapping the games, talking in chat rooms,' she said, gently.

'So that's why the Cyber Vigilante hit him?' I asked.

Scotto answered promptly. 'It certainly looks like the Cyber Vigilante's work. There was no forced entry into your mother's house so Bones knew whoever it was, he let them in.'

'Is that why you thought it could have been me?'

Clayderman was very matter of fact in her reply. 'We have to consider every possibility and every suspect. And the possibility that you are lying. That you're part of the ring.'

'Back to that again.' I said.

'What you have got to understand about this,

Clarkie,' said Scotto, 'is that, thirty years ago, child molesters were plying their sick trade in parks. Then they moved into arcades. Now they are on computers. It puts a whole different slant on the line, "Don't talk to strangers".'

'There have been five killings in Britain in the last two months and all of them were Internet users.' Clayderman added grimly. The sad thing about all of this is that at the moment the children understand the technology and their parents don't.'

I was sickened by the whole affair. The thought of Bones being involved in this kind of activity was horrifying. I didn't say a thing to them about Froggy. I wanted to get more information first. I asked Clayderman and Scotto to give me a five minute break.

# EVIL EVIL EVIL

S I D E **95**

'... Hello.'

'... Hi, Pauline it's Clarkie.'

'... Where are you? You sound distant.'

'... Outside the police station,' I said, twisting Bones' diamond stud in my ear. I wanted to take it out, but I decided to wait until I had all the evidence.

'... Are you going to go in? Do you want me to come with you? I'll bring Darren with me.'

'... No. I've already seen them.'

'... How did it go?'

'... OK. Can I ask you a question?'

'... Yes.'

'... How do you gain a child's confidence? I mean I thought I'd ask you, being that you're a school teacher, you should know.'

'... Everybody says that'

'... What?'

'. . . I'm a school teacher and I should know.' She paused. '. . . It depends on the child and the context.' She sighed. '. . . Do you mean a neighbour's child or a child in a supermarket?'

'. . . A child in a supermarket.'

'. . . Why? Why do you want to know?'

'. . . The police are telling me about paedophiles. They want me to help them get a profile on Bones.'

'. . . Have you mentioned Froggy to them yet?'

'. . . No. I wanted to speak to you first.'

'. . . A child in a supermarket would be very wary of you, unless you had something that they wanted. And that's difficult to define because different age groups like different things.'

'. . . I don't get you.'

'. . . OK, take Darren, he loves football, he thinks he's Ian Wright. I can't stop him from going, he stays awake at night thinking about games. So if someone gets talking to him about that, a stranger, he might be in danger. But, you know, a lot of the kids nowadays have been taught not to talk to strangers. There've been campaigns in schools, clinics all over the country telling children to say "No". Before school closes for holidays, the kids are all reminded. Does that help?'

'. . . Yeah, in a roundabout way.'

'. . . The thing is though, people who hurt children, I would say that one per cent are strangers. Don't quote me on that. What I'm trying to say is that the majority are people the children already know. A person down the road, in the sweet shop, someone that they wouldn't think twice about.'

'. . . What about computers?'

'. . . What about them?'

'. . . The Internet.'

'. . . Yes.'

'. . . Cyber solicitation.'

'. . . What is that?'

'. . . The same thing but this time over a computer. I mean the kid makes a friendship with a stranger, over a period of time, you know, they chat about their interests on line. If it is computer games, they get to know each other through that, then they meet and stuff.'

'. . . I've never thought about that. But yes. I suppose so. God, yes! I never thought. I mean that is real dangerous, because number one, they can build up the children's confidence over time, groom them, number two the child will never suspect they are in danger and number three, the person on the other end is a stranger but the child feels that they know them. I'll have to keep an eye on Darren.'

'. . . This shit is heavy.'

'. . . But either way there still has to be the physical thing.'

'. . . What is that?'

'. . . The meeting. And parents can still warn against that.'

'It's not that easy any more. I mean, what if the person on the other end of the computer says "Where do you live?" and the kid says "Edmonton". Then the character on the other end can say I'll be there in five minutes Or an in hour. The kid won't think twice about it, they'll just get on a bike and be over there. The parents might be out.'

'. . . Yes. Yes. I'm definitely going to keep an eye on Darren. He's always on the phone. He's part of a fantasy football league, he's got his own club, he's buying and selling players, working out strategy. The computer plays the games over the weekend, the results are on cable. He gets calls from Scotland, some of them are grown men. Next season he's playing in Europe. Is that what the police think Bones was doing?'

'... I dunno. I can't really talk about all that now, it is real complex, but thanks for listening to me.'

'... Clarkie? Is there something else?'

'... No. I'll call you later.'

'... OK, bye.'

'Bye.' My fist was clenched tight. Full of fury.

## EVIL EVIL EVIL

S I D E **96**

There was no way I could have told Pauline what had happened to me when I was about twelve or thirteen. And to think my own brother was allegedly putting other children through that made me want to vomit. I mean, at thirteen I figured that I was streetwise, I figured that I had everything locked down. But one day a guy approached me as I left my gym. I used to go there to watch the fighters and they had a junior class where they taught me basic moves. I was walking down the street and the guy said, 'You look like you're gonna be a fighter one day.'

'I am,' I said.

'I've trained some of the best. I've pictures with all of them. You got a good frame but it looks like you need work on your stomach. I can tell from the way you are standing.'

'What's wrong with it?' I asked.

'Weak lower back. I can help you get that together, make you great. I just live across the road, I'll show you.'

Now I never thought for one second that he could hurt me, I never thought that he could kill me. All I was thinking about was being a boxer, a better boxer, and here was someone who said they could make it happen.

When we got into his living room, he took out some photograph albums and showed me pictures of him and other boxers. He was winning my confidence, just like Pauline said. Looking back now, I could see all the moves but at the time it didn't register. The fact of the matter was, at that age I was considered to be one of the smartest guys on the block, but I'd been sucked in because of my desire to be a great boxer. So here

I was, with this man in his house, lying on my back, doing sit ups, with his hand on my stomach, saying he was feeling how strong my abdominals were and that he would have to go a little lower to see if they were fully developed.

I got out of there real quick, struggled with the door and got into the fresh air. I'd never told anybody about it. We moved out of that area but I can still remember the street and the house real clear. At the time I didn't really think of it as abuse, just improper behaviour, but now I knew different. Bones' case had opened up the emotional doors. I had to face up to my own past. It had only taken one little thing, just one little thing to get me to trust that man. I wanted to tell Pauline about it, but the time wasn't right.

The fact that Clayderman and Scotto were saying Bones was involved in such activities made me feel even more sick. It made me sick to think that he was like that man, that he was gaining kids' confidence and luring them into a frightening world. Maybe the Cyber Vigilante had done a good thing by wiping him out. But there was still a bit of doubt in my mind. This was my own flesh and blood, and there was something not right about it all. Froggy was doing business with

Hunter, he had his own club, he had always been jealous of Bones. Dumping rubbish on Bones' computer was just the kind of thing he would enjoy.

**EVIL EVIL EVIL**

S I D E  **97**

Scotto and I were alone in the interview room.

'The first killing in Europe was at the beginning of the year,' he said. 'I was here at the time, attending a police conference, and that was when I met Clayderman. When I went back to the States we communicated for a couple of months, and there were more killings. Then just recently it's like the vigilante went on a real spree. I was on vacation in France, so I cut it short to come and help Clayderman.'

'Were you in Chameleon the other night?'

'What's that?' he asked, leaning forward slightly.

'Bones' club.'

'No. Oh yes, of course, Chameleon, it didn't register. No, I've never been there. Why?'

'Nothing.'

He opened his notebook and read his notes. 'So you said that there was someone tailing you in a white mini?'

'Yeah, and I think it was the same man who broke into my house. He was searching through my belongings.'

'If there's somebody tailing you, I'll ask Clayderman to offer you some sort of protection if it's possible. Would that make you feel any better?'

'A little.'

'And you've reminded me,' he made notes. 'I'm going to put a flyer out on the Deadmeat web site, a notice on the late night news. I want people who were in Chameleon on the night of the murder who knew Bones to come forward. I want to find every person he spoke to.'

'Maybe Bones made contact with this Cyber Vigilante character at the club.'

'That's a possibility.'

'But why would anybody want to tail me? Break into my house? Do you think it was the Vigilante?' My insides suddenly felt hollow.

'If it was then you're in danger. It's possible the Vigilante thinks you're part of the circle, because child abusers are a very tight group. You're sure it was a man?'

'No woman I've met packs a punch like that. So if it was the Vigilante, he was hoping that I might lead them to other people? Is that it?'

'That is the only reason I can think of. I'll definitely get a police officer to be at your side for a while.'

'I still can't believe Bones was a paedophile.'

I know this has all been a lot to take in but the cold hard evidence is there. We all have dark sides and that must have been Bones'. It was a secret that he must have kept to himself, he didn't want it to ruin his career. He was most probably non-predatory.'

'Meaning?'

'Paedophiles who believe that children enjoy and can give their consent to sex acts.'

'But there's no proof that he was having sex with anybody.'

'True, but he still shows the pattern. He has over 200 games on his machines and these can be used to attract young people.'

'So what about the predatory types?'

'They are prepared to hurt children, to ignore the pain the child is expressing,' said Scotto, clicking on the computer.

### CHARACTERISTICS OF PAEDOPHILES

*—over 25*
*—no dating pattern with either sex*
*—select youngsters who are physically or emotionally neglected*
*—do not marry/ may have a marriage of convenience*
*—belong to children's organisations*
*—have high rate of re-offending*
*—groom victims to abuse, thus turning child into perpetrator, which means child is less likely to complain and give evidence in court*

'Froggy could have put that stuff on the machine.'

'Are you saying that he's a child abuser too?' asked Scotto.

I shifted in my chair. 'No, but he might have wanted it to look like Bones was one.'

'You think Froggy would be that manipulative? Why?'

'He's driven by his insecurities. He can't put his ego to bed. He's felt sorry for himself for a long time.'

'What would Froggy achieve?'

'The fame and attention that he has always craved, but first he had to get Bones out of the way. Froggy wouldn't physically kill him. He might want to, he might think about it, but dumping that garbage is the next best thing.'

'That's something to think about. We'll call him in to help us with our enquiries. He sounds like a freeloader.'

'And what if Bones was like this Cyber Vigilante character, what if Bones was playing possum? You know, he had also infiltrated this whole kiddies' network, he was also trying to track down people or expose it in his own way, and then he came across the Cyber guy by mistake?'

Scotto sighed. 'I think you're clutching at straws there.'

I continued. 'Froggy had access to this network, he finds that kind of stuff funny, you know distorting someone's image, but it all went wrong and this Cyber Vigilante hit the wrong person.'

394

Clayderman entered the room.

Scotto looked at his notes as he spoke to her. 'We've got a serious matter to deal with. Clarkie was being tailed by someone in a white mini and there's the outside possibility that it was the Vigilante.'

'Well if Clarkie's in danger we'll have to protect him, get that car checked out.' She turned to me. 'What can you remember about it?'

'I caught part of the number plate, 2029, and it had tinted windows and spoilers.'

Clayderman took the information in. 'OK, Scotto, as of tonight, you are detailed to protect Clarkie. Put his mind at ease.'

Scotto looked shocked and said, 'Me?'

'Yes, you,' said Clayderman. 'I can't spare anyone else, and in any case if it is the Vigilante you'll be in the best place.'

Scotto sighed. 'You got it.' He shook his head.

S I D E **98**

## Caption: Tuesday 2.59pm

Children were running around the playground. Pauline and a few other teachers were supervising them, making sure they played safely among themselves. Pauline noticed me standing across the road. I waved, she came over to the school gates.

'What are you doing here?' she asked, looking over her shoulder.

'I've come to see you.'

'You shouldn't be standing out here.'

'Why?'

'You might get reported by School Watch.'

A bell rang. The children stop playing. They were still, frozen just as if they'd been playing Stuck In The Mud.

'I've got to go back inside, we've got story time, then it's home time,' said Pauline.

Another bell rang. The children lined up.

'I'll see you when school is finished,' said Pauline, running back towards the kids. She took the children into the building.

S I D E

The classroom was empty.

Pauline made sure the room was tidy, then she started getting things ready for the next day. I was sitting in a low chair, about twelve inches high, the table was approximately eighteen inches. I was enjoying making displays, the job Pauline had assigned to me. When I finished one I handed it to her and she hung it up on the wall.

'You should have called first,' she said.

'I don't have your school number.'

'Well, like I said, you were lucky you weren't reported to School Watch. If a teacher sees a suspicious character standing outside a school gate, we take down a description. One is sent to the police and five are faxed to neighbouring schools, and they fax them off to another five schools.'

'Sounds sensible.'

'Last year there were reports of this transvestite hanging around the school gates, a man with a blond wig. A couple of the children, the girls, said he approached them and tried to touch them.'

'You can't be too careful.'

'Especially with other people's kids. When Darren was born, I didn't leave him with many people. I can count them on one hand. I was so frightened that someone was going to molest my child. And when he was seven I left him with a neighbour and her child, and she popped next door to see a friend. She was watching a horror film and she left it playing on the video, so Darren and her child went into the room and watched it. When Darren came back in, I was shocked because he said Mummy, Mummy I've just seen a tree raping a woman. The first thing I wanted to know was who told him about rape and stuff like that. I went over to her house and we had a steaming argument. You know, some parents have got the edges blurred.'

S I D E **100**

Pauline and I walked out of the school gates and made our way to her estate.

'So, are you still up for speaking to the kids?'

'Yeah, but I feel like a hypocrite.'

'Why?'

'Because I'm still doing some of the stuff I was doing before. Can't you get someone else to talk to them?'

'Well, maybe it's time for you to make a turnaround. Just talk to them about the dangers of crack, your experience in prison. I mean, you don't want to go back there, do you?'

'No.'

'Well that's a good start. So, you've got police protection.'

'Only at night. I can take care of myself during the day.'

A woman holding a screaming baby was knocking

on Pauline's door. Two children were standing on either side of her, who looked anywhere between four and six years old.

The woman smiled as she saw Pauline coming towards her. She opened her mouth to speak.

Pauline raised her hand and shut her eyes. 'Don't say a word,' she said, opening her purse. She took out a twenty pound note and gave it to the woman. 'Buy some food. Later on tonight I'm going to bring some typing I want done. The money is in exchange for that, OK?'

The woman nodded and pushed the money into her bra. She tugged her children and loud-mouth baby down the corridor and entered a flat a couple of doors away.

S I D E  101

Pauline plugged in the kettle. 'My mother always said show me your friends and I'll show you who you are. I think you should review your relationship with Froggy.

He's ambitious, greedy, vain, arrogant and willing to lie and cheat. It may be time to change friends.'

Darren walked into the kitchen. 'Americans do that every two years.' He grunted as he saw me, sitting at the table.

'Hello,' I said.

'Hello,' said Darren, his tone tense, his voice muffled.

'It's envy, Clarkie. That's Froggy's problem. I mean you could go out and give free ice-creams to everybody on this estate and somebody will still say . . .'

Darren finished the sentence. 'Look at him, he thinks he's so flash.'

Pauline smiled to herself. 'Then they would try to hurt you. Physically or emotionally. You could be running a corner shop and one day you're busy and you forget to say "Hello" to somebody and they'll turn around and say you're acting like that just because you own the shop.'

Darren opened the fridge and took out some yogurt. 'Mum. Don't let him twist you around his little finger.'

'When I need your advice I'll ask for it.'

'I'll always tell you what your friends won't tell you.'

'That's my line.'

'Hey who cares, it works,' said Darren, scooping a spoonful of yogurt into his mouth.

# S I D E  102

The National Gallery was slowly thinning out. Pauline, Darren and I looked at the works of art.

'I'm bringing my class here next week, so I thought I'd just look around now, work out a route.' She stopped in front of a large painting. 'This one has an interesting story behind it. The origin of the Milky Way. The canvas is smaller than the original.'

'How do you know that?'

'There is a story behind it. That's Zeus.'

'Yeah. I heard about that dude,' said Darren.

'And that is his wife, Hera. It's set in heaven.'

Darren nodded his head. 'Scene rasta.'

Pauline gave him a cutting look. He said sorry with his eyes.

'Zeus went down to earth and slept with humans.

The children he had with the humans were demi-gods. They were not immortal but they had special powers.'

'You mean like Superman and the Fantastic Four?' I asked.

'I don't know about the Fantastic Four,' said Darren.

'There should be flowers right at the bottom of it, but you can't see them, because they have been cut off. People have cut this painting to fit on the walls of their houses.'

'If I'd had teachers like you, I would have spent more time in school,' I said.

S I D E  **103**

Darren broke off some bread and fed the pigeons as Pauline and I walked slowly across Trafalgar Square. The National Gallery loomed in the background.

'What's Hunter, Bones' art dealer, like?'

'I don't trust his shoes.'

Pauline smiled.

'Can you talk to Mum and Dad for me? They listen to you. Tell them about this crazy mess.'

'When the time is right we'll do it together.'

# SIDE 104

Hunter's gallery was a spacious, well-lit property in Cork Street. Bones' statue of Melaine with the plaque KEEP OFF THE GRASS was in the centre of the room, and his computers were linked up. On one wall there were some of Bones' paintings, on another Froggy's.

Hunter sat back in a chair, talking on the phone. '... It's going swimmingly. I've just signed up Froggy.' Hunter took a sip of his drink. A young man opened a bottle of champagne and poured it into his glass. '... He's got his own unique style, an eclectic artist, what you see is what he saw last. I'm having a joint exhibition. It's worth reviewing,' he said, glancing at me. '... I've sent catalogues to all the crucial collectors, the ones that have bought Bones' work. There'll be red dots everywhere. It'll be controversial, cool, real and authentic. Don't worry. The right curators will be there. They're up for being influenced, because they don't really know what they're talking about.' His mobile phone rang. '... You know how it is, they want to follow the fashion and the trends, they want their galleries and their exhibitions to be trendy and fashionable, up to the minute. Look, I've got to go. OK. Bye,' said Hunter, putting the receiver down and the mobile to his ear.

'Hello ... Akio.' His voice lifted. '... How are you? I've got Froggy, this great new young artist turned computer art freak. I know. I know. But Froggy is different from all the others. He worked with Bones for years so he knows about the image and the myth.' Hunter crossed his legs and employed his very persuasive tongue. '... A lot of people really like his work, he's doing something completely different. He's got a really good tribal thing going on here, with a crossover. I really think you should buy some of his work, people are liking it, it's going to go up in value.' Hunter took a handkerchief from his jacket sleeve and blew his nose. '... Good, I'm glad you're interested. Yes, off course I know you're not interested in buying one or two, twenty? That's fine. We'll agree the price when I see you later tonight. You know it will be good, I'll put tags on a few of them at the exhibition, collection of Akio. No, no, don't worry, you're we'll ahead of New York, you're getting the best price. OK. Bye.' Hunter switched off his mobile. 'Yes. Can I help you?' His tone was cutting.

'Is Froggy about?'

'No. I understand you were planning to hide all these little goodies from me?' he said, pointing to the statue of Melanie and Bones' art work. 'Your mother was very kind, she thinks I am the best person to represent these. She has vested her power in me. Froggy and my assistants were kind enough to help me to get them out of the cellar. You wouldn't know what to do with them.' He went on very slowly, 'We need to have a talk now, as we're both on the same side. Now that Bones is dead the market for his work might actually collapse.'

'Why?'

'Bones' work might become very expensive for a while but then people could lose interest. He's only worked for a brief period and people are very insecure. People like the idea that an artist lives on and produces good work, because that makes a statement about this artist and his sincerity, so I needed him there to prove that his work was a good buy.'

'The only talking I'm doing is through my lawyer.'

'I'm glad you could find one you're not sleeping with.'

I stayed cool, calm and collected. I wasn't going to rise to the bait. Froggy had obviously been spreading the word.

The phone rang. It sounded very British with its two strong beats.

'Froggy was in court earlier on today. Why don't you try Willow's watering hole? Could you kindly leave my premises?' He picked up the receiver and placed a tight hand over it. 'Notify my secretary with the details of the law firm that is handling your business.' He put the receiver to his ear and turned his back on me. '. . . Yes, yes, but you should come and see Froggy's.' He fiddled with the cord. '. . . I know you don't pay those sort of prices but I'm planning Froggy's career now. I'm going to get him a flat, a studio, set him up with a couple of assistants. Yes, yes. It is very sad about Bones. No, no, I don't want to swap any of Bones' work for Froggy's. I could end up with a whole gallery full of Bones' work and that would never do.'

I shut the gallery door and left the cold, ruthless art world behind me. I felt even more determined to prove my brother's innocence.

S I D E

## Caption: Night

I glanced at my watch. I should have been at the police station or in my house where Scotto could protect me. But I had business to deal with in Zone 1 and that had to come first.

The doorway of the gambling club was open, work-men were unloading crates of drinks and carrying them down the stairs. Froggy's and Willow's voices floated up.

'How did it go in court?' asked Willow, very slowly.

'Ah tell Tina don't feel bad. Yu win SOM yu lose som,' said Froggy, laughing. 'Ah get custody AH one ah di kids. Mi LIKKLE gyal Cheyenne. An TENKS fi givin mi di CARL wen Clarkie wuz goin tu use yu lock-up.'

'You can pay me back in another way. You've signed up with Hunter.'

'Wen yu hungry yu can't hang ROUN rasta. Somtimes yu ave tu be ah devil EEN disguise tu MEK it. Dere ah DESE huge doors HOPENIN een my life. Me nah look back.'

'Like I've always told you, water seeks its own level once it has been set free. That's why I put money into your little drugs operation at the back of Howard and Shirley's place. I knew early doors that Bones was holding you back. You have to express yourself star. Build up your character. I'm here to help you.'

'Tenks. TINGS ah move now. Ah my pay day now, ah ave som serious backin.'

'The environment dictates your character. Bones is out of the way and now you've stepped into his shoes and you're moving in the right circles. If you have little pockets people are going to call your bluff. So I'm still a good person to have around. Don't forget that.'

'BUT now me is ah bonafide artist. DI article yu get me?'

'Yeah, you have to bring me in.'

'Yu een di room halready. Mi nah go no where wid hout yu.'

'So, are you going to let me buy some paintings off you in cash. So I can clean my dollars?'

'No problem. If yu want SOM EEN Bones' style ah can do dat as well, no one will ever be able tu tell di difference. Ah AVE me technique down,' said Froggy, eagerly. 'Ah need yu Jeep fi ANADA week ah so til Hunter cum TREW wid me hadvance.'

'Use it for as long as you like. What are you doing tonight? You want some rocks or plug?'

'Me ah TEK Mary HOUT. MI club ah hopen tomorrow so uh goin RELAX. Ah AVE nough plug. Ah tell yu bout Mary halready innit?'

'Yes. But aren't you frightened?'

'No. She REAL sensitive. Me like DAT bout har.'

I decided to change plan. I doubled back.

S I D E  106

Froggy slung his video camera over his shoulder. His mobile phone rang. He put it to his ear. '. . . Hunta. It's

GOIN well,' he said smoothing out his dulcet tones. '... I WON di case. I'll get som art work TU yu. No ah haven't SEEN Clarkie yet,' said Froggy getting into the Jeep. '... I'm ARN my way roun ... Don't worry bout Clarkie, ah told yu ah KNOW ow tu deal WID im.' He turned the key in the ignition. '... I'll MEK im mad from the hinside and let IM blow IMSELF up bit by bit, an I'll jus be SMILIN, what ever E says will BOUNCE off ah my shield. Yu know I'll MEK mistakes een front of im but it will hall be planned. I'm four steps ahead ah him. No, no. Yu don't need TU do dat, I've had time tu plan it ... What will ah use? Speech, of course. It is di most powerful tool een di world, forwad plannin.'

I sat up in the back seat and put the nozzle of the revolver at the back of Froggy's neck. 'Nine millimeter hand gun. Six bullets.'

Froggy coughed quietly and said, 'Rasclatt ... Hunta, ah AVE fi go. Yu get me? Ah said I've GOT TO go. I've just been given SOM info. I've got tu plan AHEAD. Bye,' said Froggy, switching off his phone.

'Drive till I tell you to stop.'

'Yu got it, BRO. Yu got,' said Froggy. 'Be careful, ah don't wanna go ova HENY bumps. DAT gun MIGHT go ARF.' His eyes were framed in the rear view mirror as he pulled off. We were in an empty parking lot at the back of the gambling club.

'Why did you put all that shit on Bones' computer?' I asked.

'Yu ave HENY evidence?'

I pushed the gun a little harder into his skin.

'OW could yu tink dat?' said Froggy. 'Sorry, yu AVE di rong person. Ah got NUTTIN else tu seh.'

I tightened my finger around the trigger.

'Yu JUS suspicious,' said Froggy quietly.

The chamber clicked and Froggy panicked big time.

'Ah don't noh why AH did it. Ah don't noh why ah did it,' he said.

'You must know.'

'Ah FINE it hamusin.'

'That's all. That's the reason? A prank, a joke. And now my brother is dead?' I said hitting him on the head with the butt of the gun.

'Ah JEALOUS.'

'So you had a score to settle?'

'Bones thief HALL ME ideas.'

Froggy slammed on the brakes. I was jerked forward by the force. The gun fell onto the passenger seat. The chamber opened, there were no bullets. Froggy elbowed me in the face with venom as he realised I had brought the gun with me just to scare him, to get a confession.

He jumped out of the Jeep and opened the boot with gusto. 'Yu TINK ah goin LEK yu stan een me way?' he said pulling out a machete. 'Yu FUCKA.'

I got out. Froggy's eyes were glassy. He raised the machete in the air and slashed it down with a vengeance. I blocked its path with my hand. I screamed as the blade cut into my flesh.

'Yu pussyclatt. Yu bloodclatt. Yu DON'T noh me. Ah go cut yu down like ah lumberjack right tu di root,' said Froggy. 'Ah go cut up yu, RARSE. Cum ere yu fucka. Where yu tink yu AH run tu?'

I was dealing with a psycho. Froggy had lost it. He delivered another strike which I ducked. I backed away as the silver cut through the thick night. I ran towards a wall and used my good hand and my legs to clamber over it. I heard the blade hit the wall and Froggy cussing on the other side as I ran across the street.

I eventually found a payphone that worked and called an ambulance. Blood was dripping from the wound and I was starting to feel dizzy. I crouched down on the floor as I saw the Jeep circling the area.

Clayderman was waiting for me as I came out of Casualty. The nurses had reported the incident and she'd got the information through the police network. The wound had been cleaned, stitched and dressed with a bandage. Clayderman took down the details. I told her that Froggy had confessed to dumping the child porn on the computer. She said that there were no witnesses at the scene, so when push came to shove he might deny it, but she asked me for a list of addresses where Froggy might be hanging-out. She couldn't do anything about his confession, but she had enough to arrest Froggy for attempted murder, and she wanted him picked up as quickly as possible. She offered to drop me home, but I told her I wanted to walk and get some fresh air. Before she pulled away she told me Scotto would be waiting for me outside my house.

### Caption: A Few Hours Later

I was hungry and tired. I couldn't go to my mother's house, because she was still refusing to speak to me. I'd called a few times but when she heard my voice she put the receiver down. I wasn't ready to go to my gates, so I rang Pauline's doorbell, because I felt there would be some emotional support behind it.

Darren opened the door and let me in.

'Where's your mum?'

'She's asleep.'

I walked into the living room. Pauline was asleep on the sofa.

'Aren't you gonna wake her up?' asked Darren.

'I'll just sit for a while.'

Darren shrugged his shoulders and walked off. I sat down next to Pauline. She turned in her sleep. I took off my jacket and laid it on the floor. I went over to a chair and picked up a cushion. I looked at my coat; it seemed miles away. I sat in the chair and closed my eyes. I felt the cushion falling from my hand.

S I D E  109

### Caption: Wednesday 8.25am

Sunlight filled the room. I was disorientated for a second. The room was unfamiliar. I was sitting in a brown armchair. Darren walked in and everything fell into place. I was still in Pauline's house.

'I hope you don't make a habit of this,' said Darren, picking up his satchel.

'Darren! You're going to be late, get a move on,' shouted Pauline from upstairs.

The sleep had been deep and trouble free. No nightmare. No Wayne. The potion Mrs Birchfield had given me must have been working.

I felt a sharp pain in my arm and held the bandage.

The arm was stiff, it throbbed and my mind replayed the dark images of the previous night.

Darren stuffed some books into the satchel. I got up and made my way to the bathroom. I had filled a sink with water and was just about to splash some on my face when Darren popped his head around the door. 'The blue toothbrush is mine and the red one is my Mum's. We don't have a spare one, so that means you'll just have to use your finger.'

S I D E **110**

Pauline was sitting at the kitchen table, eating a bowl of cornflakes.

Darren was frying some eggs, black people style, mashing up the yolk. No sunny side up business. 'Mum, yesterday a new boy joined our school and the teacher asked me to look after him. Why me?'

'Maybe she thinks you're responsible.'

'As it happens he is nice. Lives in a big house near

the park. He's invited me over there on Saturday. Is that alright?'

'I'll have to meet his parents first.'

'Great.'

I walked into the kitchen.

'You've finally woken up,' said Pauline, putting her bowl in the sink. 'I was wondering what I was going to do. You gave me quiet a shock when I woke up last night, but you looked so at peace I didn't want to disturb you.'

'I knew exactly what I was going to do, if he didn't wake up before we left,' said Darren turning over his eggs. 'I was going to poke him in that bad arm with a pencil. I'm sure that would have opened his eyes.'

'Darren!' Pauline's tone was firm. She pointed at my arm. 'Looks like you had a pretty eventful night.'

'I had a little trouble with Froggy.'

'I warned you about him. What happened?'

'He dumped the porn on Bones' computer. I confronted him about it and things didn't go as planned.'

'I've told you before, you guys live such complicated lives.' She glanced at her watch. 'Oh, if I don't leave now I'm going to be late. You can tell me all about it on my way to school. Or you can stay and Darren will fix you something to eat and you can call me later.'

'Fix who?' Darren's face was stern. 'I ain't fixing anybody nothing. I'm going to make an early start myself.' He switched the cooker off, picked up his satchel and was out of the front door before Pauline could say a word.

I smiled. 'I would have done the same thing.'

S I D E **111**

The sun was shining. The ruff necks were drinking brew and listening to music outside the barber shop. Sprinklers were out on some lawns, people were washing their windows, others were gardening, painting their fences and walls.

Two elderly black gentlemen were leaning on their garden gates having a chat.

The taller of the two said, 'The only good thing about the good old days is they've gone.'

'I remember years ago when we didn't have to lock our doors,' said the shorter and more intense-looking man.

'That's because you didn't have nothing. The people that did locked their doors.'

'But nowadays people with nothing have got locks.'

As I walked past Mrs Birchfield's house, I saw Mad Mary going inside. She was holding Froggy's dollar bill head wrap.

I decided to take a leisurely stroll down the Harrow Road. I walked past the spot where the nightmare had begun, the place where the Karmann Ghia had broken down. There were a lot of people in the Kentucky.

Then I saw it. I saw the white mini with tinted windows and this time I clocked the full registration, WAR2029. It was ahead of me caught in the traffic, it indicated and pulled into a car rental place. My luck was in. I ran up the road and I saw the back of a man going into the building. I hid behind a parked car and waited until he came out. I froze. It was Scotto, the American cop. He was wearing a false beard and moustache.

I thought about confronting him but I decided to wait. He walked up to a junction. A few minutes passed then a Harley Davidson motorbike pulled up, Scotto got on the back and they pulled off.

# S I D E 112

In the distance I saw a police officer standing outside my house. My instincts told me something wasn't right, so I used the payphone and called my digits.

Clayderman's voice boomed down the receiver. '... Where are you?'

'... What's the problem?' I asked calmly. '... Why are there officers outside my gates?'

'... You were meant to stay there last night. You were meant to come back here after I saw you at the hospital.'

'... I had a change of plan.'

'... You should have informed us. Scotto was outside all night waiting for you. You've wasted his time.'

'... I can't see what you're so hot about. I'm here now.'

421

'... I've had officers looking for you all night. And if they had found you, you would have been arrested.'

'... For what.'

'... Froggy is on a drip in hospital.'

'... What! I had nothing to do with that.'

'... Calm down. I know that now, but last night I didn't, and the fact that you didn't turn up at home as agreed meant you were the number one suspect.'

'... I had an alibi. Two people knew where I was, they were with me all night.'

'... We're pretty sure it was the Cyber Vigilante who hit him. He didn't kill him. Someone interrupted him before he delivered the final blow. We thought he'd hit you as well. I was waiting for one of my officers to report in and say they'd found your body.'

'... What hospital is Froggy in?'

'... The St Mary's Paddington. I want you to come to the house before you do anything. Froggy is lucky to be alive, but he managed to give us a description of the Vigilante. It fits the person who broke into your house. He was wearing a mask.'

'... So where is Scotto now?'

'... I've given him some time off. He was up all

night, reporting to us every hour. Just get over here as quickly as you can.'

# S I D E 113

Melanie's Citroen pulled up outside the house. We really didn't have much to say to each apart from a tense hello. She said that she had left bits and pieces in the house that she wanted to pick up. She was in a hurry because her trip had been delayed by the police questioning; she wanted to jet out of the country and relax in Paris.

I let her in. Clayderman watched her going from room to room, putting her belongings in two cardboard boxes. I offered to help her carry them to the car, but she said that she was fine and she could handle it.

Clayderman and I stood in my front garden and watched Melanie's Citroen speed off. Clayderman's eyes narrowed, she turned to me. 'Isn't that the car?' she asked.

'What car?'

'Over there, parked over there, 2029. The Mini, the one with tinted windows that was following you.'

'Yeah, that's it,' I said in a casual manner. 'It's mine for the week.'

Clayderman looked surprised. 'Yours?' Her voice was hard, almost threatening.

'Yep. I hired it, I saw it at a car rentals.'

Clayderman crossed the road, walking briskly towards the car. I followed her.

'I thought it looked familiar,' I said, 'so I hired it. I went in and tried to find out who had it before me, but everything was bogus, nothing really connected, you know false address, name. Whoever it was must have used false ID.'

'Did you get a description?' she asked, circling the car.

'Black male. Beard, moustache. Over six foot, jeans, white t-shirt,' I said. 'I'll drive you down to the hire place so you can get all the details; they'll tell you more than they told me.'

Clayderman was deep in thought, her face screwed up in concentration. 'I'll have the car searched and see if we can pick up any fingerprints.'

S I D E

## Caption: Evening 6pm

I opened the front door and took a step back inside as I was met by Scotto's smiling face. He was wearing a blue suit, white shirt, grey tie, black shoes.

'What's up, cat?' he asked, smiling. 'How you be? Looks like I came at just the right time,' he said, looking at the sports bag in my hand. 'I would have missed you.'

I touched his shoulder. 'Why don't you wait in the house until I come back, there's some beer in the fridge.'

'Where are you going?'

'To the gym.'

'That's a real sharp pair of pants you're wearing. You go training dressed so fly and with a hand bandaged up like that? It looks real bad. Looks like you should be going to the hospital not the gym,' he said flatly, a hard glint in his eye.

'I'm just going to do my stomach.'

He laughed. 'You could do that at home.'

'But it's not the same.'

'I'll come with you. I ain't worked out in a while.' He shrugged. 'I used to box myself, maybe I could show you a thing or two. What size feet have you got?'

My mouth tightened. All I could say was, 'Tens.'

'I'll be able to squeeze into that. You got a spare pair of sneakers?' He glanced thoughtfully at me. 'If not I'll just go barefoot, that don't bother me. I don't want you to go missing, like you did last night. Not after what happened to Froggy.' He sounded uncharacteristically anxious.

S I D E  **115**

Scotto moved around the ring with ease, cutting down space, jabbing and ducking, springing fast combinations. He was good with his hands and sparring with Joey Blade. They were both wearing headguards.

The only person who'd ever beaten Joey was me. He was a big heavyweight with well-toned muscles. The referee moved in and out of them but he kept the fight flowing. Scotto was doing all the right things, he was confident, hungry. Joey was blocking his punches, he was just waiting to land a big punch. I rang the bell and they both went to their corners. Joey was puffing heavily, he was not winning the fight. He'd underestimated Scotto, thought he'd tire, but he was wrong. Scotto raised his gloves and let off a flurry of punches, showing me that he still had a lot left in him. He didn't sit down on the stool, just rested his arms on the ropes.

The bell rang and Joey came out like a tornado. Scotto showed his experience, he avoided the blows, that was the most important thing, he wasn't getting hit. Joey looked the most aggressive but he was just hitting hands. Scotto spun him around and hit him with a solid body shot. Joey groaned. There was a clash of heads, it was lucky that they were wearing headguards or anything could have happened. Joey suddenly realised that Scotto could hurt him; he was getting sloppy and hitting with the insides of the gloves.

I started to shout instructions at Joey. I wanted to be in the ring with Scotto, I wanted to test him out to see if I had an edge over him. Like I said, I was the only guy who had ever stopped Joey, and it had been a hard fight.

Scotto was carving him up. There was a crowd gathered around the ring, a mixture of crooks and cunts because that was all that inhabited the boxing world. I never hung around with the cunts since that meant I would have stayed hungry. I always moved with the crooks because the crooks were simply the people who were massaging the untruth, that was all a crook was in boxing. The crooks were all wondering who the newcomer was, the guy who was giving Joey Blade a good working over. Joey was not a very popular guy, so I could tell that a couple of crooks felt that he was getting his just desserts.

One of the crooks looked at me and said, 'Good matchmaking, Clarkie. That's how you build a champion, it's about time we saw Joey matched properly.'

'Joey, make him miss with a punch,' I shouted. 'Make him miss once.'

Scotto went for a knock-out punch, Joey side stepped him. Scotto took a deep breath as he hit air.

Joey was fighting back now, and I was in there with him.

'Rip his head off! Rip his fucking head off. Rip it off his fucking shoulders!! He's so big you can't miss him. Use your left hook,' I said, jabbing with my bandaged arm. A sharp pain reminded me that I was not fighting fit.

'You look devastating. Slip and counter back. Load up and hit with bad intentions. Go up another gear! Go up another gear,' I screamed.

Scotto was getting hit in rapid succession, his gumshield flew out of his mouth. I was enjoying every second of it. Joey was venting my anger for me. Scotto was packing in mentally, Joey was on top of him, Scotto looked like he didn't want to be in there any more. And just when I thought his arms were broken, he delivered a crashing right and a left, followed by a right cross. He was landing the cleaner shots to the head and body. Joey thought he'd got it easy, now he knew he was in a fight.

'Work! Work! Joey!' I yelled at the top of my voice. 'For fucksake worrrrrrrrrk! Hold on. Hold on. Sharpen up your concentration!!' Get confident!'

The crooks cheered as Scotto came forward. They

didn't care, they just wanted to see a good fight. A couple of them placed bets amongst themselves. Some of them wanted to manage Scotto, fix him up with a couple more fights. They didn't care where he came from. This was the real world. The one thing I'd learnt was that in the industry of boxing there was no room for naïveté; if you wanted to be naïve go to church. The people in the boxing industry were capable of doing anything. Capable of doing anything, because they were people who knew or had found out what life was all about. They didn't come from privileged backgrounds, they came from under-privileged backgrounds like myself. Not that you had to come from an under-privileged background, but that was the way it was, it attracted those sorts of people.

'Throw the towel in! Throw the towel in!' shouted the crooks.

A roar went up in one corner as Scotto delivered a hammer blow to Joey's jaw. Joey fell on the canvas. He tried to get up but his legs crumbled underneath him, that was the end of the fight. The bets were paid out.

I jumped into the ring, and with the help of a

few other crooks we dragged Joey to his corner and splashed water over his face. Scotto came over and touched gloves with Joey, who was still trying to figure out where he was.

'What's your name?' I asked Joey, slapping his jaw.

'Blade,' he said, trying to focus on my face.

'Blade what?'

'Joey Blade. I'm the Blade cos I cut em down.'

Scotto put his arm around my shoulder. There were a couple of crooks congratulating him, patting him on the back, making him feel like a champion. Waiting for their opportunity to make a deal.

'You done well,' I said. 'You're better than I thought.'

Scotto picked up his gumshield. 'Do you reckon you could take me?' he asked, arrogantly. 'If your arm was better, you wouldn't have had to send in one of your boys.'

'It would be close.'

'You know why I like a good fight?' said Scotto, confidently.' Because I learn a lot, I learn a lot. Boxing is like life, there are a lot of things you need to experience, the amount of tricks in this ring is unbelievable. I learn a lot about myself in the ring, I learn what sort of person I am. You understand what

I'm saying?' he squinted, studying me. 'You were in his corner.' He pointed to Joey and pulled his glove off with his teeth. 'You were in his corner so I've learned a lot about you.'

S I D E **116**

The local Caribbean take-away was busy. I ordered sky juice, ackee and salt fish with plain rice for myself and fish soup, carrot juice, curry chicken with rice and peas, two fritters and a dumpling for Scotto. He said that he could eat a lion and I believed him.

We walked out into the neighbourhood. He looked at a gang of youths sitting on a wall outside a liquor store. They were watching people walking by.

'Superpredators,' said Scotto. 'Them youths, that's their job. That is their job, to prey. They know what time certain people leave their houses in the hood, what time they come back in. When they empty their garbage. They know the system, they can smell the cops. Undercover officers in luxury cars, but those guys can identify them. That is their job. Same shit back home.'

'There was a time when I was going sideways, now I'm going straight. I've got a fresh take on life. But I still say the police force is just as corrupt as them youths.'

He straightened up and looked at me. 'What do you mean?'

'That's why you have so many different sections.' I made a grimace that passed for a smile. 'You don't go round telling the public that you're so corrupt that you can't call it a police force, you have to call it sections, the drug squad, the vice squad, fraud squad. You're just as bad as those guys on the street corner.'

A small sigh escaped through his lips. 'I wouldn't say that. We are there to uphold the law.'

'You're outlaws.' My voice was stronger now. 'Why have you got all those different squads? I thought you were policemen?'

'It's more efficient that way, the organisation runs more smoothly.'

'You can keep that for your PR chat,' I said wearily. 'The reason you have all those different squads is because if you have an officer working in the drug squad too long they become known to certain people who deal in drugs, a friendship will develop and the officer would be susceptible to taking money. So that's the reason why the officer gets moved. Maybe that's the real reason you're in this country.'

My words burned into his brain.

'I've never taken drugs money.'

'But maybe you want to cool off for a while. Things may have been too hot for you in the States and your boss said "Take some time out, Scotto, take a longer vacation. Go to Europe. Travel, come back and we'll sort everything out, no one will know what happened."'

Scotto laughed. 'Something like that.'

I took a deep breath, my self-control was coming back now. 'After all, the police force is just human beings, they seem to forget that sometimes and try to pass themselves off as whiter than white. I know some category A ex-con niggers who are working for them. In the CIDS.'

He broke his stride and observed me. 'That's some rugged shit. Forget it. Kick that to the kerb. You know what hurts me most? And both sides have their part to play.'

'What?'

'Crack babies. It just gets to me when I see a newborn baby addicted to cocaine.' He walked on. 'It's sad when you see kids whose parents are doing two or maybe three jobs in a day just to make the rent on crack. Their parents work day and night, they're so busy they forget they got kids until Sunday comes round. I've seen it first hand, the kids feed themselves, go to school if they feel like it, or just hang-out on the block and become predators.'

'I don't think it's as easy as that.'

'Think about it. I'm telling you what the really real is. You're eight years old, your parents ain't around, and you're hungry and sitting outside a rat-infested, cockroach-lined, bullet-soaked apartment complex on 125th Street. A beat-up Cadillac drives by, the driver stops twenny yards down the street, gets out of the Caddie, runs up to you, puts a bag in your hand, says, MEET ME HEAH TOMORROW ... SAME TIME ... OR YA MAMA'S GONNA BE FOUND FLOATIN IN DA EAS RIVER ... YA KNOW DA RULES ... SO SHUT DA FUCK UP! ... NOT A WORD ... OK?' The driver gets back into the Caddie and high tails it out of the neighbourhood. What are you gonna do?'

I didn't say a word.

'Are you gonna talk? And what you gonna do if curiosity the cat tells you to open the bag? Eh?' Scotto looked at me, waiting for an answer.

I shrugged my shoulders. 'I'll open it.'

OK, you open it, and you find it's full of dollars, more dollars than your little eyes have ever seen. Are you gonna talk now?' he asked, a faint touch of sarcasm in his voice.

'No. I'll hide it, 'I answered, swiftly.

'And if the bag was full of guns?'

I paused. 'I'd definitely put it in a safe place.'

'You are now a predator. At the tender age of eight you have joined their ranks. You'll be down with the program and tunin into Channel Zero. It's as easy as that, and now you will live by the streets. The driver will return the following day to find you sitting on the kerb waiting for him. He will look over his shoulder, throw his cigarette butt on to the dirty sidewalk and say, WHERE IS IT, MUTH-AH-FUCK-AH?

'You will be really proud and lead him to the ugly black, litter-lined gutter, behind the disused railway tracks on the outskirts of the city where you've have hidden the bag. You'll tell him how smart you are and say, ONLY MY SPECIAL THINGS ARE KEPT HERE.

'The driver will be pissed off but he will wait patiently, while you dig your hands into the grimy slime and pull out his bag, which you've thoughtfully covered in plastic, so it didn't get wet. The driver will grab the bag, rip off the plastic, look over his shoulder, and open it. I DIDN'T TAKE A DIME, you'll say.

'The driver will kneel on the ground, lick his tobacco-stained fingertips and count the money. It might take him twenny minutes, but he'll count, then recount just to make sure you haven't pulled a fast one. He'll even hold some leaves up to the sunlight to check the water mark. He'll be amping and you'll be laughing. When he's satisfied, he'll say, HERE YA GO ... And put a crumpled dollar bill in your sweaty palm. ... I MIGHT AVE MO WORK COMIN UP ... YA A SMART KID ... I COULD PUT IT YA WAY ...

'He'll scratch his spotty, cocaine-worshipping nose, lick his blistered free-basing lips, rub his wax-filled ears and say: ... ME AN YA CAN GO PLACES. RIGHT FROM JUMP STREET I KNEW WE COULD BE PARTNERS

... YEAH ... MAYBE ONE DAY YA COULD BE LIKE ME ... I STARTED OFF AS A STICK EM UP KID ... AN LOOK AT ME NOW ... DON'T NOBODY SQUARE OFF WITH DA ICE MAN ... COS THEY KNOOOOW I'LL SMOKE EM ... DA ICE MAN THAT'S WHAT THEY CALL ME ... YA COULD AVE A CAR LIKE DA ICE MAN ... WEAR FANCY CLOTHES LIKE DA ICE MAN ... I'LL TELLYA SOMETHIN YA BE DOIN DA NASTY SEVEN DAYS A WEEK ... WITH TIGHT ASSED ... CHINESE AN LATINO SKEEZERS ... MACKIN AN THUGGIN WILL BE YA NEW WAY A LIFE ... I COULD TEACH YA TO AVE A BRAIN LIKE MINE ... YEAH ... YA COULD BE LIKE ME ... I WANT YA TO WAIT FOR ME ON DA CORNAH OF OCEAN AN ATLANTIC ... EVERY THURSDAY ... 10 AM ... ON DA DOT ... I DON'T KNOW WHAT TIME I'LL GET THERE ... BUT ... YA BETTAH BE THERE!!! OR I'M GONNA GET MAD ... I'LL FUCK YOU UP REAL BAD!!! NO ... MAYBE ... I'LL BREAK YA MAMA'S LEGS ... OR SHOOT YA DADDY ... WITH MY NINE.

'You'll play hooky, lie to your parents, and wait all day on that street corner. You will wait for the street to feed you. If a dollar can come that easy, why go to school? You will become a predator and take anything that comes your way, you'll learn to wheel, deal, steal. By your tenth birthday, you will be living large. You'll be the bread winner, you'll provide the turkey at Thanksgiving, you will sit at the head of the table at Christmas, elderly people will come to you to solve their petty problems. You will feel invincible, and talk big time. You are now a superpredator.'

S I D E **117**

Scotto finished his meal and helped himself to a beer from the fridge. He asked me if I'd been to the hospital to see Froggy. I held my bandaged arm and told him I needed a couple more days to cool off before I could even consider being in the same room as him.

We moved into the living room and I switched the computer terminal on and clicked into the TV channel.

Scotto smiled. 'Clayderman tells me that you did a good piece of detective work. You managed to find the Mini.'

'It was luck, really.'

'She's circulated the description of the suspect; hopefully our officers will be able to get a lead soon.'

I gave Scotto a disk.

'What's this?'

'I dunno. Bones gave it to me to look after.'

Scotto slipped it into the computer. He shook his head in amazement as he opened up the file. 'Wow! Is this the shit Bones was into?'

'What is it?'

'Object orientation programming.'

The words meant nothing to me.

Scotto turned to face me. 'The idea is to combine code and data in one capsule and that allows you to reuse the objects. For example, on the screen right now, he's got one side of a pyramid. And there is an object code for that one side.'

I pulled up a chair. 'I'm with you so far but a pyramid is four-sided.'

'So you call up that code three times and that is

called inheritance.' Scotto clicked on the screen. 'See, now we have a four-sided pyramid.'

'What's the point of it all?'

'It gives you more security, everything is encapsulated, it's reliable, it speeds the programs up, looks neat and it makes writing programs easier. It uses C++ language, like JavaScript.

'Don't get technical,' I said, pointing at the terminal. 'Why are all those international banks up there, and all those tax havens?'

Scotto eased back in his chair. 'The benefits are speed of response. If the world changes you can react. You know, if a new tax haven is created or if a loophole is found. A classic case of object computing is in derivative dealing in the City, and that might be the link with Bones.'

'Derivatives?'

'When you set up a basic dealing system, if the law changes and a new dealing system arrives it might take you three months to put it up, you won't do it in a week. It's speed of response that is important, it means that you can get in there and change things immediately.'

'Which means?'

'Make money.'

'Even the art world?'

'To begin with you'd think it was irrelevant because paintings are not a time-sensitive thing. It looks like Bones was going to use it for paintings, setting it up for the art world. It would be interesting for computer art, because with object programming you can make things, or copies of things. However I suspect using a paintbrush would be simpler. But if an art dealer has an artist who is good at copying work, he can move things around.' Scotto was in full flow. 'And if an artist dies, and his work becomes time-sensitive, and you have 200 or 300 of his pieces in storage, you can create objects for the collectors and transfer money from various tax havens or accounts at a great speed, as quick as a phone call. Or you can copy the work onto computer and sell it to customers on the Internet. So they can put it up on their screen savers and you take the money from their accounts. It is even possible to put a copyright sign or a watermark in the capsule.' Scotto leaned back from the computer screen. 'He was a smart kid.'

Scotto and I moved over to the comfortable seats.

'What part of the States are you from?' I asked

'The Bronx, that's where I'm living now. But I was raised in Bushwick, Brooklyn.'

'What's it like there?'

'Police sirens are the signature tune of New York. In Bushwick and the Bronx, they sound like a cross between a screaming child and a howling cat. If you live in New York you have to change or the city will change you. It makes you hard. If you act loose then people will take advantage. 42nd Street at night is like the rush hour in London. Count yourself lucky that you're on the right side of the Atlantic. Out there, man, brothers younger than you are selling crack, guns, women, children and themselves. Anything you want is on the streets.'

'It's the same here.'

'There's more competition in the States, that's the main difference. That's why everybody is brand-name crazy, and that's why the prices are cheaper, the drugs are cheaper, everything. You can get whatever you want by just picking up a phone. Twenty-four hours a day.'

'Americans are real different.'

'Why?'

'It's like they don't know there is a world outside their own.'

'That's cos everybody comes to us. There ain't no real American anyway.'

'But you can't dress, though.'

'Excuse me?' said Scotto, adjusting his tie. 'Are you getting personal here?'

'I'm just saying Americans can't dress. Any time you get it right it's by chance.'

'Is that right?'

'That's why you guys are always in suits and sportswear. Because it's already done for you. If you were put in a room with tops and bottoms and told to mix and match you wouldn't stand a chance.'

'You British kids follow us anyway.'

'Not any more we don't.' I paused. 'You know, it's just starting to sink in that my brother is never going to come back. Every time I walk into the house I expect to hear his voice or see him sitting in here. You know, just before you came I was listening to a record and I turned to the chair he usually sits in and started talking to him. Or I'm in the kitchen making some food and I call up the stairs and ask him if he wants anything, but there's no reply – and then it hits me.'

'I know what you're saying.'

'You do?'

'Yeah.'

'How?'

''Cause I lost my youngest sister to crime.'

'You did?' I asked.

'It hurts when they take something of yours.' His voice was cloaked in sorrow. 'She was only thirteen. I found her in an apartment in downtown Brooklyn. She'd told my mother that she was just going down the road to get some milk, she went missing and I eventually found her while I was doing routine police work. She was lying there on the floor with her throat cut from ear to ear. Her dress was raised over her face and some sick mind had broken a bottle and stuck it in her.' His soft brown eyes misted over. 'She worshipped me and she was lying dead in front of me, abused by sickos.'

'What did you do?'

'I just sat there and cried. I talked to her. Then I pulled the bottle out of her and lowered the dress.' A tear ran down his left cheekbone and crash-landed on his white shirt. 'I knew I was possibly destroying

445

good evidence, you know the killer's fingerprints and stuff, but I didn't want the other officers to see her that way.'

A news flash came up on the computer screen.

*Another victim has been found murdered by the Cyber Vigilante. A woman was found hanging from a tree, with the killer's calling card of a white rat found attached to a Harley Davidson motorbike nearby. Police are asking anybody who might have seen this bike to come forward. Also, anyone who has any information about the driver of a white mini, registration WAR 2029, please contact your local police station. The driver is described as black, with a beard and a moustache, heavily built, approximately 6'1". Do not approach him.*

I turned away from the screen and found Scotto's eyes on me. Now I knew he was the killer. I'd seen him getting onto the bike. Scotto was just sitting there staring. I picked up the plates and took them into the kitchen. Scotto stood in the doorway.

'Have you got a problem?' I asked.

'Have you got a problem?'

'No. Why are you following me? This is my house.'

'My job is to protect you so you've got to be in my vision at all times.'

'You going to follow me to the toilet?'

'Are there any windows in there?'

'Yes.'

'Can anybody climb in?'

'No.'

'OK. Then there's no problem.'

My brain was working like a super computer. Here I was in the house, with a guy I suspected of being the Cyber Vigilante, my brother's killer. Froggy was on a drip in a hospital, Scotto had just beaten the shit out of Joey Blade. My arm was bandaged up, so even if I tried to take him on I was already handicapped, my gun was in the Jeep. I didn't know what to do. I mean, I didn't like paedophiles myself so did I turn Scotto in and stop him from killing other paedophiles? He'd killed my brother. Froggy had admitted that he'd put the porn on the machines. I didn't know what to do. I thought about calling Pauline, but I didn't want to get her involved.

### Caption: Night

A black figure with a tight mask lunged towards me with a knife. It was the Cyber Vigilante. I froze, I knew my time had come. He put his hand on my shoulder to get a better grip. I screamed as the knife came down towards my chest.

I jerked and opened my eyes. Scotto was moving across the living room towards me. He put his hand on my shoulder.

'Do you want a cup of tea?' he asked.

My eyes focused on the steaming cup in front of me.

'I made some for myself, so I thought you might want one,' said Scotto.

I took the tea. 'Thanks,' I said, as I watched him walking back to his seat. He sat down, picked up a book and started reading.

Sleep had finally caught up with me. I'd tried to fight it all night, I'd dozed off a million times, but I'd managed to force my eyes open. But this time I'd sunk into it and dreamt that I was being attacked by the Vigilante. The effigy that Mrs Birchfield had given me was still under my pillow, but I had no faith in it.

The book Scotto was reading was *The 13th Valley* by John M. Del Vecchio. He lowered it and stirred his tea. 'Sounds like you were having a nightmare.'

'I'm alright now.' I bit my lip, thinking. 'I was just a little tired, that's all.'

'Yeah, we've all got to sleep sometime.' He was watching me closely.

I kept control over my voice. 'I saw you.'

'Where?'

'Getting onto that Harley, with that woman. You had a false beard. A master of disguise.'

Scotto had a crooked smile on his face as he placed the book face-down on his lap. 'You did?'

'Yeah.'

The smile still held on. 'It wasn't me,' he said, the smile tight now, deadly.

I couldn't tell what he was thinking. 'That's what you said about Chameleon,' I said. 'But you were there, baseball cap, John Lennon style glasses, a different image. That's where you made contact with Bones. It was you who broke into my house, it was you that I chased and you who got into the Mini.'

Still nothing showed, but he said calmly, 'So what are you going to do?'

'I don't know yet.'

'I do.' His eyes fixed on mine, shiny bright. 'I could kill you.' He stared at me, cold, expressionless. 'I could have done it when you dozed off, it could have all been easily explained to Clayderman. You sneaked out of the back of the house, I lost you, you were found dead somewhere. There are 100 possible reasons and 100 answers.'

When I was ready I said, 'So what's stopping you?'

His eyes came up, fastened on my face, catching every movement. 'Nothing. Nothing at all.'

'You killed an innocent man.'

'I didn't know that at the time.' His voice thick.

'My brother. Well, what are you waiting for?' I held my bandaged arm close to my chest. 'Why don't you get on with it. I'm not going to be able to fight back, not with an arm like this. And I'm not going to give you the pleasure of being scared,' I said bluntly. 'You've evaded capture so far. I'm sure you're not going to run the risk of me speaking up.'

He finally said, 'At the scene of the crime, sometimes things are not always what they seem.'

'What are you talking about?' I watched his face closely.

'My sister's murder. I removed vital evidence from the scene.'

'You've already told me that.'

'I didn't kill Bones.' His voice almost paternal.

'He was hung up?' I snarled. 'That's what you do to your victims isn't it?' My eyes crinkled at the corners and I felt tears running down my cheek.

'He fell down the stairs of the cellar he was so drunk.' His hand trembled. 'Yes, I was in Chameleon, got talking with Bones about computers, and arranged to meet him later at your mother's house. He was late and pissed, when we were going down the stairs he fell and broke his neck. I did go there with the intention of killing him. If he hadn't fallen I would have killed him, but the fact is I didn't do it.'

'Why hang him up?' I wiped the tears away with the back of my hand. 'Why didn't you just leave him then?' My breathing was quick and uneven. 'He was dead already, why do that in my mother's house?'

'I checked his machine and I found the porn, so I hung him up as a warning to other paedophiles. I threw the rat away in the garden.' His voice sounded flat and cold.

'Why? If you wanted to warn other paedophiles, wouldn't you want the rat to be found in the cellar?'

'I don't always carry the rat with me. I could be stopped and searched. Sometimes I leave them in the car. It depends on the victim. In Bones' case I jumped over your mother's wall in the back garden. I didn't want to use the front door. It was too risky. I got the rat. When I was coming back to place it, a light went on in your mother's house. I didn't want to take a chance so I threw the rat in the bushes. I knew it would be found sooner or later. I claimed the killing but, like I said, I didn't kill him.' He rose from his chair, the book fell to the ground. He pulled a black mask out of his pocket. I had a sudden horrible feeling that my life was coming to an end. I gritted my teeth and refused to squeal, fighting the fear in my heart.

# S I D E 119

## Caption: Thursday

Clayderman was excited as she led me into a room. Scotto was already in there, he was smoking a cigarette. Slow, deliberate.

'We had a good response from the news item on TV last night,' said Clayderman.

There was a two-way mirror, I saw twelve men with beards and moustaches lined up against a wall.

'Are any of those men the one you saw coming out of the car rental building? The girl who was working in there was so rushed she didn't really take a good look at him, she was no good to us when she was in here. Do you see anybody you recognise?'

I looked at Scotto, who took a hard pull on his cigarette. His shoulders were hunched over like he was feeling cold.

'No,' I said. 'I think the guy I saw was much shorter, he can't have been 6'1", I think he was about 5'9". I was a long way away, and he had dreads. I didn't say that before, but he had locks.'

Scotto glanced at me, the cigarette halfway to his mouth, his eyes expressionless. He knew I was letting him go.

He stubbed out the cigarette. 'I got a plane to catch,' he said, getting up from his seat. He left the room and shut the door behind him.

Clayderman was exasperated. She flopped into the vacant chair and sighed audibly.

S I D E **120**

The puppy in the pet shop had the most beautiful eyes. It was a silver grey Weimeraner, a ghost dog. I looked at it through the glass, it was the most active of the litter, it pushed its nose up against the window. Asking, no begging, me to take it home.

I decided to come back later that day and buy it. At least that way I wouldn't have to return to an empty house. I would have to be responsible for it, I'd have to look after it and maybe that would help me look after myself. The puppy barked.

I felt a presence behind me. It was Mrs Birchfield, Queenie was wagging her tail.

'You could both help each other,' she said.

The puppy chased its tail. I smiled and Mrs Birchfield nodded her head.

S I D E **121**

Darren let me into Pauline's flat. I had two shoe boxes in my hand. I handed one to him.

'You can't buy me, you know?' he said, as he opened the box. His eyes opened up as he saw a pair of fat trainers. 'Wow. Well, maybe in time we could be friends.'

Pauline was in the living room, watching TV. I gave her the other shoebox.

She gasped as she opened the box. 'You're really naughty.'

'Don't you like them? I can change them for something else.'

'No. No, they're lovely. I didn't really think you would go out and buy me a pair. I wasn't serious, when I said get me a pair.'

'Well, I wanted to,' I said. 'I wanted to. When I get some money I'm going to get some Capizzo's from New York. I'll get somebody to bring them over for me.'

'What's so special about them?'

'They've got soft white uppers, ornate black patent toes and heels, I think the soles are canvas. They'll be my wingtips when I'm out dancing in a salsa club.'

'Wingtips?' asked Pauline, smiling.

'My black belt. You get me? A lotta guys are gonna stay away from them shoes, because they carry a sense of respect. If you wear them, you've got to be able to live up to them. You get me.'

Pauline nodded.

Darren came into the living room, opened the window and looked out onto the street. Some of his friends were calling him to come out to play.

Darren turned to Pauline. 'Mum, that cop is down there again giving everybody tickets. I sure he ain't got nothing else to do.'

Pauline and I laughed.

S I D E

### Caption: A few days later

For one glorious day the vibrant sound of New Orleans was brought to the streets of Kensal Rise. A bunch of old time jazz musicians serenaded the hearse that carried Bones' coffin. Saxophones, trumpets, and flutes all wept joyously as the musicians walked in front of the long procession of cars and limousines. They played the blues and danced like hoofers, they spun and shuffled, twisted and clapped to the syncopated rhythms. A grey haired scats singer improvised spontaneously to any riff that floated in the air. It was rag-time, Count Basie style, and that's the way Bones wanted it.

On the pavement some members of the public muttered disapprovingly to themselves. They pointed as we slowly passed by; they must have thought we were crazy. The more polite took off their hats as a sign of respect. The younger and more adventurous amongst them joined in the entertainment and kicked their legs in the air and waved their newspapers. It was bombastic. Tourists clicked their cameras. The afternoon traffic came to a standstill, hundreds of heads popped out of buses, cabs, pubs and shops. The policemen beckoned us on, it was one of those days when everybody was in tune. Bones' coffin passed our old primary school, then the youth club where he won his first medal in a table tennis tournament. It went past the green where he met his first girlfriend, past the church where he was Christened. Mum and Dad never shed a tear, they just smiled and nodded as they looked out of the window of the limo. Humour was what the doctor ordered. Pauline, Darren, Uncle Oscar and I sat opposite them. We all knew that this was not a day to be sad. Bones had left money so that his friends and business associates could have a wild party instead of a dry wake.

Mum had arranged everything. She had got in contact with as many people as possible. So even though it was a sad occasion we all kept our spirits up, those who couldn't hold their emotions were hugged and consoled.

When we finally reached the graveside Mum made a moving speech. The majority of the congregation came from a younger generation but her words still had meaning. The peace was interrupted by the sound of James Brown's raw, rough-edged tones blasting over Kensal Rise cemetery. In the distance, I heard a train rumbling past.

The pulsating bassline and familiar voice of THE GODFATHER OF SOUL were coming from a huge ghetto blaster I was holding, a track specially remixed by 4 Hero. A melody of Drum 'n' bass tracks played as the undertakers shovelled earth into the grave. I could

almost see Bones clapping and laughing as he sat on
his throne in the sky.

*RINSE OUT!*

*IT'S TIME TO GET PHYSICAL*

*RINSE OUT!*

*IT'S TIME TO GET MOODY*

*Now that I have con**Q**uered it is time for fun!*

# GLOSSARY

| | | | |
|---|---|---|---|
| affta | .....after | dere | .....there |
| ah | .....a, at, I, of, is, to | di | .....the |
| anada | .....another | dis | .....this |
| arf | .....off, half | do-do | .....shit |
| arks | .....asks | dough | .....though |
| arn | .....on | doze | .....those |
| baas | .....boss | duppy | .....ghost |
| baddy | .....body | dutti | .....dirty |
| bahg | .....bag | dyam | .....damn |
| batti | .....bottom | een | .....in |
| bill | .....build, built | fah | .....for |
| bin | .....been | farda | .....father |
| breadda | .....brother | feava | .....favour |
| bucckle | .....bottle | fi | .....for, to |
| buds | .....birds | fine | .....find, found |
| bus | .....bust | firewall | .....a security measure acting as a barrier which stops unwanted people accessing a company's server and thus their internal network of information |
| bwoy | .....boy | | |
| carl | .....call | | |
| chirping | .....talking | | |
| coal | .....cold | | |
| cum | .....come | | |
| cumin | .....coming | | |
| dan | .....than | | |
| das | .....that's | | |
| dat | .....that | | |
| dawg | .....dog | | |
| de | .....there | | |
| deh | .....they | forrid | .....forehead |
| dem | .....them, their, they | FTP | .....file transfer protocol |
| den | .....then | gi | .....give |

| | | | |
|---|---|---|---|
| gwaan | .....go on | noh | .....know, no |
| gyal | .....girl | nyam | .....eat |
| hall | .....all | ooh | .....who |
| har | .....her | ozband | .....husband |
| heny | .....any | pom-pom | .....pussy |
| hinjoy | .....enjoy | pun | .....upon, on |
| hout | .....out | renk | .....to reek |
| houtta | .....out of | rispek | .....respect |
| http | .....allows text, | saaf | .....soft |
| | images, audio | seh | .....say |
| | and video to | si | .....see |
| | be combined | strickly | .....strictly |
| | into a single | tahl | .....tall |
| | document. URLs | tase | .....taste |
| | are prefixed by | tek | .....take |
| | http:// code | ting | .....thing |
| ina | .....in, into | tink | .....think |
| jancrow | .....vulture | tree | .....three |
| jugs | .....drugs | trew | .....through |
| ketch | .....catch | trute | .....truth |
| kru | .....crew | tun | .....turn |
| laas | .....last | udder | .....other |
| lek | .....let | URL | .....your |
| lick | .....knock, hit | | web address |
| likkle | .....little | VRML | .....Virtual reality |
| madda | .....mother | | modelling language |
| mek | .....make | WWW | .....World wide web |
| mi | .....I, me, my | waan | .....want |
| might | .....mate | wid | .....with |
| moni | .....money | wile | .....wild |
| mussi | .....must | wuz | .....was |
| nah | .....won't | wuzn't | .....wasn't |

Q would like to thank:–

All the people who bought the original DEADMEAT formats.
Your advice, support and encouragement spurred me on. I hope
you enjoy this reinterpretation. A big shout out to the night
club managers, promoters, security, guest list operators, press
and TV journalists and radio DJ's up and down the country who
picked up on the DEADMEAT LIFESTYLE back in the day
and let me into venues for free to sell my literature and gave
me airplay/time and coverage in their papers. ERNIE TURTON
– for the dynamic wood cut illustrations in the original book
(view them on http://www.deadmeat.com). The musicians who
have contributed tracks to the various Deadmeat projects.
SAMI KHAN, M.A.D. and GEORGE aka SEED – who did some
kick arse illustrations for this book but due to technical
problems they cannot be viewed on paper, but you can catch
them on the Deadmeat web site. Gary 'eye 2 eye' Innis. Lisa
I'anson. Doreen Y. Barnett. Rampage sound system – Richie P
(thanks for all the hook ups), Mike and Pyscho. Trevor at
Diamond time. Freddie M. Linda Gunnell, Edward, Marcella,
Alex and Andy. Caroline. Ken Macdonald. Anne-Marie
L'Estrange. Steven Heffer. Paul Cook. Sebastian Boyle. F1
Sisters. Normski. San Ra – space is the place. Everyone
involved in the script slam in Camden, thanks for giving your
time. Chris England. Mark Hughes. Al Digital. Wow
Foundation. Destination Moon. Ytech. Roberto. Ricky. Desmond
Johnson. Olly at DNA. Merrilee, Tracey and Al at the Writers
House. Carole Welch thanks for saying yes and editing this
novel. The Sceptre team. The Deadmeat intranet too numerous
to mention but are all involved in the millennium rinse.